**W9-DIB-190**

"A successful person is one who can lay a firm foundation with the bricks thrown at them. Life throws unexpected bricks! *Faith Beyond the Trials* will show how to catch the bricks and build life's solid foundation. **Powerful! Real life!**"

> —Dr. John Tolson, Founder and Chairman of the Board for
> The Gathering/ USA, Inc. and The Tolson Group;
> Team Chaplain, The Dallas Cowboys

"I have enjoyed reading *Faith Beyond The Trials*. It offers **tremendous insight into the legal system and life issues** such as guilt and redemption, providing a strong Christian perspective."

> —Sidney A. Stubbs, Esq., Senior Partner at Jones, Foster,
> Johnston & Stubbs, P.A., West Palm Beach, Florida

"The book is sterling. Turk manages to combine courtroom, legal, and personal drama with enough action to keep even the most casual reader reading well into the night. No human emotion goes untouched; and there is surely a **redeeming message of hope** for every person who reads this wonderful book."

> —Bette Kester Conrad, Esq. Attorney and Author,
> West Palm Beach, Florida

Acknowledgments

There are a number of people to whom I owe a debt of deep gratitude for helping me make this book become a reality. In constructing some of the scenes which take place, I was graciously and expertly assisted by Assistant State Attorney Ellen Roberts, Esq.; Allen Geesey, Esq.; and by Robert Friedman, Esq. Also, Colonel Michael Gauger; Deputy-Administrative Assistant Patrick Halperin, Ph.D.; Lieutenant Robert Tutko; and Lieutenant Delaney Haff of the Palm Beach County Sheriff's Office were all instrumental in helping me develop portions of this story. Although the novel is a work of fiction, I tried, to the best of my ability, and with the help of each of these attorneys and police officers, to keep the scenes as realistic as possible. Notwithstanding the assistance of each of them, the ultimate responsibility for the content lies with me.

After several drafts were completed, I obtained invaluable input from numerous friends. The comments and suggestions I received from them were of great benefit in preparing the final draft. Special thanks to Herb and Dorothy Achtmeyer; Mike Conrad and Bette Kester Conrad, Esq.; Wayne Gill, Esq. and Sharon Gill; Phil and Susan Holden; Burt and Teresa Nightingale, Esq.; and Bob Schuemann.

For their professionalism and sage advice, I also extend my thanks to my "Book Shepard," Karen Granger; editor and graphic designer Luann Yarrow; website developer Jamie Burns; and publisher Grif Blackstone and Blackstone Media Group. They provided the necessary expertise, support, and encouragement from start to finish, and I appreciate each of them.

As always, my children were with me every step of the way. Starting with my eldest daughter, Diana Stanbro, and son-in-law Jeffrey Stanbro; my son Gregory and daughter-in-law Amber; and my youngest daughter, Carolyn, I could have not have asked for more support or love from any of you. My love to all of you and to my new grandson, Aaron Stanbro.

I never could have retired from the practice of law at the age of 54 to pursue my long-time ambition of writing Christian novels without the agreement, encouragement, and assistance of my wife of 35 years, Katherine. You are truly my partner in this life journey we've been on together since high school, and I give thanks to God for the soul mate He created for me. Thank you for always being there.

"Without faith a man can do nothing;
with it all things are possible."
-Sir William Osler

Chapter 1

"All rise," bellowed Bailiff Peter Magorie. "The Circuit Court of Palm Beach County, Florida is now in session, the Honorable Hubert Johnston presiding."

With that announcement, Judge Johnston appeared through a side door adjacent to the bench and looked across the courtroom. A smile crossed his face as he saw that only a few attorneys were present for calendar call; that meant the trial docket would be quickly resolved. He'd be able to spend most of the morning reading the pretrial motions and briefs submitted to him by the attorneys for a murder trial starting next Monday. For a change, it looked like his Friday would be put to good use catching up on paperwork. Although tedious, it was still better than spending hours trying to get cases scheduled for trial, especially when some of the attorneys were less than cooperative with the court.

Taking his place on the bench, Judge Johnston proceeded to read the docket sheet and, with the experience of a trial judge who had been trying cases for nearly thirty years, he began calling the docket. The first case on the docket was the State of Florida versus John Taylor. The judge asked whether the parties were ready to proceed.

"The State is ready," replied Assistant State Attorney Paul Del Garden, "and we anticipate the case will take three days to try."

"I seem to recall from prior court hearings that this matter involves a felony charge against Mr. Taylor for driving under the influence of alcohol, resulting in serious bodily injury. Is that correct?" inquired Judge Johnston. "Yes, your Honor, that is correct," answered Del Garden.

"Does counsel for Mr. Taylor agree that the case can be tried in three days?" asked the judge.

"Actually, your Honor, this case ought to be dismissed by the Court in one day, after the State puts on its evidence. But in an abundance of caution, in the event the Court does not rule in our favor, we agree that three days will be sufficient for the jury to hear and decide the case," replied Donald Brisbane, counsel for John Taylor.

"I appreciate you letting me know how I should rule, Mr. Brisbane. Out of an abundance of caution, and in the event that I do not dismiss this case but let the jury decide, we'll set the case for three days. I want all of you here one week from this Monday morning at eight o'clock for preliminary matters. We'll call the jury panel up at nine o'clock. Mr. Del Garden and Mr. Brisbane, both of you may be excused while I go on to set other cases. Have a good weekend, gentlemen."

Both attorneys packed up their briefcases and began to leave the courtroom. One matter remained for Brisbane before he returned to his office: dealing with John Taylor, who was sitting in the last row of the courtroom and not looking very happy.

John left the courtroom first and waited outside for

Brisbane. Retreating to a deserted corner of the hallway, John let Brisbane know, in no uncertain terms, about his unhappiness at what had just taken place.

"Why in the world didn't you try to have the Court rule on our motion to suppress evidence before the trial begins? If not today, then why not shoot for next week? When I have civil cases with significant evidentiary issues, I always try to get those issues resolved in advance of trial, not on the day of trial."

"Listen, John. I realize you're an experienced civil trial attorney, and a very good one at that. But you're not a criminal defense attorney, and you don't know Judge Johnston because he has served on the criminal bench for the past twenty years. It was clear to me, based on his comments today, that he was in no mood to entertain legal arguments on evidentiary issues in this case—either today or next week—in light of the murder trial he's starting next Monday. The Judge gave us one full hour on the day trial begins, before he calls the jury, and I'll be able to more than adequately raise our evidentiary issues with him that morning. So my advice to you, my friend, is to chill out and let the lawyer you're paying big bucks to make the strategy calls. Okay?"

"Well, I do agree that I'm paying you big bucks. Five hundred dollars an hour is nothing to sneeze at. But I know you're worth it. You've done a very good job for me so far, and I know you'll continue to do so at the trial. So I apologize for second-guessing. It's just the thought of possibly going to jail and losing my law license is driving me nuts."

"Apology accepted. Go home to Anna and try to relax. I'll call you first thing next week so we can go over your trial testimony and our strategy."

At that, John said goodbye to Brisbane and headed to his car to begin the trek from the courthouse in West Palm Beach to his home in Palm Beach. More important than his home was his wife of twelve years and high school sweetheart, Anna Taylor, who was there waiting for him, waiting to hear the outcome of the day's proceedings. John dreaded telling her the trial was only a little over a week away. The nightmare continued.

Chapter 2

As John made the drive home, vivid memories of his life with Anna engulfed him. He still recalled with great delight the first time he met Anna. It was a crisp autumn day, one that was destined to leave an indelible mark in his memory bank. Even though it was twenty years ago, when John was 17 and a high school senior in Downers Grove, Illinois, he still remembered in great detail how he and Anna met. John attended St. Peter's High, an all-male Catholic high school and was dating Bonnie Hopkins, who attended an all-female Catholic high school in the same town. Bonnie wanted to go to a football game between two local powerhouse high schools, neither of which was St. Peter's.

Although John was tall, muscular, and very athletic, he did not care for football and rarely went to any games. John was a baseball and basketball star, and he preferred to have people watch him play, rather than go see a bunch of guys he didn't know play a sport he disliked. Reluctantly, John agreed to go with Bonnie, which was perhaps the best decision he had ever made in his life. While at the game, Bonnie and John ran into six of her girlfriends from school. John didn't know any of them, although he could hear the girls making not very subtle comments about how good-looking he was.

Out of the six girls, one stood out above the others: Anna. She was so cute, not just from a physical standpoint but also in her actions. Her bubbling, effervescent personality really caught John's attention. But John was loyal to Bonnie and never thought anything would come of his attraction to Anna. How wrong he was. When Bonnie's former boyfriend saw the error of his ways and reconciled with her, John was a free man. Anna quickly entered the scene, and she eventually became John's new girlfriend. It was a relationship made in heaven—and one that would eventually be put through the fires of hell.

As John thought back about their relationship, he fondly recalled their post high school days, when they both attended the same community college outside of Downers Grove. John earned his degree in retail business management, and Anna received hers in liberal arts. After community college, they both graduated from the University of Illinois, where John majored in business administration and Anna in education. Anna wanted to become a teacher and quickly found a job outside of Downers Grove in a local elementary school. John decided a career in law was his best option, and, with Anna's agreement, headed off to the University of Michigan to obtain his law degree.

Although John and Anna were apart while John attended law school, their relationship grew stronger, and after his first year was completed, John proposed to Anna. She immediately accepted. Plans were put in place for a wedding following John's graduation from law school. John worked hard while in law school and graduated near the top of his class. He was also an editor on the law review and won a school competition for the best student in trial advocacy. As a result of John's efforts, he was awarded a full scholarship for his last two years. That was a blessing for both John and Anna, as John's parents did not have the financial resources to contribute to his law school expenses.

As hard as John worked in law school, Anna was with him every step of the way. She took a part-time job as a bookkeeper at a local grocery store to supplement her teaching job. The extra money would help her parents pay for her and John's upcoming nuptials. She also saved money for the wedding by living at home with her mom and dad.

During John's last year in law school, he interviewed with many different firms. He was highly sought after because of his impressive credentials and down-to-earth personality. Although John wanted to earn a good living, he wasn't focused on the money. Ultimately, and in agreement with Anna, he decided against taking a job in New York, although he was offered several lucrative positions in that area. Instead, John opted to accept a position at a small, prestigious Palm Beach law firm, Smith & Patterson. George Smith and James Patterson, the two senior partners in the firm, had graduated from the University of Michigan several decades before. When they decided to hire someone to work with George in high-end real estate and trust litigation, they interviewed several Michigan law students for the position. John and the partners hit it off immediately, and John was offered the job.

Although John was definitely interested, he first called Anna to see if she would relocate to Florida. She agreed. Anna had made several trips to the east coast of Florida for family vacations, and she absolutely loved the area. She also relished the opportunity of starting a new life with her husband-to-be. John struck a deal with Smith & Patterson and began working with them that summer, after his graduation and wedding.

As John drove along the ocean stretch of Palm Beach toward his home, he could hardly believe it had been twelve years since he had exchanged vows with Anna and moved to Florida. Memories of their wedding flooded his mind. It had been a grand event. Following a breathtaking wedding ceremony at St. Peter's Church, a wonderful reception attended by two hundred guests took place at the local country club. The band was rocking and rolling, the drinks were flowing, and the party continued into the early morning hours. A great time was had by all! It marked the beginning of a new life for John and Anna—a life that until one year ago had been a storybook fairytale.

As John drove along the beach, he pondered the irony of the waves slamming across the rocks, sending ocean spray high into the air. At one time they were magnificent reminders of the sea's power, a glorious sight he and Anna enjoyed. Now they only served to remind him of how his fairytale life was crashing in around him—and threatening to drown him.

Exiting the scenic beach road, John turned west on Reef Road and drove the last two blocks to home. Pulling into his driveway, John bit his lip and grimaced as he thought about what he was going to tell Anna about the morning's events. As the garage door rose up, he saw Anna waiting for him. *My God, what will I tell her?* John thought.

Chapter 3

"Well, what happened? Did Don's motion to not allow the jury to hear the State's expert's testimony get ruled on by the Judge?" asked Anna, in a voice strained by stress.

"No, it didn't. Initially I was really ticked off at Don for not pursuing it more aggressively. But, he convinced me that he was right in letting it go until the morning the trial begins, which is a week from Monday," replied John. He was hoping his short answer would curtail any further interrogation by Anna. No such luck.

For the next ten minutes, Anna cross-examined John about the morning's proceedings and the impending trial in a manner that would have made famed trial lawyer Clarence Darrow proud. John, however, was not pleased and stormed into the kitchen for a can of diet soda. He badly needed to pump some caffeine into his system. He was struggling to choose the right words to say to Anna.

"Listen, Anna. I know you mean well, and you're very concerned about this mess I've gotten into, but please, you need to leave the details of the case to Don and me. We'll get this thing straightened out. Just arrange with the school to get three days off beginning a week from Monday so you can attend the trial. Okay, Sweetheart?"

"Well I can't do that today seeing how school is closed, but I'll talk to the principal next Monday. I just hope and pray to God that Don and you get this mess straightened out like you said. I don't know what I'll do if you go to jail, and I lose you!" With that, Anna started crying, first softly, then uncontrollably.

Taking her hands into his, John tried his best to reassure her that she wouldn't be losing him. Grabbing him, Anna squeezed John with such force that for a second or two he thought he might black out. Fortunately, she let go and walked out of the kitchen into the adjoining family room, where she paused in front of the wedding picture of the two of them. John came over to Anna and, looking at the photo, realized how little she had changed in their twelve years of marriage. She was still beautiful with her long blonde hair, green eyes, and infectious smile. But John hadn't seen much of that infectious smile during the past year. The strain of events had taken their toll on both of them, and he was struggling not to break down and cry with her.

Gazing at the delicately framed wedding photo, Anna asked, "When can we go back to that time and place? That time and place where we were so happy, and life was so full of promise and hope? It feels like it's been replaced by nothing but sadness and dread of the future. Although I keep praying to God for a change and hope for the future, my prayers just don't seem to be answered."

Mustering every ounce of courage in his body, John answered, "You know how hard I'm struggling with my faith and trying to believe that a good God does exist out there, and things will get better. Let's just pray for the best and hope that God comes through for us so this nightmare will end."

Looking at his wife once more, he changed the subject. "On the way home I noticed the waves were breaking really well for a good board ride. I'm going to change, head to the beach for some surfing, and then come back and go to the office." With that, John headed to the bedroom, quickly changed, grabbed his surfboard, and headed out of the house for the two-block walk to the Atlantic.

Although a bit miffed at John's sudden departure, Anna realized it was a form of stress relief for him, as were the barbells, weights, and punching bags in the garage. The physical activity kept John in good physical condition, and it was his way of dealing with the pressures of the trial. Anna had no desire to hamper John in that area. He was barely keeping his head above water, as was she, and the activity provided a good outlet.

Anna knew that she, too, ought to get back into her exercise regime. It had been months since she'd ran or played tennis, and that needed to change. Weight gain hadn't been a problem, as she carefully watched everything she ate, but she really needed to burn off some stress. She promised herself that tomorrow morning she'd go for a long, slow jog—and call her best friend, Tess, for a Sunday tennis game.

Deciding to take a nap while John was surfing, Anna headed to the master bedroom, which was on the other side of their spacious, upscale, four-bedroom, four-and-a-half bath home. At nearly 5,000 square feet of air-conditioned space, it was quite large, but certainly not close to a mansion by Palm Beach standards. With an expansive outdoor entertainment area, complete with an oversized pool, spa, and barbeque pit, their home had been the perfect place for John and Anna to host numerous dinner gatherings and parties in the three years they'd lived there. Entertaining clients, co-workers, and friends was something they both thoroughly enjoyed and were quite skilled at, although no parties or functions of any kind had taken place within the last year. Both Anna and John missed entertaining, but neither of them had the disposition or energy to do so since the night from hell occurred.

As she headed down the hallway to the master bedroom, Anna stopped outside the doorway to the first bedroom. Going inside the sweetly decorated room, she stood at the foot of the hand-carved wooden crib that looked like something from a designer catalog. Above the crib on the wall was the picture of an angelic looking baby, taken when the child was six months old. Adorned in a long, white dress with a hat on her tiny head, the little girl was the epitome of beauty and sweetness. At the top of the picture frame was the baby's name, Maria Taylor. At the bottom of the frame was a miniature wedding photo of John and Anna. As she gazed at Maria's picture, Anna began to feel faint and left the room to go lie down on her bed.

While Anna rested in bed, her mind went back to Maria's birth some eighteen months ago. Anna's neighbor had taken her to St. James Hospital in West Palm Beach. They arrived before John, who was tied up in a court hearing. By the time he arrived, Anna was in the natural delivery birthing room almost ready to deliver the baby, and the doctor and supporting staff were all with her. In walked John with a hideous Frankenstein mask over his head and a video camera in his hand. It was John's comic idea that when the baby came out, he would scare the little squirt with his mask and then videotape her jumping into Anna's arms. *Real cute,* Anna thought, but not at all surprising for John, who had a tendency to be a hard-core practical joker.

Actually, that escapade was nothing compared to what John had pulled off at their wedding. While greeting guests standing in line at the wedding reception, John suddenly had to go to the men's room. When John returned, he stood behind Anna's grandmother and tapped Granny on the shoulder. When she turned around, Granny nearly fell down on the floor from seeing some lunatic wearing a wolf man mask and holding an axe in his hand. After a couple glasses of wine and some profuse apologies by John, Granny relaxed and joined the festivities on the dance floor. Luckily Anna knew what she was getting into when she married John and never begrudged his practical jokes. She realized they were never intended to be mean or vindictive, and some were actually quite funny.

Anna grinned widely as she recalled bringing Maria home from the hospital. What a spectacular day it had been! John and Anna finally had a precious little child to share life with. Although the two of them had tried for several years to have a baby, Anna had difficulty conceiving, much to their disappointment. Finally, their prayers were answered, and their adorable infant captured their hearts.

On the day Maria came home with Anna, John had decorated the house with balloons and banners, and Anna's friends from work had come over earlier in the day and whipped up a gourmet feast for dinner. John and Anna had purchased a bassinet for Maria and kept her in their room to sleep with them for the first three months. It was only after Maria began to wake up at one o'clock and four o'clock every night to be fed that John asked Anna to put the baby in the crib in her nursery, which Anna reluctantly agreed to.

Oh how Anna had enjoyed putting Maria in her stroller and walking down the pedestrian pathways in Palm Beach! She enjoyed showing Maria off to anyone she encountered. It often took her an hour or more to complete a one-mile jaunt with the baby because she was continually stopping to let people see her precious cargo. Those walks, however, paled in comparison to the Sunday rides to Wellington to see the polo matches. In late winter, soon after Maria was born, John began representing a wealthy polo player from Columbia who lived in Wellington during the playing season. They had a standing invitation to attend the Sunday polo matches, and after going to church at St. Gregory's, where Maria also drew much attention, the three of them proceeded along Southern Boulevard into the prestigious village of Wellington. Their host spared no expense in entertaining them at the polo games and afterwards at his home for dinner. Little Maria was always the focus of attention on those outings, and John and Anna were as happy as could be.

As she continued to rest in bed, cherishing her thoughts of Maria, Anna remembered how she had returned to her job at St. Gregory's Elementary School three months after Maria was born. Although Anna didn't need to return to teaching for financial reasons, she enjoyed working with the children immensely, and so she decided, with John's agreement, to resume her career. A full-time nanny was hired, and both Anna and John were very satisfied with her care of the baby. Although Anna missed the baby while at school, the evening reunions were so much the sweeter.

John was totally enamored with the baby as well. He made a big effort after she was born to arrive home by seven o'clock each night, rather than his usual time of eight. John was always talking of getting to work on their second child so that Maria would have a sibling to play with, but Anna convinced him that they needed to wait until Maria was at least a year old before they'd try again.

Anna managed to fall asleep before those sweet and wonderful memories were transformed into the continuing and inevitable waves of terror and dread. At least she was at peace this time while sleeping, unlike numerous other occasions when her nightmares would cause her to awaken in a cold sweat.

While Anna was getting a much-needed rest, John was battling a strong surf and big waves—just as he liked it. He had been in the water now for about two hours and was ready to come out. He decided he wouldn't go to the office today and would instead catch up on work tomorrow. The weekends were always quieter and more conducive to productive legal work, which translated into more billable hours. Catching his last wave into the shore, John picked up his board and began the walk home. There were a lot of surfers in the water today due both to the favorable conditions and the popularity of this location. This beach was known for having some of the best breakers in the state. John felt more relaxed now and was hoping to convince Anna they should go out to dinner this evening, something they hadn't done in a long time. Having tried civil cases for nearly twelve years, he knew the importance of distracting yourself from the litigation, at least temporarily, if you were going to have any chance of succeeding. And Pronzi's Italian Restaurante on Brazilian Avenue in Palm Beach was just the ticket.

Arriving home, John looked for Anna and found her sleeping in their bed. Being careful not to disturb her, he called his office, informed his secretary that he would be in tomorrow, and proceeded to shower and change. When he came out of the bathroom, Anna was awake.

"How was the surfing?" she asked.

"Couldn't have been better. I worked up quite an appetite out there. I'm not going into the office today. I'll go tomorrow. I'd really like to go to Pronzi's tonight for some lasagna. Okay with you?"

"Sounds good. We haven't been there in a long time. I'll make a reservation for seven o'clock, if that's all right with your stomach."

"Wonderful, thanks." John was greatly relieved it didn't take an act of Congress to get Anna to agree to go.

Dinner that night at Pronzi's was delicious as always, perhaps more so due to the prolonged period of time since the two of them had last been there. They were home by nine o'clock and went to bed early. Fortunately, the two of them each had a good night's sleep, which was not the norm these days.

Chapter 4

On Saturday morning, Anna woke up at six. It was still dark outside, and she was tempted to roll over and go back to sleep. Her commitment to get in shape prevailed, however, so she got up and changed into running attire. John was still sleeping when she left the house. Stepping outside, Anna saw that the sun was just beginning to rise over the Atlantic. She decided to run along the ocean road to fully take in the magnificent view of the sun slowly ascending over the water. It had been much too long since she'd last done this. As she ran along the gorgeous coastline, Anna checked her watch and saw that she was clipping along at a nine-minute-per-mile pace. Not bad considering how long it had been since she last ran, but still nowhere near the seven-minute tempo she had consistently achieved when working out regularly.

As she headed south into central Palm Beach, Anna began to tire and looked at her watch. It had been forty minutes since she began running, so she had covered around four-and-a-half miles. Heading west to the Intercoastal bicycle and pedestrian path, she ran for another fifteen minutes before walking the rest of the way back home. Anna estimated she had run nearly six miles and felt a sense of exuberance over her accomplishment. Exercise, as she knew, was a great form of stress relief and clearly needed to be a part of her daily routine again.

Strolling along the Intercoastal route, she thought about her best friend, Tess Milan. Sunday morning tennis matches with Tess had been an important part of her conditioning program—as well as a source of emotional venting—and Anna wanted to reestablish that connection. Tess lived only a mile from the Taylors, and knowing that Tess was an early riser, Anna decided to walk by her house to see if Tess would be available tomorrow for a game. As Anna approached the Milan's home, she could see Tess in the driveway loading her van with boxes.

"What's up so early on a Saturday morning?" shouted Anna.

Spinning around from loading her van to see who was hollering at her, Tess saw that it was Anna, dropped a box, and ran to her with outstretched arms.

"Be careful, Tess. I just finished running six miles, and I'm soaking wet."

Not caring, Tess hugged Anna and gave her a kiss on the cheek. Then realizing just how sweaty Anna was, she recoiled in mock disgust and exclaimed, "You weren't kidding! You really stink!" Both of them started laughing. When she was able to regain her composure, Tess asked Anna if she really did just run six miles.

"I sure did, and I'm very happy about it. In fact, I felt so good doing it that I came by to see if you're up for a tennis game tomorrow morning at seven—but only if you promise to take it easy on me. You know it's been a long time since I've played."

Tess swallowed hard, knowing how difficult life had been for Anna in recent months, but she smiled and responded cheerily,

"You better believe I'm up for a game tomorrow, but there's no way I'm going to take it easy on you. This may be the only time I'm able to beat you!" They both laughed, looking at each with knowing eyes.

Not wanting to become emotional, Anna began walking away, explaining that she left the house while John was sleeping and didn't leave a note as to where she was going. "I need to get home before he worries," Anna said.

Tess called after her, wishing her a good day and confirming she'd see her the next day for their big match.

Anna entered the code on the garage door opener, and as the door lifted, she noticed John's car was gone. She found a note on the kitchen counter. John said he had woken up, noticed her running shoes were missing, and figured she'd gone for a run. He was headed to the office and hoped to be back home by three or four in the afternoon. Anna knew from past experience that three or four likely meant five or six. No matter. She had plenty of test papers to grade today and would likely still be at it whenever he returned.

Meanwhile, John arrived at his firm's law offices located in the heart of Palm Beach just after eight. He noticed George Smith's car was already there. *Nothing unusual about that,* John thought. The "Old Man," as his coworkers referred to George— although never to his face—was as much a workaholic now, even at the age of 65, as he was when John first started working for the firm some twelve years ago. In fact, as incredible as it seemed, the Old Man billed out more hours during 2008 than any of the other ten lawyers in the firm—with the exception of John, who was consistently at the top of the billing pyramid. The firm had done amazingly well over the years. George and his partner, James Patterson, had excellent rainmaking abilities as well as a forte for hiring bright and energetic lawyers and law students who put their noses to the billing grindstone. Even John, who had refused some lucrative Wall Street offers because he didn't want to sell his soul to the corporate gods, had become more and more acclimated to the rigors and demands of the prestigious law practice over the years. Eventually, John had reached the pinnacle of the billing and collection hierarchy.

Although the Old Man and Patterson still controlled the financial pay-out to all the firm attorneys, they had been financially generous to the lawyers who produced monetary dividends, either through their own blood, sweat, and tears; rainmaking results; or some combination of the two. In John's case, they had been very generous monetarily. John had succeeded at not only the acquisition and retention of firm clients, but also at becoming a top-flight civil trial lawyer, and had won several major cases for firm clients.

The Old Man himself was one of the top-rated estates and trusts trial lawyers in the State of Florida, and John had learned well from him. John's legal success and resulting financial compensation did not come without personal cost, however, as he had regularly worked sixty- to seventy-hour weeks. Despite Anna's frequent reminders that he should come home earlier, John rationalized his work decisions on the basis that he was providing security and a nest egg for his family. Over the course of the past year, however, John had frequently, and occasionally bitterly, second-guessed his career decisions. What had once seemed the most appropriate course of action now appeared questionable and unfulfilling, and his sense of significance and purpose was rapidly eroding. But here he was at the office on another Saturday, this time for different reasons. Working allowed him to focus on something other than his upcoming personal criminal trial, the outcome of which held the keys to his future. But, at least for today, he could focus on clients' legal matters and not his own. Or so he thought.

Walking into his office, he turned on the lights and sat down at his desk. A moment later the Old Man appeared with a deeply concerned look on his face. Closing the door behind him, he sat on the leather sofa and unfolded the newspaper in his hand.

"Have you seen this morning's paper?" the Old Man asked.

"No. What's going on?"

"I'll tell you what's going on. There's an article on the front page of the local section about an attorney's upcoming felony DUI trial, and both your name and this firm's name are very prominently mentioned in a less-than-complimentary fashion. I've already received two calls on my cell this morning from clients wanting to know what's going on."

John's face fell. "Did you tell them I was railroaded by an out-of-control legal system and that I'm fighting every step of the way to disprove the State's absurd and frivolous charges?"

"I didn't express it in those terms. I told them generally that we viewed the charges as having no real merit, and we fully expect you to be exonerated."

"So why the worried look?"

"I'll tell you why. We both know there's no telling what a jury will do, and if this thing goes the wrong way, you're looking at losing your law license and going to prison. If that happens, not only will it be unfortunate for you and Anna, but this firm will also have to weather the storm. Frankly, I don't believe you've properly transitioned your cases to other attorneys in case this goes badly. I spoke with Steve Archibald yesterday, and he told me you hadn't met with him, despite my request that you do so. What have you done to get your cases lined up for other attorneys to handle in the event you can't?"

Struggling to control his emotions, John thought hard for a moment and replied, "Look George, I really don't believe I'll be convicted, so I've done no transitioning so far. Even if the trial goes badly, the sentencing won't occur for several weeks after the trial, and in the interim, I'll arrange for the cases to be handled by other lawyers."

"Sorry, John," the Old Man said awkwardly, "but we can't wait that long. I've seen too many unpredictable and unfortunate events transpire over the course of my legal career. I want you to give top priority to transitioning all your cases this week, and I expect a full report from you no later than this Wednesday as to the status. Is that clear?"

"Loud and clear. You've made your point. Now why don't you leave and let me get started on accomplishing your mandate?" John retorted with more than a hint of sarcasm.

The Old Man got up without speaking, let himself out of John's office, and closed the door behind him. John was fuming. He thought of just leaving the office but realized no good would come of that decision. Instead he called Anna to let her know not to wait up for him. He got voicemail as she was in the shower. Later, when Anna heard the message and John's irritated voice, she decided not to call him back.

Anna graded test papers until ten that night. There was still no sign of John, so Anna went to bed. She lay in bed praying, asking God to bring John safely home and to rescue them from this nightmare. She desperately hoped her prayers would be answered.

John did arrive home safely around midnight, but Anna's prayer for deliverance from their ordeal would be answered in a way she neither expected nor was she prepared for.

Chapter 5

The next morning Anna was awakened by her cell phone alarm at six thirty. She had set the alarm on a low tone so it would not disturb John, but he was already up and in the shower. Anna quickly changed into her tennis outfit and headed to the kitchen for a glass of orange juice. As she finished her drink, John appeared, looking very agitated.

"What's wrong?" she asked.

" Well, I didn't get home until midnight last night, and I'm headed back to the office now for another fun day of dictating case status and strategy memos to some of the other lawyers in the firm—all courtesy of George ordering me around like I was some associate. Just because he saw an article in the paper yesterday about the trial starting up next Monday, he started flipping out and began issuing directives about making sure all my cases were transitioned properly."

"What did the newspaper article say to make him act like that?"

"Nothing much. Just that the DUI case against me for hitting Anthony Luciano's car was going to trial. What I think set him off was that the story said I worked for the 'prominent Palm Beach law firm of Smith & Patterson,' and that Luciano was a quadriplegic as a result of the collision. George got some calls from clients wanting to know what was going on. He told me that he low-keyed it with them, but he really freaked out on me."

"I'm not getting why George is making you transfer cases to other lawyers. Does he think you're going to be convicted?" With that question, tears started to stream down Anna's cheeks.

"Listen Anna, don't you start with me again about this conviction business! You know how conservative George is. He's always got to have backup plans for everything and is constantly driving all the lawyers nuts with his emergency contingency plans. If Smith & Patterson didn't pay big bucks to the attorneys who work for them, no one would put up with that bull! And besides that, he's not a criminal lawyer and knows nothing about how DUI cases work."

John was obviously becoming agitated. Anna knew that no good would come from further discussion along these lines and decided to change the subject.

"I'm headed over to meet Tess at the Club for a tennis match. After that, I'm coming home to change, and then I'll head to St. Gregory's for the 9:30 Mass. Do you want to meet me there?" Anna already knew what the answer would be, but she asked anyway.

"No," John said. "I've got too much on my plate right now. Don't hold me to it, but maybe I'll go with you next Sunday. I guess it can't hurt to ask for help with the trial outcome."

A tiny step in the right direction, but Anna would take it. John had not been to church for several months, and she didn't know if she would ever get him to go back. For years they had faithfully attended Sunday Mass, but now faith, or the lack of it, was a big issue—especially for John. He had been very religious throughout his life. In fact, when John was twelve years old and first became an altar boy at St. Peter's Church in Downers Grove, he was so enthused about his role that he thought for several years of becoming a priest. Although John eventually decided becoming a priest was not what he was called to do, he maintained a faithful and trusting relationship with God and had accepted Jesus as his Lord and Savior. Over the course of the past year, however, John's faith and trust in both God and Jesus was becoming more and more questionable. Anna's faith and trust were also under attack, but so far she was managing to hold on to her beliefs in the goodness and righteousness of God and His Son with the help of her pastor at St. Gregory's Church.

Anna decided not to verbally respond to John's comment regarding going to church next Sunday. Instead, she gave him a hug and a kiss and left for the match with Tess. When she arrived at the Club, Tess was already there warming up and had hit several dozen balls across the court from her serving position. At 5'10" tall and 140 pounds, she was 4 inches taller and 20 pounds heavier than Anna and could easily outmuscle her on the court. Although stronger than Anna, however, Tess didn't have Anna's quickness and agility, which usually resulted in close games. Both of them were extremely competitive, and although Tess knew she should take it easy on Anna today, it would be hard to do if Anna started succeeding. No issue there, as Anna was so rusty that she didn't come close to taxing Tess. After about an hour of mediocre play on her part, Anna decided to call it a day.

"Sorry about the poor performance today," said Anna. "I had a great run yesterday, but just couldn't get it going out here today. I don't want to quit though. Next Sunday I can't make it because I want to go to church with John, and I'll need to keep him focused in the morning. How about two weeks from now?"

"Sounds good. You've got a match." Tess said. Pausing, she looked down for a moment, and then asked hesitantly, "Anna, I saw in the paper yesterday that John's trial is starting next Monday. How's he doing?"

"Not very well. George Smith also saw the article yesterday and gave him a hard time at the office. We were very lucky the press never picked up on the accident or charges before. This whole issue of negative publicity never came up until now. At least John and the law firm didn't have to deal with that over the past six months."

Putting her arm around Anna's shoulder, Tess squeezed her and said, "I want you to know that I've been praying every day for the two of you. With the terrible grief that you've already been through, I hope and pray that John will be cleared at the trial and the two of you can put these terrible tragedies behind you."

With that comfort to warm her, Anna replied, "I want you to know how much I appreciate your friendship and support. You've been a wonderful friend to me, especially over the past year. Thank you so much for everything you've done. I don't think I could have made it without you." After embracing each other for what seemed like several minutes, they said their good-byes and got in their cars to return to their homes.

When Anna arrived home, she quickly showered, changed, and got back into her car to head to St. Gregory's Church for Mass. Located on the south side of West Palm Beach, the drive to church only took about twenty minutes. She arrived just as the service was beginning. Father James Anderson, the pastor at St. Gregory's, was celebrating the Mass. He had been a priest for the past forty years and the pastor of St. Gregory's for five years. Tall and slightly overweight, with gray hair and oversized brown spectacles, Father Anderson was well liked by the parishioners both for his humble, godly ways and his short homilies. The pastor had been a godsend to Anna and provided her with words and acts of encouragement and comfort. Father Anderson had also reached out to John, but with little, if any, success. That troubled the good pastor deeply, and with great resolve he continually looked for ways to bring some peace and comfort to John. Admittedly, it was a tad bit difficult to do when John declined to attend services.

As he greeted the parishioners following Mass, he saw Anna and warmly inquired about John. Anna said she was hoping John would join her at Mass next week. She also told Father Anderson that John's trial was starting the following Monday and asked for his prayers for a successful outcome. Father Anderson was already aware of the charges against John, based upon past discussions with both Anna and John. He assured her he would keep John in his thoughts and prayers.

Before heading home, Anna had one more stop to make. She headed west on Southern Boulevard for about five miles, toward Wellington. Pulling into her destination, she followed the narrow, stone covered road until just before it came to a dead end. Pulling her car off the road and onto the grass, she exited the vehicle and slowly made her way up a slight incline to an area filled with many types of beautiful flowers. Although she hated being here, she was more upset that John had only been here one time—the day they buried Maria! As she stood in front of Maria's grave, she was again overwhelmed with grief. Sinking down to her knees, she wrapped her arms around the gravestone and prayed to Jesus for strength and hope in dealing with her unimaginable, tragic loss.

As she knelt in front of Maria's resting place, her mind returned, as it had hundreds of times in the past, to the night just barely over one year ago when she found Maria cold and limp in her crib. It was two in the morning, and Anna had awakened. Maria had not been up for her one o'clock feeding, which was very unusual. Anna hurried to Maria's room. Turning on the light, she saw Maria lying on her stomach motionless. Picking Maria up, Anna saw that she was not breathing or responding in any way. Screaming at the top of her lungs for John, she carried their precious, lifeless child into the living room where John literally

32

sprinted to her, taking the baby in his arms. By now, they were both hysterical. John frantically called 911, and the paramedics were at their home, along with the police, within ten minutes. Nothing could be done for their tiny, six-month-old infant. She had already slipped from this life into her eternal existence.

After a police and medical investigation, the cause of death was listed as sudden infant death syndrome. None of the medical authorities were able to pinpoint an exact cause for Maria's death, although any suspicion of foul play was immediately ruled out. And although John and Anna each spent countless hours doing their own medical research on the internet, neither of them ever reached a satisfactory conclusion in their own minds as to what caused Maria's death. The suddenness of her death, along with the lack of a precise reason as to why she had died, weighed heavily on each of them. The past year since her death had been a nightmare. In fact, after Maria's burial John vehemently refused to return to the cemetery. He was emotionally distraught at the thought of her body lying there under the ground, in the tiny coffin where she had been laid to rest. He swore never to return to the cemetery, and that served as a continuing source of friction between the young couple.

Although Anna disdained her visits to Maria's gravesite, not going was simply no option. So Anna reluctantly made her weekly visits to the cemetery solo. She tried her best to rejoice in the knowledge that her precious baby's eternal soul was in heaven with her Maker, and she prayed for a new dawn to arrive for both John and her. A new dawn filled with peace, joy, and hope for the future. So far, her prayers for a new beginning had not been answered.

Standing to her feet, Anna reluctantly said goodbye to her beloved daughter. As she made her way back to her car, she wondered how John was doing at the office. John had been very successful as a lawyer at Smith & Patterson, both from a legal performance and a financial standpoint. Although John worked too many hours, and even more so since Maria's death, Anna had to admit—somewhat shamefully—she had enjoyed the monetary benefits of his labors. Anna made a good living with her fifty thousand-dollar-a-year salary, but it was barely a tenth of John's compensation when you added in his bonuses. In addition, John had a lucrative retirement account with the firm and took advantage of very astute investment advice George Smith gave to him. Over the past several years, John and Anna had taken fabulous vacations to many locations abroad including China, Italy, Australia, and Africa. Their home on Palm Beach was worth at least three million dollars after all the renovations they made. At the young age of 37, their net worth already exceeded five million dollars. Anna realized the two of them had made a very rapid ascension up the financial ladder over the past twelve years, and they wanted for nothing from an economic standpoint.

Although Anna always gave thanks to God for their financial blessings, she would gladly and wholeheartedly have given up all their monetary wealth if she could take back her daughter's death and her husband's car accident. But such a deal was impossible, so Anna struggled mightily each day to deal with the realities of life—as they now existed.

Back at the office, John was also struggling. Dictating the case memos was not an easy feat. Psychologically, the task was daunting; the thought of other lawyers handling his cases because he was incarcerated made him want to vomit. Plodding along, he slowly and methodically worked on his task in a manner that would leave no question about him being a team player, especially by the Old Man. If he was convicted, he wanted the other lawyers to be prepared. He shuddered at the thought.

There was another matter that weighed heavily on John as he worked on his case reports. Opening up his desk drawer, he removed a file and flipped to a letter he had received last month from Robert Mayberry. Mayberry was a local personal injury attorney whom Anthony and Elizabeth Luciano had retained to represent them in their claims against John for injuries sustained in the auto accident. John knew Mayberry by reputation only, and that reputation was not flattering from any of the people Mayberry sued or their attorneys. Mayberry was known in local legal circles as being a very high profile, pit bull-type lawyer, who would stop at nothing to get what he considered fair compensation for his clients. Mayberry had made tens of millions of dollars in legal fees on personal injury lawsuits and was generally disliked and not trusted by members of the local bar whom he litigated against. Several attorneys who had defended cases against Mayberry told John he was extremely difficult to work with and always attempted to intimidate them and their clients in order to force a settlement.

Reading Mayberry's letter for the umpteenth time, John did not find anything about the letter to be intimidating or coercive. He did recognize, however, that the letter was really nothing more than a form letter seeking information relating to the insurance policies John had in effect at the time of the accident. John had already sent the letter to his insurance carrier and was told by his agent several days ago that the information sought, as well as copies of the policies, were being sent out to Mayberry. There were two different policies John had in effect at the time of the collision: his underlying auto policy, with liability coverage of one million dollars, and an umbrella policy with a five million dollar coverage cap. Now that Mayberry had been sent the insurance coverage information, John fully expected and was prepared for a civil lawsuit to be filed against him. At least he had a total of six million dollars in coverage, and the carrier also had to provide him with a legal defense, so he wouldn't be incurring any more legal bills. John had registered the car involved in the accident solely in his name and was the only named insured on the policies, so Anna wouldn't be joined in the lawsuit. Although he was concerned about the impending civil litigation, at least that case couldn't affect him like the criminal case could. Or so he thought.

Looking at his watch, he saw that it was already three in the afternoon. Putting the file with Mayberry's letter back inside his desk, he decided to leave so he could catch a few waves on his board. There had been no interruptions on this Sunday, and he had finished about 75 percent of his reports, so he felt justified in leaving. Besides, no one else had made an appearance today. On the way back to his home, he noticed the waves were breaking perfectly for surfing. He couldn't wait to get in the ocean.

Anna wasn't home when he arrived. She had left a note on the kitchen counter explaining that she was grocery shopping and should be back around five. Changing quickly into his swim trunks, John headed to the beach and arrived just as two female surfers were leaving. Neither of them was very subtle in checking him out, and John knew exactly what they were doing. At 6 feet 2 inches tall and 210 pounds, with hardly an ounce of fat on his body and an olive skin complexion to match his dark brown hair and eyes, John was quite the physical specimen. Although he had to admit he enjoyed it when he saw women looking at him, he was totally loyal to Anna and never put himself in a compromising situation. Admiring looks from the ladies were a boost to his ego—something he needed these days.

After about an hour in the water, John decided he'd had enough and headed home. Anna was already there making dinner. She was cooking John's favorite dish, fried chicken with mashed potatoes and homemade gravy. Smelling the fragrant aroma, John snuck up behind her and planted a big kiss on the side of her neck. Anna's heart skipped a beat. She turned around and kissed John passionately. Several minutes passed before they noticed the chicken was burning. It had been too long since they'd kissed each other like that, and it felt wonderful to both of them!

A big smile came across Anna's face. "I guess I hit a home run with this dinner?"

"You sure did. But you hit a grand slam with that kiss," John replied, a look of mischief in his eyes. "My goodness, Anna, how I miss kissing you like that."

"Ditto. Let's not wait so long again."

"Thanks for making this for me. It smells dee-li-ciousssss!"

Anna hadn't heard John pronounce *delicious* that way in what seemed like forever. He had gotten it from his grandfather, who was quite the practical joker and storyteller. John inherited his penchant for frivolity from Pops, as he was affectionately known. How John and Pops used to love playing practical jokes on each other! Anna's favorite memory of their shenanigans was the Christmas when John put a battery-operated chirping bird behind Pops while he dozed in the living room chair. Pops awoke with a start and clamored around the room searching for the crow he thought was in the house. Finally looking behind his chair, he saw the mechanical bird and turned around to see John grinning widely and mouthing, "Gotcha." Realizing his grandson had gotten the better of him this time, Pops laughed so hard he looked like he would explode. When he finally calmed down, Pops congratulated John on his trick and gave him a kiss on the cheek.

"My gosh, John. When you pronounce *delicious* like that, it makes me think of Pops and the way you two were always trying to outdo each other with your practical jokes. It's so good thinking back on those happy times," Anna said.

John managed to smile at her comment but said nothing in response. She could see that the jovial moment was over. Although short in duration, she silently thanked the Lord for the passion and laughter and prayed for more joyous moments.

John asked if she wanted a glass of wine with dinner. Although John hadn't drank any kind of alcohol since the accident, he didn't mind pouring her a glass of wine and occasionally asked if she would like some with dinner. She sometimes said yes, but tonight Anna wanted to savor the moment they just experienced without any possible influence of alcohol. Besides, she was never much of a drinker. She politely declined his offer, asking instead for a glass of iced tea.

After dinner, John thanked Anna again for the awesome meal, cleaned up the table, and told her he needed to get some more work done in the den. She decided to watch some TV in their bedroom and fell asleep around ten. John came in shortly after, shut the TV set off and laid in bed, his thoughts vacillating between his upcoming trial and the work week ahead, which he dreaded almost as much. Finally, around eleven thirty, he fell into a deep sleep. For a short time he escaped from his troubles and what lay ahead.

Chapter 6

Monday morning rolled around too quickly. Both John and Anna left the house precisely at seven. It only took John about ten minutes to arrive at the office. He was the first one in, and he hoped he'd get some quiet time before the morning's craziness began. No such luck. Steve Archibald soon appeared at his door. Steve started at the firm around the same time as John and was also a partner. At the moment, John and Steve were the only other partners in the firm besides the Old Man and Patterson. The other seven lawyers were associates, and the partners kept them busy. Steve, although much smaller in stature than John, was every bit as tough and formidable a litigator. As Steve closed the door, the look on his face and the amount of files in his hands led John to believe this would be no quick conversation. He was right.

Taking a seat in one of the leather chairs in front of John's desk, Steve sighed deeply and hesitated for a few moments before speaking. "First, John, let me say how sorry I am for all the trouble you've been going through. I know that with everything that's happened, it's put a terrible strain on both Anna and you. That being said, I need to let you know I got a telephone call yesterday from the Old Man complaining about what he thought was your cavalier attitude in arranging for the transition of your cases."

Saying nothing in response, John sat forward in his chair with his best trial lawyer poker face, staring directly into Steve's eyes and just waiting for the next words out of his mouth. At this point their friendship teetered on the border of extinction.

"Apparently, the Old Man's biggest concern is the Abernathy litigation. He was in the office Sunday night going through the files and felt the case wasn't properly set up to go to trial in three months. He knows the client won't tolerate any delays, but with $25 million bucks on the line, he's worried we're not ready to go to court. He wants me to take over this case immediately." Motioning towards the stack of files in his lap, he continued. "He left these files on my desk to go over with you today. I need to get a sense of where we stand and report back to him."

At this point, John had heard enough, and he let Steve know it.

"Listen, Steve. What you heard from George is absolute bull! You know as well as I do that he always overreacts when cases come close to trial. I've been on top of this matter for the past two-and-a-half years, and I can assure you the case is ready for trial. Have you ever known me to be unprepared when a case is scheduled to go to Court?"

"No," admitted Steve sheepishly.

"Well here's the proof!" John thrust a fifteen-page case status and strategy memo regarding the Abernathy litigation that he had dictated over the weekend into Steve's hands. Jayne had typed the memo for him on Sunday evening and e-mailed it to his home for review so it'd be ready first thing Monday morning. Silently gloating to himself that he had one-upped the Old Man,

John watched with some enjoyment as Steve pored over the document. After about fifteen minutes, Steve put the memo down and looked directly at John.

"Well, it certainly seems thorough to me, and based on what you've said in here, the case appears ready for trial. Let me go through the report and files in more detail, and I'll let George know his worries are unfounded."

"Please do," replied John, with more than a touch of sarcasm in his voice.

Ignoring his comment, Steve indicated that the Old Man also wanted him to prepare to assume responsibility for John's other fifteen active files—just in case. John thought it was interesting how Steve would find the time to supervise those matters in addition to the very full plate of litigation cases he was handling, but decided not to ask any questions.

"When can I expect to see the other case memos?" inquired Steve.

"You'll have them this Wednesday, just like I told George."

"Okay, good enough. Thanks." Steve got up with his copy of John's memo and the Abernathy files and left the room. John started thinking that Archibald had failed to show any real concern over his and Anna's plight and began to see him as just a puppet of the Old Man and Patterson. Twelve years of friendship seemed ready to go straight down the drain!

Changing the focus of his thoughts to the two senior partners, John decided to give both of them a piece of his mind. How dare they not trust him after the twelve years of hard labor and great legal results! But, his vindication would have to wait.

Jayne Sayers, his secretary of ten years, walked into his office. "I've been trying to get in here for the past hour. I can't believe Steve was with you that long. What did he want? And did the memo I sent you last night come out all right?" She was better than John at quickly firing off compound questions and demanding an immediate response. He always told her she'd make a dynamite attorney, but she wanted no part of that scene. At forty-seven years old, she had worked as a legal secretary for twenty-five years and knew full well how stressful it was for trial lawyers like John.

Dressed impeccably in an expensive outfit purchased on Worth Avenue, Jayne was the picture of sophistication—and an outstanding legal secretary. John recognized what an important asset she was to his practice, and his clients often reminded him of it. He and Jayne enjoyed an excellent working relationship, and John was very generous in paying her monetary bonuses from his own pocket to supplement the more modest ones she received from the firm.

Responding to her questions in reverse order, John replied, "The memo came out excellent as always. Thank you. As to Steve, the Old Man sent him in to make sure I wasn't dropping the ball on getting the other attorneys up to speed if I get sentenced to jail."

"That will be quite enough of that kind of talk, John Taylor." She always called him by his full name when he made negative comments or needed to be reeled back in from some other less-than-gracious response to a stressful situation. "In another two weeks, this whole unfortunate event will be behind us and you'll be as busy as ever, driving me crazy as always." A big grin was on her face. Jayne really was a master at handling John, and he knew and greatly appreciated it. Her use of the words this whole unfortunate event will be "behind us" not "behind you" wasn't lost on him. How he wished he could believe the other three partners felt that way—that it wasn't just about them or the firm but about "us."

As Jayne was leaving, Donna Hughes popped in. His office was starting to feel like a parade stop. He'd never finish the rest of those case reports if this kept up. But there was no way he could be less than hospitable to Donna. She was the most senior associate in the firm, coming straight from law school to Smith

& Patterson seven years ago. When she arrived, Donna had been assigned to work with John, and he had served as her mentor since then. Donna was on the verge of being named a partner and deservedly so. She had progressed from being a raw associate to an experienced and talented trial attorney, one who was respected and trusted by all the judges. All this was due in no small part to John's training and guidance, much in the same way John had developed into an A+ lawyer based on the Old Man's tutelage. The comparison, however, was lost on John, at least under the present set of circumstances.

"What's up, Red?" asked John. Donna had shoulder-length, flaming red hair, and John had nicknamed her "Red," just as he had coined the nickname "Old Man" for George. Unlike George's sobriquet, the attorneys and staff frequently referred to her directly as "Red" because she viewed the name as a term of endearment. Red was married to George Hughes, a Palm Beach dentist, and they lived only a couple miles from the Taylors. The two couples frequently socialized with each other, at least they had before Maria's death, and John and Donna maintained an outstanding working relationship. They each trusted the other implicitly.

"I just wanted to come by and see what I could help you with this week," replied Donna.

"I'm in the process now of preparing and forwarding to Steve copies of case status and strategy memos on all my cases. I'll send you copies to look over to see if you're in agreement with my thoughts."

"Why in the world are you doing that now? Of course we all hope and believe you'll be acquitted next week, but even if you aren't, which is highly unlikely, why couldn't that be handled in the interim before sentencing? You're certainly no flight risk, and the Court would allow you to remain free on bond at least through sentencing."

Although she was dead on with John's thinking, and he

wanted to scream out that it was because the Old Man was an idiot, he restrained himself. "We're trying to be especially cautious and prudent in representing our clients' best interests. That way, if something goes wrong, the firm will be prepared for the change. And if everything goes according to plan, the memos can still be used in proceeding forward on the cases."

Although he disliked taking this bullet for George by saying something he really didn't believe, he didn't want to alienate Donna from the other partners. She had worked much too hard to be passed up for partnership because of any dispute over how he should be treated. This was his battle, not Donna's. She would be facing plenty of her own in the future and didn't need to be involved with this one.

"Okay, if you say so. I'll read the memos as soon as you get them to me and send Steve and you my thoughts." John thanked her, and she left his office still uncertain and uneasy about why they were proceeding this way.

John still had unfinished business. He needed to meet with the Old Man and Patterson, and he asked Jayne to set up a meeting as soon as possible. Five minutes later, she let him know that the conference would take place at three o'clock. This gave him a few more hours to work on the case reports. Not much was accomplished as the remainder of the six associates each stopped in to see him during that time. They all wanted to express their support and well wishes with the trial. All of them offered to assist John in any way possible, which came as no surprise because he was very well liked and respected by all the associates. However, his popularity with the three other partners was now suspect, at least in John's eyes.

At precisely three, John headed for the Old Man's office. Punctuality was a virtue he had learned from both senior partners. The Old Man's door was closed, so he vigorously rapped on it. Being invited to enter, he went in and saw that James Patterson was already there. Both Patterson and the Old

Man were sitting at a table on one side of the office, and George motioned for John to take a seat. The table was covered with files, some of which John recognized as cases he was handling. But there were also other files there that didn't look anything like Smith & Patterson files. John wondered what they could be.

"John, I'm glad you set up this meeting. Jim and I have a number of issues we need to discuss with you," said the Old Man.

"Likewise," replied John.

"First, let me say that we've already spoken with Steve, and he advised us that he's reviewed your status report and the Abernathy files, and everything appears on track for the case to be tried in three months. Thank you for that." Seeing the irritated expression on John's face, the Old Man stopped for a second to ask what was wrong.

"I'll tell you what's wrong, George. Your coming in here Sunday night to review the files, after I already told you everything was on track and that I'd provide you with a case status report. Steve told me all about it and how you felt the case was not ready to be tried. Since when don't you trust me?" John was livid.

At this point, Patterson intuitively injected himself into the conversation. He was well aware that both John and George were extremely strong willed, and the last thing Patterson wanted to happen was for this meeting to degenerate into a shouting match for the entire office to hear.

"John, please calm down. I don't disagree that George overstepped his bounds; but come on, he does the same thing to me, and I'm almost thirty years older than you. So this isn't about a lack of faith in you. It's about George being George."

Smooth as silk. Good cop versus bad cop. John knew exactly what was going on, but he had to acknowledge, at least to himself, that Patterson was right. Smith & Patterson had made quite a team over the years. Both were similar in appearance—tall and lean with senatorial white hair. George wore contacts while Patterson preferred his designer eyeglasses that made him look like a law school professor. The Old Man had the exterior gruffness of a well-seasoned trial lawyer, but he could turn on the charm at the drop of a hat. Patterson, on the other hand, was always suave and polished. John had learned well from each of them.

"Okay, Jim. I'll accept that George was being George." John was now much calmer, and both Patterson and the Old Man were much relieved. At this point, Patterson assumed control of the discussion. "John, we both want you to know we don't lack faith in you. It's just that we have some very tough business decisions to make, decisions that we have thought long and hard about."

"Such as what?" asked John.

"Such as how this firm is going to continue to go forward in the event you're convicted on the DUI charge and can't practice law anymore. As hard as it is for us to think about such a thing, we have a business to run here and need to have contingency plans in the event of an unfortunate outcome. You can understand that, can't you?" asked Patterson.

"I don't understand what you're talking about," replied John, although he suspected what was coming next.

At this point, the Old Man responded. "If you can't practice with us any more, that leaves a huge void in our litigation and trial capabilities. You have responsibility for about 40 percent of our litigation business. Both Steve and I have extremely full plates, and Jim doesn't practice in that area. That leaves only Donna as someone who can assist with the overall management of the cases, but she's not experienced enough yet to handle some of our larger matters without the assistance of a more seasoned trial lawyer. We're very concerned about being able to effectively run this firm without you, so we've had some preliminary discussions with a very experienced and highly regarded estates and trusts and business litigator who could jump in if you're no longer with us."

John was speechless. He couldn't believe what he was

hearing. How could this be? They already had him convicted, sentenced, and replaced!

Patterson jumped back and continued. "All of this is only on a contingency basis. If you're exonerated at trial, this potential acquisition will never occur. No one knows anything about this except George, Steve, and me. And of course, the attorney who may come here. A strict confidentiality agreement has been signed. We just thought we should alert you to the possibility that this acquisition might happen."

"I want to know who the lawyer is," demanded John.

"John, I just got through telling you that a strict confidentiality agreement is in place. Besides, if you're found not guilty and continue with us, what good would come from you knowing who it was? The possible deal will never happen, and we'll all be one big happy family again. That's what we're all hoping will happen."

"And if I do go to jail?"

"Well, eventually you would find out; but at that point, what difference would it make?" Patterson meekly replied.

"Well, if you don't know, I'm afraid I can't help you." With that John stood up, turned around, and started to leave the office. As he opened the door to let himself out, he turned back and said in a very calm, straightforward voice, "The rest of the case status memos will be sent to Steve and Donna by this Wednesday. I'll be here Thursday all day to answer any questions. I won't be here Friday because I'll be with my attorney preparing for trial." He then left the office for the day, stopping only briefly at Jayne's desk to let her know he was leaving and would see her tomorrow.

John decided on the way home that he wouldn't relay any of the day's events to Anna. He was having a hard enough time digesting what had just happened and didn't want or need to further stress her. Fortunately for her, Anna's day was relatively peaceful. Other than a skinned knee on one of her students who fell during recess, the day was quiet and uneventful. Anna had even been able to arrange, without any fanfare from the school administration, for time off the following week to attend the trial. Easy days like this were greatly appreciated in these turbulent times.

Chapter 7

The rest of the week up to Friday came and went without any new problems for John or Anna. On Friday, Anna left for school around seven and enjoyed a quiet day at work. All the arrangements for a substitute teacher for her fifth grade class were put into place for the next week. Although John had told her the trial was expected to take three days, she had been around the legal system long enough to know that delays in court proceedings were not unusual and had her substitute prepared to handle the class all week.

John's appointment with Brisbane to go over his testimony and trial strategy was set for one o'clock in the afternoon. In the morning, John reviewed his deposition as well as those of the other witnesses in the case. While reading his deposition, his thoughts went back to the accident. That fateful night had occurred almost six months ago on a Monday night around eleven thirty. John was in a softball league, and the game ended at eight fifteen. A bunch of the guys wanted to go to O'Shea's Restaurant and Bar for a late dinner and drinks. Although he ordinarily would have gone straight home, he decided this time he'd join in. After calling Anna to let her know of his plans, he headed down Congress Avenue until he arrived at O'Shea's. Going inside, he joined the other players and ordered a steak dinner with a baked potato and broccoli. Although he hadn't planned on consuming any alcohol, the beer was flowing and the guys were all having a good time. Soon he was also enjoying draft Irish beer with the crowd. Time flew by, and around eleven thirty he called it a night and said his good-byes.

As John headed home, he traveled through the intersection of Summit Boulevard and Congress Avenue. Suddenly, and seemingly out of nowhere, a dark-colored car appeared. John slammed on his brakes and did his best to avoid a collision. Unfortunately, he was unable to do so and hit the car straight on the driver's side door. The impact of the collision sent both cars spinning wildly out of control, and the other vehicle flipped over and landed on its roof. John's car remained upright but was also a total wreck. There were no witnesses to the accident. The first person on the scene appeared about two minutes after the collision and called 911. Shortly after, the police and paramedics arrived. Anthony Luciano, the other driver, was unconscious. The paramedics transported him to West Palm Community Hospital via a trauma hawk helicopter. John sustained no injuries other than minor bumps, cuts, and bruises and was able to get out of his car unaided. But after a crash scene investigation, John was charged with driving under the influence of alcohol resulting in serious bodily injury, a third-degree felony, due to the severity of the injuries sustained by Luciano.

After the accident, John retained Donald Brisbane as his attorney. Brisbane had a reputation as being one of the best and toughest criminal defense attorneys in Palm Beach County. He had represented hundreds of clients charged with various drinking and driving offenses during his twenty-five-year legal career. Although John had never litigated against Brisbane personally because they practiced different areas of law, John knew him from various bar association functions and had always respected him for his charisma and grit. Brisbane was doing an excellent job in representing John so far in the case, and John was optimistic he would be found innocent of the charges against him. The optimism stemmed partly from having Brisbane on his team and partly because John didn't believe he was under the influence of alcohol at the time of the crash—or otherwise responsible for the collision. John believed, and testified at his deposition, that Luciano was at fault in the accident because he had run a red light. Luciano had no memory of the accident, and there weren't any independent eyewitnesses, so the case was shaping up to be a battle of the experts and the trial skills of the attorneys.

John finished his trial preparations and headed over to Brisbane's office for their meeting. Brisbane was in the conference room, just wrapping up his meeting with Dave Jones, their expert witness. Brisbane's secretary brought John into the conference room, and he was immediately impressed with what he saw. Standing at the side of the conference room table were a series of exhibits prepared by Jones, all designed to prove John's innocence to the jury. Carefully studying each of the exhibits, John could tell the work product was outstanding. He frequently used demonstrative exhibits in his civil practice, and they proved valuable in convincing judges and juries of the merits of his clients' cases. He was confident these exhibits would be a tremendous help in obtaining a positive jury verdict.

"So, Don, these are the exhibits you told me about. They look great," remarked John.

"Dave did a great job in preparing them. We just finished going through his testimony, and I think we've got this lined up for trial just like we want. We believe the jury will be favorably impressed when they see the exhibits and hear Dave's testimony. Now, you and I need to go over your testimony and put the final touches on what will be our shining moment of exoneration with the jury. Of course, that's if the case even goes that far," replied Brisbane in his best trial lawyer bravado.

John really appreciated Brisbane's enthusiasm and confidence in his case. How he wanted to put this sad chapter in his life behind him! Things had to start looking up. How long could adversity keep slapping him in the face?

"Dave, I really appreciate all your great work on my case. I've worked with expert witnesses on my legal cases for many years, and from what I've seen, read, and heard about you from Don, you've really done a yeoman's job. Thank you so much!"

"My pleasure," replied Jones. "I think we've got the better case, and we should get a jury ruling in our favor. We're going to give it our best shot. But as you know John, there are no guarantees with a jury."

The comment irritated John. Jones sounded like a lawyer, a lawyer like himself or even Brisbane for that matter. Always making sure, that at some point, they covered themselves with the "no guarantee as to outcome" statement. He decided to let it go. It was a fact of life that there were no guarantees. No guarantees about anything, as he had fully come to learn.

"Okay Dave, let's call it a day so John and I can get going. I'll call you next Monday at the end of the day to let you know where we stand and when we'll need you. If things go well with our motion with the Judge, we may not need you at all."

"I'll be waiting to hear from you. Best of luck with the Judge. Nice to see you again, John." With that, Jones got up and left, taking with him a bunch of documents for continued review over the weekend. It was a double-edged sword for John. He wanted his expert to be well prepared, but it was costing him big bucks financially, although nothing compared to what he was paying Brisbane. John figured that by the time trial was completed, he would have spent well in excess of $100,000 in legal and expert fees and other defense costs. What choice did he have? He was fighting for his legal career and financial future.

"All right, John. Let's go over your direct testimony first, then cross-examination. After that, we can discuss trial strategy and anything else on your mind."

"Sounds like a plan."

For the next two-and-a-half hours, the two lawyers carefully and methodically proceeded through John's direct testimony. They covered every possible cross-examination question Assistant State Attorney Del Garden might throw at John. Brisbane had fully briefed John on Del Garden's unique and potentially devastating method of cross-examination. Although a small man physically, Del Garden possessed a booming voice, which he could lower to a barely audible whisper or raise to the sound of a roaring lion at the drop of a hat. Del Garden also had great ability to disarm his adverse witnesses by luring them into a false sense of security. He would start out by asking a series of questions that allowed the witnesses to fully explain their answers and provided them with an erroneous impression that they were getting the better of him. Then, when the questions became important, he would change his interrogation style and go for the jugular. Brisbane had seen more than one witness crumble on the stand, and he was determined that John would not fall victim to Del Garden. Of course, the fact that John was an experienced trial lawyer made Brisbane breathe easier.

Just as they were finishing the cross-examination preparation, the phone rang. Brisbane's receptionist said Judge Johnston's judicial assistant was on the line and wanted to speak with him. He put the phone on speaker so that John could hear the conversation.

"Hey, Cathy, it's Don. How are you?"

"Great, thanks. The Judge wanted me to call both Paul and you to let you know that his murder trial is taking longer than expected. It won't be over until the end of next week, and then he's out on a two-week vacation. So he decided, with the Chief

Judge's approval, to have your case tried next week by Senior Judge Jeff Stacey. Judge Stacey doesn't know your client or any of the witnesses the parties might call, so there don't appear to be any conflicts. The file has already been sent to Judge Stacey to start reviewing. Judge Stacey would like the lawyers and Mr. Taylor to be in the courtroom at seven thirty Monday morning so he can hear any outstanding matters before the jury panel is called up around nine. I've already spoken with Paul to let him know."

"Okay. You're as thorough as always, Cathy. Thanks for the information. We'll be there Monday at seven thirty," replied Brisbane.

After he hung the phone up, he saw John sitting there with his eyes closed and his head bowed. Before he could say anything, John stood up and said, "Isn't Judge Stacey an old, crusty, conservative judge who is pro-prosecution? I don't know any of this personally, because I never had any cases in front of him, but that's the rap I've heard."

"I agree that Stacey is old, crusty, and conservative, but I don't agree he's pro-prosecution. Before he went on senior status, I had many cases in front of him and never felt he was biased in favor of the State. The rap you're really talking about was that he was known to be pretty tough on defendants who were convicted in terms of sentencing, but I never had any issues with him giving both sides a fair shake in the trial process."

"Well, I guess I better hope the jury sees the light of day and finds me innocent. What's our chances he'll rule in favor of our motion to suppress the State's expert's opinion?"

"I knew you were going to ask me that. I'll give it to you straight. I will still give it my absolute best shot. But Stacey is a conservative guy who's just coming into the case, and the safer course of action, as you know, is to let the jury decide."

"That's what I thought you'd say. With the way everything's been going for me, why should I expect anything different?"

John was really dejected, and Brisbane knew he needed to bring him back up.

"Listen, John. I know this comes as a last minute surprise that neither of us wanted. But I also know that as an experienced civil trial lawyer, you've had cases where nothing seemed to go according to plan, and you had to roll with the punches."

"That's true."

"Besides, think back to just a few hours ago when you walked in here and saw Dave's exhibits. You remarked on how great they were, and you're absolutely right. Between Dave, you, and me, we'll give Del Garden the fight of his life. He'll never know what hit him, and when he wakes up, you'll be a free man, walking out of the courtroom with all this behind you. So cheer up, my friend. We will prevail."

"Thanks for the encouragement. I've delivered a similar message to many of my clients when we were preparing for trial and they felt intimidated by the whole process. It's just that now *I'm* the client, with *my* butt on the line. But you're right—all of us need to keep a positive attitude. For me to go to court Monday with a sad-sack look or attitude would be suicide. So I'll step up to the plate, and we'll give Del Garden the fight of his life."

"That's exactly what I wanted to hear. Now go home and get some rest this weekend. And please give my best to Anna."

When John arrived home, Anna was sitting in the living room intently reading something. In fact, she was in such a state of concentration that she didn't acknowledge John's presence.

"Hey, Anna. What's got you in such a hypnotic state?"

"About twenty minutes ago I heard the door bell ring. When I answered, I was served a summons. It's a civil lawsuit filed against you on behalf of Anthony and Elizabeth Luciano. I've been sitting here reading it since then. It says they're suing you for in excess of ten million dollars in compensatory and punitive damages. How much insurance coverage did you tell me that you had?"

"I have a total of six million in coverage. May I see those papers?"

Anna got up, handed him the papers, and walked into the kitchen. John could see she was deeply troubled and struggling to keep her composure. He quickly glanced at the Complaint and could now see why the lawyers he had spoken with had such a low opinion of attorney Mayberry, who had prepared and signed the document. It was full of derogatory, incendiary comments against him. In the Complaint, John was being accused by Mayberry of being a drunk attorney who callously and intentionally severely injured Luciano, devastating his family.

The Complaint claimed that because of John's heinous actions, he was responsible not only for money damages to financially compensate the Lucianos and reimburse them for medical expenses, but also for punitive damages to punish John for his drunken driving. Although John realized that the Complaint had been designed to intimidate and attempt to coerce a quick settlement with his insurer, there were two matters that were of deep concern to him. The first was the amount of compensatory damages being sought, which far exceeded his coverage limits. The second was the demand for punitive damages, because any such award would not be covered at all by his policy.

At this point, other than quickly getting the lawsuit papers to his insurance carrier so that a lawyer could be appointed to defend the proceedings on his behalf, John had no desire or ability to focus on this latest segment of the continued nightmare. He had all he could do to deal with the trial starting in two-and-a-half days. This would have to wait but for one other pressing matter! Anna! He needed to go and immediately reassure her that the insurance company would cover the suit and any damages awarded, without conveying his reservations.

Walking into the kitchen, he took Anna in his arms and tightly embraced her for several minutes without either of them talking. Then, taking her face into his hands, he told her how much he loved her and how sorry he was for getting them into this mess.

"John, I love you too, and I don't blame you for anything that has happened. So please don't worry about that. But I do want to know what your feelings are about the awful statements made in those papers, and whether or not you're concerned about the amount of money they're claiming."

Although John hated being dishonest, he felt he had to reassure her.

"Anna, based on what every lawyer told me, I'm not at all surprised about Mayberry's claims and statements against me. He's trying to intimidate me and force the insurance company into a fast settlement. I feel like this suit will be resolved by our carrier paying money to settle within the limits of the policy. First thing Monday, I'll see that the suit gets sent to the insurance company to appoint a lawyer for me. At least we won't have any legal fees to pay because the carrier will pay the lawyer directly. Then, when this trial is over next week and I'm free of that, I'll get with the insurance company lawyer and plan our strategy. So to answer your question, I'm really not concerned about this suit, and you shouldn't be either."

"That's what I needed to hear. Thanks, Honey."

John hoped his words wouldn't come back to haunt him. But for now, there were more pressing matters to focus upon.

Chapter 8

"Okay, John. Let's get moving! We've only got thirty minutes until church begins, and it takes us twenty minutes to get there. I don't want to be late." Although somewhat aggravated at John's tortoise-like movements, Anna was relieved she was able to get him to go to Sunday Mass.

"I'm coming, Dear. I just had to brush my teeth, and now I'm ready to roll. We'll be there with time to spare. Where are my keys?"

"Right where you left them. On the kitchen counter. Let's go!"

Traffic was light on this early Sunday morning, and the Taylors arrived at St. Gregory's with time to spare, just as John had predicted. Father Anderson was standing in the back of the church greeting the parishioners as they walked in. A big smile came across his face when he saw John and Anna.

"Welcome! It's wonderful to see the two of you today." He embraced Anna and then extended his hand to John and asked,

"John, would you mind waiting for me after Mass? I've got something I'd like to give you."

John really didn't want to stay and talk or get something religious from Father today. He was having a hard enough time even being there, but he didn't want to embarrass Anna or himself by refusing.

"Sure thing, Father. See you then."

Taking their seats in the middle of the church, in the row where Anna always sat on Sunday mornings, John looked around and saw that the building was full of people, just as it had been last time he was here several months ago. Father Anderson was very popular with the congregation, and it was standing room only once again. As the Mass progressed, John became more and more involved in his own thoughts and didn't hear a word of the sermon.

"Dear God," he thought, *"how has this happened to Anna and me? First our daughter was taken from us in the middle of the night for no reason. Then this awful car crash that wasn't my fault, and now I'm facing possible jail time—which means not being with Anna and losing my career. On top of that, some guy who lives for bleeding people dry sues me for millions and millions of dollars. I know I'm far from perfect, but why did all these terrible things happen to me? And what about Anna? She is one of your most loyal and obedient children, yet you've chosen to devastate her like this. How could you?"*

Tears started rolling down John's face, and he did his best to wipe them off without attracting any attention. Anna, however, saw him out of the corner of her eye. She was careful not to let him know. Anna didn't want to do anything that would give John reason to not attend church. Although she was waging a continual battle with her own demons, Anna knew John was becoming more and more alienated from God, and this worried her greatly. Anna silently thanked God for John's presence at church and asked Him to protect them. She prayed they would be able to overcome this ever-present state of adversity and that he would be found not guilty at the trial. Anna was placing her hope and trust in the Almighty once again. She wondered if her prayers would be answered, and if so, how. Only time would tell.

As they walked out of church, Anna reminded John that Father Anderson wanted to give him something. She had seen the priest disappear into a side room at the back of church and assumed he had gone to get his gift for John. At that very moment, the door swung open, and the pastor appeared with a plastic, laminated card in his hand.

"John, this is what I wanted to give you." With that, he handed John the card.

"A dear friend gave me this prayer several years ago. It's helped me through some very difficult times, and I pray it provides you with peace and comfort. Rest assured that both you and Anna are, and will continue to be, in my daily thoughts and prayers."

John wondered to himself what "very difficult times" the priest had been through. After all, Father Anderson had no family, wanted for nothing monetarily since the parish paid all his expenses, and, as far as John knew, had never faced the prospect of losing his liberty or profession. How could he possibly identify with what John was going through?

John managed a weak thank you. Anna gave Father a kiss on the cheek and told him how much they appreciated all he had done for them.

On the way back to the car, Anna asked John what he thought of the homily.

"Wonderful," he replied.

Anna knew John didn't hear a word of the Father's message but thought back to the tears she saw him shed and decided not to press the issue. Instead, Anna decided she had nothing to lose by asking John to go to the cemetery to see Maria's grave. After they got in the car she asked, "How about if we take a trip to the cemetery? We don't have to stay long, but it would be nice for the two of us to go together."

"Anna, please don't do this to me. There's absolutely no way I can go there with this trial starting tomorrow. It would only make me more stressed than I already am. Maybe after I get a jury verdict in my favor, we can go next week. Don't hold me to that but maybe, okay?"

"Okay. Can I see the prayer card Father gave you?"

Anna began reading the words silently and paused part way through. "Oh my gosh, John! This prayer is awesome. Let me read it out loud to you."

"Go ahead," John replied half-heartedly.

Anna started reading the prayer verbatim as it appeared on the card:

"In Times of Trouble and Doubt"

Dear God, it is now that I need You most during these turbulent and dark hours.

Please help me to remember Your plans are not to harm Your children but to prosper them.

Please help me to remember that with faith as small as a mustard seed, nothing will be impossible for me, and I will be able to move this mountain of trouble that stands before me.

Please help me to remember that I should not be concerned with storing up riches here on earth, as money will never bring true happiness and cannot be brought to eternity.

Please help me to remember that this life, with all its trials and sufferings, is only a temporary and transitory gateway to a new and eternal existence with You, where all tears will be wiped away and peace, joy, and hope will reign.

Please help me to remember that all my prayers are heard and are never ignored, and are acted upon by You based on an eternal and heavenly perspective and not an earthly one.

Please help me to remember that although I may not hear You speak directly to me in response to my calls for help, that You often speak to me through Your other children here on earth.

Finally God, please help me to not only remember but to believe all of these petitions and to trust in You for my well-being and eternal salvation.

Amen.

"What a wonderful, beautiful prayer! That's what we need to think about and focus on now, John. That God is with us now and will carry both of us through these terrible times."

"I'd really like to believe that, Anna. I really would. Let's wait and see what happens this week. If God really is with us, then justice will be done, and I'll be found not guilty."

Anna decided not to respond. Instead, she silently prayed that God would carry both of them through John's trial, no matter what the outcome.

As they traveled home along the ocean road, a fierce storm raged far out at sea, not unlike the storms of life that had engulfed the two of them during the past year. When and how would they find shelter from the storms? The answers to those questions just might determine their destinies—not only on this planet, but also for their eternal existence.

Chapter 9

At precisely seven thirty on Monday morning, Judge Jeff Stacey began his interrogation of counselors Del Garden and Brisbane. He had recently celebrated his seventieth birthday and was compelled by law to retire from the full-time position of Circuit Court Judge. He was, however, allowed to elect Senior Judge status, which got him back into the courtroom on a part-time basis. After only a few minutes, John was wishing Judge Stacey had never returned to the bench. The rap about him being crusty and conservative was already ringing true, based on his verbal exchanges with the attorneys. John hoped Brisbane was right about him not being pro-prosecution in trial proceedings.

After nearly thirty years of serving as a judge, Stacey was accustomed to having total control over his courtroom. If an attorney strayed from the decorum the Judge expected to be observed, the lawyer would promptly be admonished, and an instruction would be given that the offending conduct not be repeated. Although he was only an average-sized man and didn't possess a booming voice, Stacey nonetheless managed to assume and maintain command of the proceedings. Both Del Garden and Brisbane were well aware of the Judge's insistence on courtroom etiquette and knew just what he would and would not tolerate. The trial was already shaping up to be a cat and mouse adventure.

"Now that we've got the game rules established, I want to proceed to Mr. Brisbane's motion to suppress evidence," advised the Judge. "I spent the weekend reviewing the Court files and have thoroughly read the motion, the State's response in opposition, and all the cases and other legal authorities cited by the parties. Additionally, I've read all the deposition testimony cited by either party. Based on that, I'm prepared to issue my ruling at this time."

"But your Honor," injected Brisbane, "what about oral argument on those issues?"

"It's not necessary," replied Stacy. "The written materials were more than adequate for me to understand and rule upon the motion. My ruling is that the defendant's motion to suppress evidence is denied, and the State shall be allowed to present expert testimony at trial regarding its position as to Mr. Taylor's blood-alcohol level at the time of the collision. That ruling is without prejudice, Mr. Brisbane, to your right to subsequently make any appropriate motions directed to the expert testimony which is presented by the State."

"Thank you, your Honor." Brisbane knew it was worthless, as well as dangerous, to try to argue with the Judge at this point and made no attempt to do so. At least he had brought the Court's attention to an anticipated legal battle over the State's evidence. He might still get a favorable ruling from the Court.

At this point, all the preliminary matters had been completed, and Judge Stacey instructed the bailiff to go downstairs to the jury room and bring the jury panel to the courtroom. Both Del Garden and Brisbane returned to their seats. Sliding his chair next to Brisbane's, John whispered to him, "Do you still think the Judge is not pro-prosecution?"

"Yes, I do. I told you last Friday that under the circumstances he was not likely to grant our motion. We still have a shot later on in the case to attack their expert's testimony. Let's not worry about that right now, and let's focus on getting the best jury we can, okay?"

"Okay, okay. You're right. I'll focus on the jury panel." Turning around, John saw Anna enter the courtroom. She took a seat in the center of the second row of the spectator seats, just as the two of them had discussed. John looked around the courtroom, and although there were several other people present, he didn't recognize any of them. Suddenly, the back courtroom door sprung open and Bailiff John Simon led in what appeared to be a mass of humanity, some of whom were the arbiters of John's future. Staring intently at all of them, he wondered what he'd gotten himself into.

After the jury panel was seated, Judge Stacey spoke to them for an extended period of time about the jury trial system, their role in it, and the nature of the case some of them would be chosen to decide. The panel had filled out questionnaires given to them by the Court Clerk's office, and the attorneys and John were busy studying them. As strict as Judge Stacey was on most matters in his courtroom, he did not try to control the *voir dire* process and allowed the attorneys wide latitude in questioning the jury panel.

Del Garden started first and took about one hour to question the panel. John thought his questioning was straightforward and businesslike but lacked any personal empathy. He was more like a robot, devoid of any personal bonding with the jury. Although John knew from experience that you could not be overly ingratiating or patronizing toward a jury, there was an emotional chord that needed to be struck, and he didn't think that Del Garden came close to establishing personal rapport with the prospective jurors. That was a good thing for him. He was certain that Brisbane would be much more effective.

Brisbane was next and took about an hour and a half to conduct his *voir dire* questioning. John thought he was more thorough than Del Garden and much better at bonding with the panel. John got the feeling the jury liked Brisbane, which hopefully translated into their trusting him. His spirits were lifting, and he started to feel a tiny release of pressure. Meanwhile, Anna didn't know what to think. She was a novice at the whole jury selection process and was overwhelmed to think some of these people would decide her husband's fate. She thought back on the prayer Father Anderson had given to John yesterday and recited it mentally, as best she could, from memory.

Once the interrogation by the attorneys was completed, John and Brisbane consulted with each other regarding who they thought would make the best jurors for their case. Surprisingly enough, both John and Brisbane positively viewed the six jurors and one alternate who were selected for the trial. This was a good sign! It made John think maybe there was a good God who was looking out for him. How he wanted to believe that!

Judge Stacey thanked the jury panel members who were not selected and sent them back to the Court Clerk in charge of prospective jurors. The six jurors and one alternate were seated in the jury box, sworn in by the Court, and given preliminary instructions. Of the six primary jurors, three were female and three male. All of them were Caucasian. One of the female jurors was a retired banking executive, one was a teacher, and the third was a certified public accountant. The male jurors consisted of a truck driver, an airline pilot, and a retired civil engineer. The alternate juror was a Hispanic female who worked as an aerobics instructor.

Looking at his watch, the Judge saw that it was now twelve forty-five. He decided it was time for a lunch break and dismissed the jury until two. At that time, he advised, the attorneys would make their opening statements and the State would put on its case. He also reminded the jurors they were not to discuss the case with anyone during any of the Court recesses.

Anna met John and Brisbane in the cafeteria during the lunch break. Brisbane grabbed a candy bar and soda loaded with caffeine. John and Anna settled for bottled water. Anna really wanted to know how they thought the *voir dire* went and what they thought of the jury. "I'm very pleased with our jury. This is actually one of the best I've ever had on a DUI case. The Judge was great in giving us free reign over the questions and time he allowed, and that really helped."

"I agree," replied John. "After the way he conducted the *voir dire* and ruled in our favor on your challenges to some of the jury panel, I started to breathe a little easier. You might be right; he may not be pro-prosecution. Anyways, I also think we got a good jury, and I'm comfortable with them."

"Well, I'm relieved both of you feel that way," Anna said. "Never having gone through any of this, I really didn't know what to think." Looking at her watch, Anna excused herself to make a phone call to her substitute at St. Gregory's because she was concerned about how the children were doing. She knew first-hand that teaching twenty-five fifth-graders was no easy task. After speaking with her substitute, Diana Jenkins, she felt relieved everything was going smoothly. Anna headed back upstairs to the courtroom. When she opened the door, she saw that the Judge and jury were all seated, and Del Garden was at the podium ready to begin his opening statement.

After plodding through the standard speech about the jury trial system and their role in it, Del Garden moved on to acquaint the jury with the State's theory of the case and the facts as seen by the State.

"The State has a number of witnesses it will call in support of its case. You will hear from both the investigating officer and the traffic homicide investigator who was called in to assist in the examination of the crash scene, and the circumstances surrounding the collision due to the severity of the injuries sustained by the other driver. You will also hear from the paramedic who was called to the scene to take a sample of the Defendant's blood for purposes of determining his blood-alcohol level at the time of the crash. Also, the State will present expert witness testimony regarding its position as to the Defendant's blood-alcohol level being at 0.08 when the collision occurred. Finally, you will hear the testimony of Anthony Luciano, the driver of the car struck by the Defendant."

John shuddered at both the mention of Luciano's name and the thought of him being wheeled into the courtroom to testify. The State's whole case here, he thought, rested on the State evoking sympathy for Luciano as the helpless victim of a drunk driving attorney. But the truth of the matter was that he wasn't drunk, and he didn't cause the accident. Luciano caused the crash by running the red light. He couldn't wait to take the stand to tell the jury what really happened. He desperately needed to clear his name from the storm cloud that had been hanging over him the past six months. As he had told Anna the day before, if there was a good God watching over them, then justice would be done and he'd walk out of the courtroom a free man.

Del Garden continued with his opening statement for another ten minutes. He finally wrapped it up by telling the jury, "The State will prove to you beyond a reasonable doubt that at the time of the collision, Mr. Taylor was under the influence of alcoholic beverages to the extent that his normal faculties were impaired—or that Mr. Taylor had a blood-alcohol level of 0.08 or greater."

Returning to his seat, Del Garden looked over at Brisbane as though to convey, "Okay, let's see what you've got." Ignoring him, Brisbane got up from his seat and slowly walked to the podium with a look of disgust on his face. The theatrics weren't lost on John, nor was he surprised, as he had pulled quite a few acting stunts of his own during the course of his trials. The real question, as John knew, was what the jury thought. They would all know that soon enough.

As Brisbane delivered his opening statement, John reflected on the difference in appearance and style between the two attorneys. Del Garden stood about 5'5" and couldn't weigh more than 140 pounds. John knew from Brisbane that Del Garden was 55 years old and had worked in the State's Attorney's office for his entire career. Although not physically large, his voice was capable of resonating throughout the courtroom. His salt-and-pepper hair and gray spectacles made him look like a college professor. Brisbane, on the other hand, was a big bear of a man. At 6'5" and 250 pounds., he looked more like a former linebacker than an attorney. His blonde hair and smooth skin made him look much younger than his 52 years. When he spoke, his voice was normally low-pitched, yet very pleasant and soothing. He was clearly capable of verbally expressing his anger, however, and he was about to do so right now.

"Ladies and gentlemen of the jury, the evidence in this case will *never* establish that Mr. Taylor was driving under the influence of alcoholic beverages at the time of this unfortunate accident," Brisbane began. "Rather, the evidence will demonstrate to you that at all times he acted in a very lucid, coherent manner and fully cooperated with the police investigation, even to the point of voluntarily allowing his blood to be drawn at the accident scene. The evidence will further show that the State's investigation in this case is fatally flawed, and their expert witness testimony has no viable basis. It's based on false assumptions that should never have been made by their expert.

"Clearly, the accident that occurred was very tragic." Brisbane continued. "But, Mr. Taylor is not responsible for that accident. The evidence will show that the accident was caused by Mr. Luciano himself, running a red light."

For the next fifteen minutes Brisbane waxed eloquent, laying out for the jury a road map of the events that would take place over the next two days. John was very pleased with his opening statement, and while he continued to be optimistic about the ultimate outcome, he was acutely aware of the uncertainties of the litigation process. During his career, there were trials he'd won that he should have lost, and there were trials he lost that he should have won. The ultimate outcome of this present trial remained to be seen. In the interim, the roller coaster ride with all its peaks and valleys continued.

"All right, Mr. Del Garden. Call your first witness," exclaimed Judge Stacey.

"The State calls Deputy Thomas Greer to the stand," replied Del Garden.

Bailiff Simon quickly exited the courtroom in search of Deputy Greer. Finding the Deputy waiting just outside the courtroom door, Simon led him to the stand where the circuit clerk swore him in. Del Garden then began his direct examination of Greer, initially establishing for the jury that Greer had been a Deputy Sheriff for the past twelve years and had been called to the scene of the accident.

"Describe for us what you saw when you arrived at the scene," Del Garden said.

"Both cars appeared to be totally wrecked. One of the cars had flipped over and landed on its roof. The other car remained upright but had sustained very heavy damage."

"What did you do at that point?"

"I first called for the paramedics, then positioned my vehicle in the middle of the intersection between the two accident vehicles with my lights flashing. I got out of my car and went first to the car flipped over on its roof. With my flashlight I could see that there was one occupant, and he appeared to be unconscious and bleeding heavily."

"Were you able to determine who that person was as a result

70

of your investigation?"

"Yes, his name is Anthony Luciano."

"What did you do next?"

"I went over to the other car and saw that the occupant had exited the vehicle and was standing near it. I asked him if he was okay and if anyone else was in the car with him."

"What was his response?"

"That he had some bumps, cuts, and bruises but didn't think he had any broken bones or serious injuries. He also told me that he was the only person in the car."

"What is the name of the person to whom you just referred?"

"John Taylor."

"Do you see Mr. Taylor in the courtroom here today?"

"Yes," Deputy Greer stated, pointing at John. "He's sitting at the table right there with the blue suit on." John could feel the eyes of all the jurors upon him.

At this point in the proceedings, Del Garden asked the Judge to have the record reflect that Greer had identified the Defendant as John Taylor. After Judge Stacey granted the request, Del Garden continued on with his direct examination of Deputy Greer.

"While you were speaking with Mr. Taylor, did you notice whether or not he appeared to have been drinking alcohol?"

"Yes, there was definitely the smell of alcohol on his breath."

"What did you do after noticing the smell of alcohol on Mr. Taylor's breath?"

"Well, by this time the paramedics had arrived and were attempting to get Mr. Luciano out of his vehicle. They were having a hard time getting him out and had determined he was very seriously injured. So I decided to call a traffic homicide investigator in to conduct the investigation."

"Did a traffic homicide investigator come to the scene?"

"Yes, Bill Hutchins, a traffic homicide investigator with the Sheriff's department came and conducted the investigation."

"I have no further questions of this witness."

"Okay, you may cross-examine the witness, Mr. Brisbane," instructed Judge Stacey.

"I have only a few questions of this witness, your Honor," asserted Brisbane.

"Officer Greer, other than the smell of alcohol on Mr. Taylor's breath was there anything else that Mr. Taylor did or didn't do to cause you to believe he'd been drinking alcohol?"

"No, not really."

"In fact, you never conducted any roadside field sobriety tests of Mr. Taylor, did you?"

"No, I did not."

"So you have no way of knowing whether or not Mr. Taylor was under the influence of alcohol at the time of the accident, do you?"

"No, I don't."

"And Mr. Taylor did tell you that the accident was caused by Mr. Luciano running the red light, didn't he?"

"Yes, Sir. He did."

"Thank you, Deputy Greer. Your Honor, I have no further questions of this witness."

Del Garden had no re-direct questions, and the Court excused Deputy Greer. *So far so good,* thought John. Deputy Greer had not done anything to hurt his case and in fact had helped it. Hopefully that trend would continue.

The next witness called to the stand was the traffic homicide investigator, Bill Hutchins. Del Garden established for the jury that Hutchins was a twenty-five-year veteran of the Sheriff's Department and had worked as a traffic homicide investigator for the past fifteen years. Although there was no death involved in this crash, Hutchins was often called in to conduct an investigation when serious bodily injury was involved and alcohol or drugs were possible factors.

Del Garden also established for the jury that Hutchins had

conducted his investigation and determined that John had been drinking and that a blood test should be performed. Hutchins called in another paramedic because the ones already there were busy trying to remove Luciano from his vehicle and attending to his physical life-support needs. Hutchins testified on direct examination that Luciano had to be transported via trauma hawk helicopter to West Palm Community Hospital. As a result of Hutchins investigation, and the blood test results of 0.08 received from the blood drawn from John, Hutchins told the jury that the Sheriff's Department, in conjunction with the State's Attorney's office, had decided to file Driving Under the Influence of Alcohol charges against John.

During Hutchins testimony, John noticed most of the jurors were busy taking notes of the testimony. This made him feel uneasy, although he did realize that Brisbane had not yet begun his cross-examination of Hutchins. Hopefully, they would again score points with the jury as he felt had been done with Greer's cross. His training as a trial lawyer also caused John to observe the difference in physical characteristics between Greer and Hutchins. Greer was in his early thirties, of average size, with curly brown hair. He spoke softly and was very passive in his demeanor. Hutchins, on the other hand, looked like a professional wrestler with his bald head and bulging biceps. He spoke forcefully and convincingly.

Rising up from his chair, Brisbane slowly approached the podium to begin his interrogation of Deputy Hutchins. Brisbane knew this would be a key moment in the trial and was determined not to let his emotions run away with him. Although he needed to be tough with Hutchins, he didn't want to go overboard with his questions and risk having the jury feel sympathetic toward him.

"Deputy Hutchins, when you arrived at the accident scene, what did Deputy Greer tell you?"

"That there had been a two-car collision. The two drivers were the only occupants in the vehicles. There were no eyewitnesses. One of the drivers, Anthony Luciano, was unconscious and the paramedics were attempting to extricate him from his car. The other driver, John Taylor, did not appear to be injured other than minor bumps and bruises. Deputy Greer also told me he smelled alcohol on Mr. Taylor's breath and decided to have a traffic homicide investigator called in to make an investigation at the scene."

"Deputy Greer never conducted any roadside field sobriety tests of Mr. Taylor, did he?"

"No, he did not."

"And you never conducted any roadside field sobriety tests of Mr. Taylor, did you?"

"That's correct, I did not."

"The reason that you did not conduct any roadside field sobriety tests was because of Mr. Taylor's emotional state after the crash—that you felt the tests might be skewed due to the trauma which he had just experienced. Correct?"

"Correct."

"But you decided to have blood drawn from Mr. Taylor at the accident scene for purposes of having a blood-alcohol test run on the amount of alcohol in Mr. Taylor's blood, did you not?"

"Yes, I did."

"Tell us, please, what made you decide to run a blood-alcohol test on Mr. Taylor?"

"I smelled alcohol on Mr. Taylor's breath. I had already read Mr. Taylor his rights and asked him if he had been drinking. He admitted that to the best of his recollection, he had about four or five draft beers. Mr. Luciano appeared to be very seriously injured as a result of the crash. Taking all of that into account, I decided to call in a paramedic to take a blood sample from Mr. Taylor. The paramedics at the scene were busy attending to Mr. Luciano, so I called for another paramedic."

"Mr. Taylor voluntarily agreed to the blood sample, didn't he?"

"Yes, he did."

"In fact, Mr. Taylor voluntarily cooperated with you in all aspects of your investigation, didn't he?"

"That's correct."

"He was never belligerent at any time during your investigation was he?"

"No, he was not."

"You didn't arrest Mr. Taylor that night, and, in fact, you let him go home, didn't you?"

"Yes, he had cooperated with us in the investigation. We knew he wasn't a flight risk, and his wife came to pick him up."

"You said in your direct examination that the Sheriff's Department, in conjunction with the State's Attorney's office, decided to file Driving Under the Influence of Alcohol charges against Mr. Taylor after the results of the blood-alcohol test came back, correct?"

"Correct."

"Now, if the blood-alcohol test results from the Sheriff's Department toxicologist had come back showing a blood-alcohol level of 0.05 or less, no charges would have been filed against Mr. Taylor, would they?"

Jumping up from his seat, Del Garden roared out, "Objection, that question calls for speculation and a legal conclusion."

Before Brisbane could respond, Judge Stacey replied. "Overruled, the witness may answer the question from his perspective as the lead investigator and arresting officer."

"Your Honor, may we approach the bench?" inquired Del Garden.

"No, you may not. The jury is entitled to hear his answer from his perspective as the lead investigator and arresting officer. Now sit down, Mr. Del Garden." Although fuming, Del Garden knew better than to challenge the Court on the ruling and reluctantly took his seat.

"Deputy Hutchins, do you understand the question and my ruling?" asked the Judge.

"Yes, your Honor."

"Then please answer the question."

"Although I don't know what the State Attorney's office would ultimately do, from my perspective I'm uncertain about what course of action I would have recommended be taken. On the one hand, Mr. Taylor did admit to me that, to the best of his recollection, he had consumed four or five beers. He also showed some signs of impairment with his speech and walking. But as I also mentioned earlier, I elected not to perform any roadside field sobriety tests due to the emotional trauma of the crash. So to answer your question, if the blood-alcohol test had come back in at 0.05 or less, I'm not sure what action I would have recommended be taken. I'd have to discuss that with the State's Attorney's office."

"Thank you, Deputy Hutchins. I have no further questions." With that, Brisbane returned to his seat.

"Any redirect, Mr. Del Garden," asked Judge Stacey.

"No sir."

"All right then. Ladies and gentlemen of the jury, I see that it's almost five o'clock. Rather than start another witness now, we'll break until tomorrow morning at eight thirty. Please remember that you are not to discuss this case with each other or with anyone else. Also, please refrain from reading any newspaper accounts of this case that may appear. Court stands adjourned."

After the judge and jury left the courtroom, Brisbane took the occasion to poke a little fun at John. "Well John, not a bad ruling today with Hutchins from a pro-prosecution Judge, huh?"

"I knew I'd hear that from you; but you're right, it was a great ruling. Let's hope we get some more tomorrow." Turning around, John saw that Anna was still in the courtroom waiting for him. Sitting down next to her, he put his arm around her and gave her a kiss.

"Well, sweetheart, I thought everything went as well as it could today. Don thought so also."

"I'm glad to hear that. It didn't seem like they had a very strong case today, but I'm no lawyer. I just hope that the jury thinks the same."

"I made arrangements with Don to meet him at seven tomorrow morning at his office. You can just plan on being here at eight thirty."

"I'll be here. I've got to run to the grocery store and pick up a few things. See you back at the house."

Chapter 10

As John sat in his car in the parking lot of Brisbane's office, he looked at his watch. It was now 7:05 a.m., and there was no sign of Brisbane or anyone else. Several minutes later, Brisbane pulled his car next to John's and got out carrying two cups of coffee and a bag of bagels.

"I thought we could use a shot of adrenaline before we resumed doing battle, so I picked up some high-test coffee and bagels."

"Good plan. You're always prepared, Don. Just like yesterday. That was a great job in court."

"Let's hope it goes as well today. I can't wait to get their expert on the stand."

After they sat down at Brisbane's conference room table, the conversation turned to the jurors.

"John, I noticed yesterday that four of our six primary jurors were taking copious notes of the testimony. Jayne Hagan, the retired bank officer, and Amber Smith, the certified public accountant, were both writing away. I didn't see Linda Hartford, the high school teacher, taking any notes nor was our alternate, Maria Alvarez, the aerobics instructor. Of the male jurors, I saw Brad Bailey, the airline pilot, and Rob Perkins, the retired civil engineer, both taking detailed notes, but I didn't see Greg Chatsworth, the truck driver, taking any notes."

"I agree, but what's your point?"

"When you take the stand to testify, I'd like you to make certain that you're establishing eye contact and speaking to Hagan, Smith, Bailey, and Perkins. I don't want you to ignore Hartford or Chatsworth, but right now I see those two as going along with whatever consensus is reached by the other four. So focus on those four. Also, at this point, I see Hagan as probably being the foreperson based on her age, job experience, and personality. If that's the case, it will be really important for you to establish a connection with her, so keep that in mind. If anything changes between now and when you take the stand, I'll let you know."

"I knew I was paying you the big bucks for good reason. Excellent advice. I'll make sure I follow it."

"Also, when Luciano is wheeled into the courtroom, please make certain you keep your best poker face on during his entire testimony. Please ask Anna to do the same. We both know that Del Garden will use him to close his case and try to elicit sympathy from the jury. That's the strongest part of his case."

"That's been my biggest fear in this whole mess. That the jury sees Luciano as the innocent victim of an attorney who had some beers and decides that justice calls for a conviction. I'll do as you ask and so will Anna. I'll talk to her as soon as I see her at the courthouse."

"Depending on how Luciano's direct comes out, I may not ask him any questions. If I do, it will be short and sweet because I certainly don't want to alienate any jurors. I just wanted to let you know my thoughts."

"I appreciate that and fully understand. That's why I hired you to make these strategy calls, and I'm with you all the way."

"One last thing," Brisbane said. "Yesterday, a local newspaper reporter named Cassandra Brown called my office looking for some details on the case. Of course, my secretary told her nothing. I think she is going to show up to cover the rest of the trial. Let's have an agreement that neither of us, nor Anna, speaks to her about the case."

"Of course. I don't know her, but I'll talk to Anna and neither of us will talk to any reporters about the case."

"Okay, let's head over to the courthouse. I'll meet you there."

When John arrived at the courtroom, he saw Anna was already there, standing outside the door waiting for him. He immediately told her Brisbane's advice about Luciano's appearance in the courtroom as well as his instructions on the newspaper reporter. As he finished talking to her, a smartly dressed young woman approached the two of them with an inquisitive look on her face.

"Hello, my name is Cassandra Brown, and I'm a reporter with the Palm Beach Daily Chronicle. Are you Mr. and Mrs. Taylor?"

"Yes," replied John. "Why do you want to know?"

"I'm doing a story about your DUI trial and was wondering if I could speak to the two of you about it."

Before John could respond, Brisbane appeared behind the reporter and tapped her on the shoulder. Turning around and recognizing him, she smiled at Brisbane and grabbed his hand. "I was just introducing myself to Mr. and Mrs. Taylor and asked if I could talk with them about the trial."

"Sorry, Cassandra, but you know the routine. Neither the Taylors nor I can talk to you about the case right now. After it's over, I might speak with you. We'll see what happens."

"That's what I thought, but it never hurts to try. I look forward to watching you in court." She then walked into the courtroom and took a seat in the first row.

Following her into the courtroom, Brisbane and John both took their seats at counsel table, and Anna again sat in the middle of the second row. Exactly at eight thirty, Judge Stacey appeared and had Bailiff Simon bring the jury in from the jury room. Judge Stacey then instructed Del Garden to call his next witness. Del Garden called Jessamine Turner to the stand. He progressed through a detailed and methodical direct examination of Turner. The jury learned she had been a paramedic for ten years and had taken hundreds of blood samples in connection with DUI investigations. She also testified to being called to the crash scene to obtain a blood draw from John Taylor. Turner also gave testimony regarding the procedures she had followed in obtaining the blood draw and preserving it. At the conclusion of her direct examination, Turner described how she had brought the blood sample directly to the Sheriff's Office crime laboratory for testing.

During his cross examination, Brisbane questioned Turner regarding both the reliability of the blood draw and the probability John's blood sample had been tampered with. Brisbane's goal was to show that the process by which the blood was drawn and preserved was not scientifically reliable, and thus, the integrity of the results obtained from the sample were compromised. Brisbane got Turner to admit that she could not remember whether there was anything in the blood sample tubes when she took the blood sample from John. However, she did recall that the tubes had a gray stopper. During the cross-examination of Turner, John thought Brisbane did a good job, but he noticed that none of the jurors were taking many notes. He didn't view that as a good sign.

Del Garden's next witness was Peter Dell, a forensic toxicologist with the Sheriff's Office crime laboratory. Dell had worked with the Sheriff's Office for seventeen years and had testified in hundreds of cases. Today he was being questioned as an expert witness regarding the results of John's blood-alcohol test and the effect it would have on his normal faculties, including his ability to drive an automobile. He explained in great detail the testing procedures that he used and the calculation of John's blood-alcohol level through use of the "Widmark Formula."

He then interpreted the test results and testified that John's blood-alcohol level was 0.08 at the time of the crash. Dell also testified that John would have had to consume at least eight beers to have such a blood-alcohol level and that the effect would be a loss of mental acuity, a decrease in good judgment, an impairment of eyesight, and a decrease in distance perception.

At the conclusion of Dell's direct testimony, Judge Stacey called a mid-morning recess. John and Brisbane huddled at counsel table to discuss Dell's cross-examination. Although John was concerned with Dell's opinions, he remained confident that Brisbane would be able to discredit his testimony. After discussing Brisbane's strategy, John turned around and saw Anna at the back of the courtroom motioning for him to come outside. Stepping into the hallway, the two of them took a walk down the corridor.

"John, I'm concerned about that expert's testimony. The jury was definitely focused on him, and many of them were taking notes on what he said. What did you and Don think of him?"

"Don and I were both prepared for what he said. It's consistent with his deposition testimony. I think Don should be able to get him unglued on cross. We'll wait and see."

"I certainly hope so, John. I know I've never gone through anything like this before, but I'm getting really nervous."

"I understand, Sweetheart. Just keep hanging in there. I noticed you were wearing your best game face in the courtroom. Thanks."

Looking down the hallway, John saw Brisbane motioning for them to return to the courtroom. Before entering, John noticed Cassandra Brown, the newspaper reporter, sitting on a bench in the hallway, banging away on her laptop. *No good going on there,* he thought.

Brisbane began his cross-examination with a flourish. He proceeded to attack the reliability of John's blood draw with gusto.

"Mr. Dell, you were not present at the time of the blood draw, were you?"

"No, I wasn't."

"Paramedic Turner testified earlier today that she could not remember whether there was anything in the blood sample tubes when she drew blood from Mr. Taylor. You also don't know whether there was anything in the blood sample tubes when Mr. Taylor's blood was drawn, do you?"

"Well, I do know there was a gray stopper on the tubes and that blood kits with gray stoppers contain an anticoagulant."

"Other than the anticoagulant, you don't know whether there was anything else in the tube before Mr. Taylor's blood was taken, correct?"

"Correct."

"As far as the anticoagulant, there was evidence of that being in the blood tubes, correct?"

"I assumed that there was because the blood from Mr. Taylor was not clotted."

"The anticoagulant could have affected the reliability of the blood samples, correct?"

"No, I don't believe so."

"Why not?"

"The only way the anticoagulant could affect the reliability of the blood samples is if there was none at all in the tubes."

"On direct examination today, you stated it was your opinion that Mr. Taylor had a blood-alcohol level of 0.08 at the time of the accident, correct?"

"Yes, that's correct."

"It's also correct that the time of the blood draw was one-and-a-half hours after the accident?"

"That's right."

"And I believe it's also your opinion that Mr. Taylor had probably consumed at least eight beers in order to cause his blood-alcohol level to register a 0.08?"

"Yes, that is my opinion."

"But you don't know if there was anything else in the tubes, other than the anti-coagulant, when Mr. Taylor's blood was drawn?"

"No, I don't."

Brisbane continued on with his cross-examination for another fifteen minutes. John thought it was very effective and noticed that most of the jurors, particularly Jayne Hagan, were busy taking notes. He felt relieved they were paying such close attention to Dell's cross. There was one other person in the courtroom who appeared to be consumed with note taking—Cassandra Brown. John wished she had never come to cover the trial.

Del Garden had called everyone except one witness. Just as Brisbane and John had anticipated, Anthony Luciano was called and wheeled into the courtroom by his wife, Elizabeth. As she pushed the wheelchair down the aisle, total silence enveloped the room. All eyes of the jury were focused on this man in the wheelchair with his neck brace on, and the woman taking him to testify. John had not seen Luciano since the accident, and he was taken aback at the scene that was developing. Anna was doing everything possible to maintain her composure. Even Judge Stacey, with all his years of courtroom experience, had a concerned look on his face.

With Bailiff Simon's assistance, Luciano's wheelchair was positioned in front of the witness stand, and his wife took a seat in the back row of the courtroom. Del Garden took his place at the podium and began asking him questions.

"Sir, would you please tell us your name and home address?"

"Anthony Luciano and I live at 5896 Cypress Court, Greenacres, Florida."

"Are you married, Mr. Luciano?"

"Yes, to Elizabeth Luciano."

"Is she here now?"

"Yes, she just brought me in."

"How long have you been married to Mrs. Luciano?"

"For fifteen years."

"How old are you, sir?"

" I'm 36."

"Do you have any children?"

"Yes."

"What are their names, and how old are they?"

"Tony Jr. is 12, and Rosie is 10."

"What is your occupation?"

"Right now I'm unable to work. Before the car collision I had my own business as a marble and tile supplier and installer."

"You mentioned an automobile collision. When did that happen?"

"It was around six months ago. I have a hard time with the details because I was knocked out and don't really remember what happened."

"Is there anything you can tell us that you remember about the collision?"

"Well, I've gone through this many times in my mind since then, and there are a few things I do recall."

"What are those?"

"I remember I was working at one of my jobs over in West Palm Beach. The owners were away, and I was trying to get it finished before they came back. So, I was working really late and finished it up. I locked up the house and headed home—west over Summit Boulevard. After that, I really don't remember anything until I woke up in the hospital. I'm sorry, but that's all I can tell you."

"Do you remember anything about how the vehicle collision occurred?"

"No, I can't remember."

"You mentioned earlier that you were unable to work. We all see you sitting in the wheelchair. What happened to you as a result of the collision?"

"Now, I'm a quadriplegic. My spinal cord was severely injured in the accident, and I'm not able to use my arms and legs. The chances of my walking or working again in my business are slim to none."

"Thank you, sir. I have no more questions."

Throughout Luciano's testimony, John noticed all of the jurors seemed spellbound. Although none of them took any notes, it seemed as though each of them were hanging on every word coming out of Luciano's mouth. At this point, he didn't even expect Brisbane to ask any questions.

"I just have a few questions, your Honor," said Brisbane.

"You may proceed," replied the Judge.

"Mr. Luciano, because you don't remember the circumstances of the accident, you personally don't know who was at fault, do you?"

"No, I don't personally know who was at fault."

"And because you don't remember any of the circumstances of the accident, you don't know whether or not you might have run the red light, do you?"

"No, I don't know that."

"Thank you, Mr. Luciano. I have no further questions."

"I have no more questions, your Honor," replied Del Garden. "The State rests."

"Mr. Luciano, thank you for coming. You may be

excused." Luciano nodded his head to the Judge in response and his wife wheeled him out of the courtroom. Once again, all eyes of the jury remained fixated on the two of them. After they left, Judge Stacey addressed the jury.

"Ladies and Gentlemen of the jury, it's twelve fifteen; so, we'll go ahead and take our lunch break. The attorneys and I have some legal matters to take up at this point, so I'm going to give you an hour-and-a-half for lunch. Please be back at one forty-five. Thank you."

The jury left the courtroom, and the lawyers approached the bench.

"Okay, Mr. Brisbane, now that the jury is gone, I assume that you have some motions you want to present," stated the Court.

"Yes, your Honor, I certainly do." For the next fifteen minutes Brisbane tenaciously argued that Peter Dell's expert opinion should be stricken, and the Court should enter a judgment of acquittal in favor of John. The basis was that the blood draw sample had been tampered with, and as a result, should be stricken from evidence and the case dismissed. Additionally, Brisbane claimed that without the blood-alcohol level testimony from Dell, there was no evidence that John was driving under the influence of alcohol to the extent that his normal faculties were impaired. He cited in detail the testimony given by Officers Greer and Hutchins as a basis for acquittal. John thought Brisbane did an excellent job in presenting the motions to the Judge, but noticed the Court did not appear to be buying the arguments. The Judge had a skeptical look on his face and kept drumming his fingers on the bench. After Brisbane finished, Del Garden returned to the podium and ably presented the State's position why the Judge should deny the motions and allow the case to go to the jury.

"Okay, gentlemen. I appreciate the arguments being raised by both sides. It's my ruling that the defendant's motions are denied and this case shall proceed forward for a decision by the jury. In terms of the argument raised on behalf of Mr. Taylor that the blood sample had been tampered with, I find there is insufficient evidence to show a probability that the sample had been tampered with. At best, there is a mere possibility that the blood draw was tampered with, which is an inadequate showing under the law of this State, as set forth in the cases cited by Mr. Del Garden. Also, as to the defendant's argument that there is insufficient evidence that Mr. Taylor was under the influence of alcohol to the extent that his normal faculties were impaired at the time of the collision, I find that there is, in fact, sufficient evidence to go to the jury and allow them to make that determination. Let's break now for lunch. Please be back at 1:40."

Brisbane, John, and Anna got on the elevator to head to the cafeteria. Before the doors closed, reporter Brown slipped in and flashed a big smile at Brisbane.

"Don, I was really impressed with your arguments. You really are as good as everyone says. I thought the Judge was going to rule for you. Too bad he didn't."

"Thanks. Why don't you put that in your article?"

"I don't think so. Good luck this afternoon." The elevator door opened, and Brown disappeared into the crowd in the hallway. John wished she would vanish forever.

No one really wanted any food. All of their nerves were beginning to get frayed from the pressures of the trial. Anna went and got each of them a bottle of water. When she returned, she looked Brisbane directly in his eyes. He knew what was coming.

"Don, it seemed to me, based on my very limited experience, that you did a wonderful job trying to have the case thrown out. But the judge refused to dismiss it and said the jury has the right to determine whether or not John is guilty." Looking pained, she went on, her words spilling out quicker and quicker. "Does that mean he thinks John is guilty, and if so, does that mean the jury thinks that, too? And what about Anthony Luciano being in that wheelchair? It seemed like the jury was totally absorbed with him. What did you think?"

Brisbane could see she was distressed. He needed to give her confidence, and John as well. John was about to take the stand to testify, and there could be no mistakes. Everyone needed to be calm, cool, and collected. So much depended on John's testimony—and the demeanor of John and Anna.

Taking Anna's hands into his, Brisbane replied, "Look, just because the Judge ruled that way doesn't necessarily mean he thinks John is guilty. I wish he'd ruled in our favor, but the safer course of action for him, considering an appellate court is likely to review this case, was to let the case go to the jury. He's less likely to get reversed if he lets the jury rule. It doesn't mean he thinks John is guilty."

Brisbane took a deep breath and continued. "I also don't think the jury thinks John is guilty. I've been getting good vibes from them, and I feel great about that. As far as Luciano goes, John and I always knew that was our biggest hurdle. But when John takes the stand and they the jury hears what really happened, I think we'll be able to overcome any sympathy they may have for Luciano. So don't worry," he said with a sincere smile. "Your husband—and all our witnesses—are going to do a great job, and we'll prevail. Now let's head back upstairs and knock the State's case right out of the courtroom."

Anna breathed a big sigh of relief. Her eyes filled with tears as she said, "Thank you for everything you're doing for us. I can't begin to express how grateful we are." John nodded his head in agreement.

Now that Brisbane appeared to have picked up both their spirits, he hoped there wouldn't be a valley he'd have to climb out from. It was times like these that he wondered why he'd gotten into this line of work.

Chapter 11

"All right, Mr. Brisbane, call your first witness," said Judge Stacey.

"We call John Taylor to the stand."

As John made his way to the witness stand, Anna silently prayed. "Dear God, please help John convince this jury of his innocence. Be with us now, and remain with us through these dark and terrible times—especially if John's found guilty. Without your help, I'm afraid neither of us will be able to endure what may lie ahead." She ended her prayer just as the questioning began.

"Sir, please tell us your name and address."

"John Taylor, 280 Reef Road, Palm Beach, Florida."

"What do you do?"

"I'm a civil trial lawyer with the Smith & Patterson law firm in Palm Beach."

"Are you married?"

"Yes, to Anna Taylor. She's sitting right there," John said, pointing to his wife.

The attention of all the jurors turned to Anna. She managed a small smile in response and then forced her facial muscles to express her best "game face," as Brisbane had requested. As John's testimony continued, she noticed all the jurors were carefully listening to him, and most were taking notes. She also saw that John was making eye contact with the jurors and talking to them in an easy, pleasant manner. Some of the jurors were even nodding their heads at John's answers to Brisbane's questions. Anna viewed their interest in John's testimony and their body language as a positive sign. She hoped it would continue.

"Mr. Taylor, let me focus your attention on the day that the accident with Mr. Luciano happened. Did you go to work that day?"

"Yes, I was taking some depositions at my office and finished around five thirty."

"What did you do after that?"

"I was playing in a softball league in West Palm Beach on Monday nights, and after finishing the depositions, I changed into my playing clothes at work and headed to the field."

"What time did the game start?"

"Around six."

"What time did the game end?"

"Around eight fifteen."

"Either before the game or during the game, did you consume any kind of alcohol?"

"No, absolutely not."

"What happened at the end of the game?"

"Well, usually at the end of the games, a bunch of the guys go out to have a late dinner and some beers. I didn't usually go, but on this particular night I had hit a game-winning home run, and all the guys were on me to go out with them. So I called Anna to tell her what I was doing and then headed to O'Shea's Restaurant and Bar on Congress Avenue in West Palm Beach."

"Were you alone in your car?"

"Yes."

"Did you have any alcohol of any kind while driving to O'Shea's?"

"No, I didn't."

"What happened after you arrived at O'Shea's?"

"When I walked in, there were already a bunch of guys there. They were at two large tables in the back of the restaurant."

"What time was it when you arrived?"

"Around eight forty-five."

"How many guys would you say were there when you arrived?"

"At first, maybe ten or twelve. Eventually, I would say around twenty. They were from both teams that had just played each other. We've got a pretty friendly league, and the players like getting together and socializing."

"Were any of the ballplayers drinking alcohol when you got there?"

"Yes, there were several pitchers of draft beer being passed around."

"Any other types of beverages being served besides the draft beer?"

"Not alcoholic beverages. There were a few pitchers of ice water and soda."

"Once you arrived, did you start drinking any of the draft beer?"

"Not at first. I wasn't really planning on having any beer because I had more depositions to take the next day and needed to be in the office early to meet with a client. So initially I was just drinking ice water."

"At some point, did you drink any beer?"

"Yes. One of my teammates, Joe Casperson, poured me a beer and made a toast to salute me for the game winning home run. That was probably about a half hour after I got to O'Shea's."

"So that would be around nine fifteen?"

"Yes, that's right."

"Did you have any other beers while you were at O'Shea's?"

"Yes, but not right away."

"Would you explain that answer, please?"

"Around nine thirty, dinner came out. I remember looking at my watch because I was really starved. I had ordered a sirloin steak with a baked potato and broccoli. I didn't drink any beer with dinner and had several glasses of ice water. Later on, I did have several more beers before I left."

"When would that have been?"

"Well, I left O'Shea's around 11:20. So I would say that between 10 and 11:20."

"Now, you said you had 'several' more beers. How many do you mean by 'several'?"

"To the best of my recollection, I had a total of four or five beers, counting the first one I drank shortly after arriving. So I believe I had three or four more between 10:00 and 11:20."

"Is there a reason you don't know the exact number of beers you drank?"

"Well, I didn't pay for anything because the guys on my team were treating me for winning the game. I wasn't sitting there counting the beers, but I don't believe I was drinking a 12-ounce beer any faster than one every 20 minutes, which would make a maximum of four more beers after my initial one, and it may have been three."

"When you left O'Shea's to go home, did you feel as though you were under the influence of alcohol?"

"Absolutely not. If I'd felt that way, I wouldn't have gotten behind the wheel of my car. I would have called a taxi. I could have left my car in the parking lot and gotten it the next morning. But there was no reason for me to do that because I was not under the influence of alcohol."

"Tell us what happened on the way home."

"As I pulled out of the parking lot, I looked at my watch and saw that it was 11:25. I headed north on Congress Avenue toward Palm Beach. As I approached Summit Boulevard, I saw that the light was green and started to go through the intersection. All of a sudden, out of nowhere, a dark-colored car approached. I slammed on my brakes and did my best not to hit it, but I couldn't avoid it. I remember there was a terrible screeching noise, and my car was spinning around. Finally, I got it under control and managed to bring it to a stop. At that point, I was in a daze. I had hit my head against the driver side window, and the airbag went off."

"Were you hurt?"

"Physically, I wasn't too bad. I had a big bump on the side of my head, and my left arm was cut up a little. There were a few other bruises but nothing major. Emotionally, I was shook up from the force and suddenness of the collision, especially when I got out of the car and saw the other vehicle lying on its roof."

"After you got out of the car, did you talk with anyone?"

"Yes, Deputy Greer came over and started asking me questions."

"What did the two of you discuss?"

"First he asked if I was okay and if anyone else was in the car with me. I told him I was alone and only had minor bumps and bruises, but that I was really shook up. He also asked how the accident occurred. I told him the other driver had run the red light. I tried to avoid hitting his car, but I couldn't. Then he asked me how fast I was going, and I told him I was driving at the posted speed limit of 40 miles per hour."

"Is there anything else you remember discussing with Deputy Greer?"

"I recall asking him how many people were in the other car and whether they were hurt. He told me the driver was the only person in the car and that he was unconscious. He said he was waiting to hear from the paramedics about the extent of the driver's injuries."

"What happened next?"

"I saw Deputy Hutchins pull up, get out of his car. and start talking with Deputy Greer. After that, both deputies went over to Mr. Luciano's car. They talked to the paramedics who were trying to get Mr. Luciano out of the car, and then Deputy Hutchins came over to talk to me."

"What did he say to you?"

"He told me that the paramedics had advised him that Mr. Luciano appeared to be very seriously hurt. He also asked me how the accident happened, and I told him the same thing I told Deputy Greer about the red light. I also told him about my bumps and bruises and how emotionally distressed I was."

"Was there any other discussion between Deputy Hutchins and you?"

"Yes. He told me that Deputy Greer had smelled alcohol on my breath, and he said he also smelled alcohol on my breath. He then read me my rights and asked if I wanted to consult with a lawyer. I told him no, that I was a lawyer, and that I would answer his questions and cooperate with him."

"So, what did Deputy Hutchins ask you?"

"He wanted to know if I had been drinking alcohol. I told him about my going to O'Shea's after the game and having some beer and food, just as I previously testified."

"Did you tell him how much beer you had?"

"Yes, I told him that to the best of my recollection I had four or five 12-ounce glasses of draft beer, and I had no other alcohol of any type."

"Did Deputy Hutchins ask you any other questions?"

"Yes, he wanted to know if I would voluntarily agree to a blood draw. He wanted to call another paramedic to the scene to take a blood sample from me so they could determine my blood-alcohol level."

"What did you tell him?"

"I agreed to a blood draw, and he called for a paramedic."

"Did a paramedic come to take a blood sample from you?"

"Yes. It took awhile for her to get there, but eventually Ms. Turner, who testified here today, came and drew some of my blood for the sample."

"Mr. Taylor, did you fully cooperate with Deputy Greer and Deputy Hutchins in their investigation?"

"Yes, I did. I answered all their questions and did everything they asked me to do."

"You didn't have anything to hide, did you?"

"I had nothing to hide. I had done nothing wrong."

"Your Honor, I have no further questions for Mr. Taylor."

All of the jurors instinctively turned toward Del Garden, waiting for his questioning of John. As Del Garden approached the podium, John took a deep breath. Testifying as a witness in court was something he had never done, although he had been a trial lawyer in dozens of jury and non-jury trials. This was an infinitely harder role, compounded by being a defendant in a criminal case where so much was on the line.

For a few brief seconds, his eyes locked with Anna's, and it was as though he was looking into the windows of her soul. He could feel her pain. He wished he had never had any beers at O'Shea's. The charges would never have been filed, and she would have been spared this turmoil. Even though he still fervently believed Luciano was at fault and the case against him was baseless, he recognized that his consumption of alcohol had put them in this terrible and potentially life-changing position. There was nothing he could do to change the past, but he was determined to not let Del Garden score any points against him with cross examination.

Del Garden began his cross exam just how Brisbane had predicted. For the first twenty minutes, his questions were mostly meaningless and designed to lure John into a false sense of security. John didn't bite on any of them, and Del Garden knew it. He started to become aggravated and decided that it was time to go for the kill.

"Mr. Taylor, as I understand it, your position is that Mr. Luciano was at fault for the collision between the vehicles because he ran the red light. Is that correct?"

"Yes, that's correct."

"And it's your position that the alcohol you drank had nothing to do with the collision, correct?"

"Yes, that's correct."

"Are you aware there is no evidence of Mr. Luciano driving under the influence of alcohol or any other substance?"

"Yes, I am."

"And you also heard Deputy Hutchins testify that there is no evidence Mr. Luciano was speeding, didn't you?"

"Yes, I did. There was no evidence I was speeding either, because I wasn't."

"So, I guess this all comes down to either Mr. Luciano or you running the red light and causing the collision, correct?"

"I guess, but you know my position is that he did."

"I know that's your position, but your perception as to who ran the red light was affected by your consumption of beer that night, wasn't it?"

"No, I don't believe so."

"Speaking of believing, you believe you consumed either four or five beers before you got in your car to drive home, correct?"

"Yes, to the best of my recollection."

"Now you've qualified your answer by saying that 'to the best of your recollection' you drank four or five beers, haven't you?"

"No, I don't believe I've qualified my answer."

"But you never told us you knew for a fact that you drank four or five beers, because you've already testified that you were not counting the beers and did not pay for anything that night.

Isn't that fair to say?"

"I said that I could not give an exact number because I wasn't counting them and didn't pay for them, but I believe I did not have more than four or five beers."

"Let me ask you this, Mr. Taylor. We've already established that Mr. Luciano was not speeding and was not under the influence of alcohol or any other substances at the time of the collision. So, that being the case, why do you think he ran the red light?"

Brisbane jumped out of his seat like a jackrabbit. "Objection, your Honor. Speculation!"

Before Del Garden could respond, Judge Stacey interjected. "Normally, Mr. Brisbane, I would agree that the question calls for speculation. Under the circumstances, however, I believe the jury is entitled to hear Mr. Taylor's answer as to why he thinks Mr. Luciano ran the red light, so I'm going to allow it. Please answer the question, Mr. Taylor."

"Well, I can't say I know the exact reason why he ran the red light. But it seems to me he wasn't paying attention, was tired, or was anxious to get home. He said he worked late to finish one of his jobs and was just coming home at 11:30 p.m. So that was a very long day, and you could see how he would be tired and in a hurry to get home. Maybe he thought he could make the light."

"Thank you, Mr. Taylor. I have no further questions."

Brisbane replied, "I have no redirect, your Honor."

"Ladies and Gentlemen of the jury, I know that it's only 3:30 and we would normally have at least one more witness testify before we stopped for the day. But the Chief Judge has asked if I could hear an emergency matter in another case this afternoon, assuming that it would not delay the conclusion of our trial tomorrow. I've conferred with Mr. Del Garden and Mr. Brisbane, and they have advised me that the evidence will be concluded by noon tomorrow. After that you will hear their closing arguments and receive instructions on the law from me. Then you will retire to the jury room to deliberate. So we will have plenty of time tomorrow to conclude the trial, even with breaking early today. Please plan on eating your lunch in the jury room tomorrow. Bailiff Simon will provide you with menus, and we'll arrange for lunch to be brought to you. So, that being said, we'll adjourn for the day. Please remember not to discuss this case with each other or anyone else, and do not read any newspaper articles about the trial. Have a good afternoon."

Speaking of newspaper articles, John turned around and saw that Cassandra Brown was still there. She had been there all day, and he knew she'd be back tomorrow for the grand finale. He couldn't wait to see his name splattered all over the front page of the local news. Win or lose, it was a very bad way to make the headlines.

As Brisbane packed up his briefcase, John watched about a half dozen people exit the courtroom. He didn't know any of them and figured they were here for some sort of entertainment. Although that thought really aggravated him, he knew there was nothing he could do about it. After all, this was the land of the free, and people were free to do almost anything they wanted. Except, of course, when their actions infringed on others rights. Such basic ideas that once seemed so straightforward to him were now anything but that. Life had degenerated into a muddled haze that was making less and less sense to him as each day dragged on.

"Listen, John. Why don't you and Anna head home and relax. I'm meeting with Dave one last time to go over his testimony and then finalizing my closing argument. I really don't need to take up more of your time, and it would be wise for the two of you to rest."

"Good idea, Don. We'll do that. See you tomorrow and thanks again for everything."

"You're welcome. By the way, your testimony today was

great. You did a wonderful job holding Del Garden at bay. I couldn't be more pleased."

John wondered to himself whether or not Brisbane was being sincere. After all, he had given the same speech to many clients after they had testified, even when he thought they were awful. "Thanks. Let's see what the jury thinks."

After John and Anna arrived home, they both collapsed on the living room sofa. The rigors of the trial and the anticipation of the verdict had caused each of them to be physically and emotionally exhausted. Both of them were in a deep sleep on the couch when the phone rang. John woke up first and went to answer it. Not recognizing the number on the caller ID, he let it go into voicemail and turned the phone volume up so both he and Anna could hear any message that was left.

"John and Anna, this is Father Anderson at St. Gregory's Church."

Anna was frantically motioning John to pick up the phone, but he refused to do so.

"I just wanted to let you know that you're in my thoughts and prayers. Tomorrow morning after I say Mass, I will stay in church for the rest of the morning praying for you, asking God to watch over and protect both of you. God bless you. Good-bye."

"John, why didn't you pick up the phone?" Anna sounded irritated.

"Because, Anna, I just can't deal with Father Anderson right now," John snapped. "Anyway, I didn't hear him say anything about praying for the jury to find me innocent."

"Well, if you had picked up the phone and given him a chance, I'm sure he would have."

"Anna, stop it! He's praying for me. You're praying for me. I'm sure there are others out there who are praying for me. Let's just wait and see if God answers those prayers. If that happens, then we'll know there is a good God out there who truly does care for us. Why He took Maria, I will never, ever understand; but there was no chance to pray for her because no one knew anything was wrong. Now we've got all these people praying for me, so let's see if the prayers are answered."

Anna sighed. Her voice softened as she tried to de-escalate the tension in the room. "John, please don't decide whether a good God exists based on the jury's decision. I know it's hard. I struggle with the same thoughts. But as I've talked with Father Anderson, I've come to realize those dark thoughts are Satan's attempt to separate us from God. What really matters is that God watches over and protects us, even if the jury comes back with a guilty verdict."

John couldn't believe what he was hearing. He stood up and shook his fist, as though he wanted to punch something.

"Are you saying you don't care if the jury finds me guilty?" he screamed. "I can't believe this!"

Anna was in no mood to take his temper tantrum. She had tried her best to comfort and encourage her husband, but he had twisted her words and only heard what he wanted to hear.

"John, I'm telling you right now to stop yelling at me or I'm leaving," Anna said, her voice starting to rise. "You're being ridiculous to even question whether I care if the jury finds you guilty! How could you say such a thing?"

John fell backwards onto the couch and said nothing in response. After about thirty seconds of silence, Anna decided she'd had enough. As she headed to their bedroom, frustration getting the best of her, she yelled, "I'm going to bed. Sleep on the couch!"

Chapter 12

"Sir, please tell us your name and address," said Brisbane.

"Joe Casperson, 5858 Wiltshire Village Drive in Wellington, Florida."

"What is your occupation, sir?"

"I run my own electrical supply company in Wellington."

"Do you know John Taylor?"

"Yes, that's him sitting right there," answered Joe, pointing to John.

"And how do you know Mr. Taylor?"

"John and I have played together on the same softball team for the last five years. He's our center fielder, and I'm the shortstop."

"Are you aware that Mr. Taylor was involved in an automobile accident six months ago after one of the softball games?"

"Yes, he told me about the accident the following Monday."

"Were you with Mr. Taylor on the day the accident

occurred?"

"Yes, we played together at the game and then went out with a bunch of other guys to O'Shea's Restaurant and Bar on Congress Avenue in West Palm Beach."

"To your knowledge, had Mr. Taylor consumed any alcohol during the game?"

"No, I don't believe so. We're not pros or anything, but we do take the games seriously. One of our rules is no drinking alcohol during the games."

"Were you at O'Shea's when Mr. Taylor arrived?"

"Yes, I was actually the first player to arrive, and I do remember seeing him come in."

"Were there alcoholic beverages being consumed by the players that evening?"

"To the best of my knowledge, the only alcoholic beverages being consumed were glasses of draft beer. There were also pitchers of water and soda on the two tables we had."

"After Mr. Taylor arrived, did you notice if he drank any beer?"

"As a matter of fact I did. After he got there, he sat down next to me and was drinking ice water. He had hit the game-winning home run, and I tried to get him to have a beer to celebrate. But he put me off, saying he had to be to work early the next day."

"To your knowledge, did Mr. Taylor drink any beers that night?"

"At some point, after I saw him continuing to drink ice water, I decided to pour a beer for him and toast him for winning the game. So I did, and I handed him the beer."

"Did he drink it?"

"Yes."

"After that initial beer, did you see Mr. Taylor drinking any more beer that evening?"

"Yes, he was. But I wasn't sitting there counting them, so

there's no way I could tell you how many he drank."

"Did the other players pay for Mr. Taylor's drinks that evening?"

"Yes, they did. We have a tradition that the player who hits the game-winning run gets treated by the other guys."

"Were you there when Mr. Taylor left?"

"Yes. He again mentioned he had to be to work early the next day, and he said good-bye."

"When he left, did he appear to be under the influence of alcohol?"

"Well, I'm not sure what that means, but he didn't appear to be drunk if that's what you're asking."

"Was his speech slurred?"

"No."

"Was he staggering?"

"No."

"Was he belligerent or aggressive in any way?"

"No."

"Thank you, Mr. Casperson. I have no further questions."

"Any questions of this witness, Mr. Del Garden?" asked the Court.

"Yes, Sir," Del Garden replied.

"Mr. Casperson, you've just told us there's no way you know how many beers Mr. Taylor had on the night of the collision, correct?"

"Yes, that's correct."

"And you don't know what Mr. Taylor's blood-alcohol level was at the time he left, correct?"

"No, Sir."

"And when Mr. Taylor left the bar, you really weren't focused on whether he was drunk, were you?"

"No, I wasn't."

"Thank you, Mr. Casperson. I have no other questions."

"Okay, Sir. You may be excused," stated Judge Stacey.

Brisbane's last witness was Dave Jones, the expert toxicologist. Jones walked into the courtroom with an air of confidence and nodded ever so slightly to the jury as he walked past them. John had never seen a witness so immaculately dressed—so polished–and yet so down to earth. As he testified, there was no sign of arrogance about him, but he conveyed his expert opinions with professionalism.

Brisbane slowly and methodically walked Jones through all the trial exhibits he had prepared. The exhibits included diagrams showing standard drink equivalents among beer, wine, and distilled spirits plus alcohol absorption and elimination rates. There was also a chart showing the effect of food on the absorption rate, and when asked, Jones explained in detail how John's dinner would have affected the alcohol level in his bloodstream. Brisbane also had Jones explain an exhibit that depicted blood-alcohol concentration levels as they related to the time elapsed since the alcohol had been consumed.

Brisbane then asked, "Mr. Jones, let's assume for the sake of argument that Mr. Taylor had consumed as many as eight beers before he left the bar—as the state expert suggested he had. You stated that it is your expert opinion that Mr. Taylor's blood-alcohol level at the time of the accident would not have been higher than 0.05. Please explain to us how you arrived at that opinion."

"My opinion is based upon Mr. Taylor having consumed all but one of the beers during the last hour-and-a-half or so of being at the restaurant. The accident happened within five minutes after he left, but the blood draw was not taken until one-and-a-half hours after the accident. Mr. Taylor had a full stomach; he had eaten a steak dinner with a baked potato and broccoli. Therefore, it is my opinion that at the time of the accident, the alcohol had not fully absorbed and did not peak until the time of the blood draw. This means that at the time of the accident, even if Mr. Taylor had as many as eight beers, his blood-alcohol level would be at no more than 0.05 and not 0.08."

"What affect would a blood-alcohol level of 0.05 or less have on a man of Mr. Taylor's build?"

"Based on his height and weight, and the other factors I previously discussed, Mr. Taylor's normal faculties would not have been impaired. He would not have experienced any appreciable loss in his mental acuity, judgment, distance perception, or motor skills."

"Thank you, Mr. Jones. I have no further questions, your Honor."

"You may proceed, Mr. Del Garden," replied the Judge.

John breathed a sigh of relief. He thought that Jones' direct had gone as well as it could. Now it was time to see how he withstood the fire of cross-examination.

Del Garden started out with his usual routine of asking insignificant questions for about fifteen minutes. Then he started questioning Jones regarding his testimony relating to the blood draw taken from John.

"Now, Mr. Jones, it's fair to say that you don't know for certain that Mr. Taylor's blood draw was tampered with, isn't it?"

"Yes, that's fair to say."

"In fact, based on your testimony on direct exam, you really can't state that it's probable that the blood draw had been tampered with while in the custody of the sheriff's office. The most that you can tell us is that there is a possibility that the draw had been tampered with, isn't that correct?"

"Well, it's my opinion that there is a very strong possibility the blood draw's reliability had been compromised. That's due to the fact that no one knows whether there was anything, other than an anti-coagulant, in the blood sample tubes when Mr. Taylor's blood was drawn. But I can't say that it's probable."

"Your opinion that Mr. Taylor could have drunk eight beers and not have a blood-alcohol level higher than 0.05 is based upon all but one of those beers being drunk within approximately the last hour-and-a-half before he left the restaurant, correct?"

"Correct."

"Well, drinking seven beers in approximately an hour-and-a-half is going to cause an impairment of Mr. Taylor's normal faculties, isn't it?"

"First of all, I don't know that Mr. Taylor drank seven beers in the last hour-and-a-half or so before he left the restaurant. In fact, Mr. Taylor told me that to the best of his recollection he only had three or four beers during that time period. Secondly, even assuming for the sake of argument that it was seven beers, I don't believe Mr. Taylor's normal faculties would have been impaired at the time of the accident because the blood-alcohol level would not have peaked by that time, particularly when he had eaten as large a meal as late as he did. So to answer your question, I don't believe his normal faculties would have been impaired."

"Mr. Jones, I want you to assume for a moment that at the time of the collision, Mr. Taylor's blood-alcohol level was 0.08. Would his normal faculties be impaired then?"

"If at the time of the accident, his blood-alcohol level was 0.08, which I don't believe it was, then yes, his normal faculties would likely be impaired."

"Thank you, Sir. No further questions."

"I have no redirect, your Honor. The defense rests."

After excusing Jones, Judge Stacey advised the jury that they would take a recess, and when they returned, the attorneys would make their closing arguments. He would then instruct them on the law before they went to the jury room to deliberate.

After the recess, Judge Stacey told the jury that the closing arguments by the attorneys were not evidence, but simply the lawyers' recollection of what the evidence had shown. He also told them that if their recollection of the evidence was different from what either counsel stated in closing arguments, they should rely upon their own memory.

"All right, Mr. Del Garden. You may proceed," instructed the Judge.

John glanced back at Anna. She was still managing to keep her best game face on, but he knew the inner chaos she was feeling. He also knew he had really blown it last evening by refusing the phone call from Father Anderson and yelling at Anna. Despite his sincere apologies this morning, he was playing in his mind the "if only" tape of his life's events. "If only" he or Anna had woken up and checked on Maria earlier that dreadful night. "If only" he hadn't drank beer at O'Shea's. "If only" he could accept Father Anderson's and Anna's prayers of protection for him. The psychological torture he was inflicting upon himself was becoming more and more unbearable. When and how would it stop?

Del Garden got out of his chair, approached the jury, and started speaking. "Ladies and gentlemen, on behalf of the State of Florida, I want to express my appreciation for your time and efforts on this case. It certainly has not been an easy case to sit through, particularly when you saw the effect the collision had upon Mr. Luciano. The evidence over the past two-and-a-half days has clearly shown, and the State has proven beyond a reasonable doubt, that at the time of the collision Mr. Taylor was either under the influence of alcoholic beverages to the extent that his normal faculties were impaired or that he had a blood-alcohol level of 0.08 or higher. There is no dispute that at the time of the collision, Mr. Taylor was in actual physical control of the vehicle that struck Mr. Luciano's car. There is also no dispute that as a result of Mr. Taylor's car striking Mr. Luciano's vehicle, Mr. Luciano sustained serious bodily injury. So, what I want to do right now is go over how the evidence has shown beyond a reasonable doubt that Mr. Taylor's normal faculties were impaired at the time of the collision or that he had a blood-alcohol level of 0.08 or higher when he struck Mr. Luciano's car," Del Garden said.

Del Garden continued. "Judge Stacey will be instructing you shortly that, under the law, 'normal faculties' include, but are not limited to, the ability to see, hear, walk, talk, judge distances, drive an automobile, make judgments, act in emergencies, and, in general, to normally perform the many mental and physical acts of our daily lives. Now, let's apply what the evidence has shown in the case."

For the next thirty minutes Del Garden took the jury through a road map of what he believed the evidence had shown and why John should be found guilty. He then looked back at John and pointed his finger at him. "Mr. Taylor has refused to be accountable for his actions on the night of the crash. Rather than admitting any responsibility, he claims Mr. Luciano ran a red light and caused the accident. Other than Mr. Taylor's self-serving and baseless claim, there is no evidence that Mr. Luciano was in any way at fault for the collision. Mr. Taylor even refused to acknowledge that his perception as to who ran the red light might have been influenced by his consumption of beer that evening. Ladies and gentlemen, the State asks that you hold Mr. Taylor accountable for the collision and the serious bodily injury he inflicted upon Mr. Luciano by finding Mr. Taylor guilty. Thank you for your time and hard work on this case."

"Accountable, why should I be accountable?" John thought to himself. He continued to ardently believe he had done nothing wrong, that his supposition of Luciano running the red light was not influenced by the beer—and was, in fact true. He silently prayed to God that justice would be done through the jury finding him innocent. After all, God owed him at least that much. Didn't He?

Meanwhile, Anna was also praying. Although she was fervently pleading with God that the jury set John free, Anna was also praying for protection of both of them to weather any storm that might occur as a result of the verdict.

As Brisbane approached the podium to counter Del Garden's

arguments, John noticed the total silence in the courtroom. It was a stark contrast to the fireworks about to explode.

"Ladies and gentlemen, Counsel for the State conveniently overlooks the facts when he asks you to hold Mr. Taylor accountable for a crime he never committed!" Brisbane roared out. "All of you heard Deputy Hutchins testify how Mr. Taylor had voluntarily cooperated with him in the investigation—even to the point of agreeing that a blood draw could be taken at the accident scene! Mr. Taylor did nothing wrong and had nothing to hide. Roadside field sobriety tests were never performed on Mr. Taylor, as Deputy Hutchins admitted. The only basis for the State even bringing DUI charges against Mr. Taylor was the blood draw. But as the evidence has shown, that blood draw was flawed, and so is the testimony of the State's expert!" For the next forty-five minutes, Brisbane explained in great detail why he believed the State had failed to show beyond a reasonable doubt that John was guilty of the charges brought against him.

"In conclusion, the defense asks that you *not* hold Mr. Taylor accountable for a crime he *didn't* commit, as Mr. Del Garden wants you to do. I respectfully submit to you that to do so would be a travesty of justice. There was no crime committed the night of the accident. What happened was just that, an unfortunate accident—not caused by my client being under the influence of alcohol. On behalf of Mr. Taylor, I want to thank each of you for the attention you have given this case over the past three days."

"Any rebuttal, Mr. Del Garden?" asked the Court.

"Very briefly, sir," responded Del Garden.

"Ladies and gentlemen, counsel for Mr. Taylor just spent forty- five minutes reinforcing what I told you earlier. Mr. Taylor refuses to be accountable for the collision, which he caused, that resulted in serious bodily injury to Mr. Luciano. The evidence is crystal clear. The State has proven beyond a reasonable doubt that Mr. Taylor was driving under the influence of alcoholic beverages to the extent that his normal faculties were impaired—

or that Mr. Taylor had a blood-alcohol level of 0.08 or higher at the time of the collision. Therefore, the State asks you to hold Mr. Taylor accountable and return a verdict of guilty."

"All right, ladies and gentlemen, that concludes the closing arguments of Counsel," stated Judge Stacey. "I will now instruct you on the law that you must apply in reaching your verdict. You will also be provided with a written copy of these instructions when you retire to the jury room for your deliberations."

The Judge spent the next twenty minutes reading the legal instructions to the jury. Included within the instructions was the definition of "normal faculties" which Del Garden had told the jury about during his initial closing argument. The Judge also advised the jury that to prove the crime of driving under the influence of alcohol which caused serious bodily injury, the State must prove, beyond a reasonable doubt, that 1) the Defendant was driving or was in actual physical control of a vehicle. 2) While the Defendant was driving or in actual physical control of the vehicle, the Defendant was under the influence of alcohol to the extent that his normal faculties were impaired or the Defendant had a blood-alcohol level of 0.08 or higher. 3) As a result of the Defendant's actions, the Defendant caused serious bodily injury to Anthony Luciano.

Judge Stacey also told the jury that "serious bodily injury" was defined as a physical condition creating a substantial risk of death, serious personal disfigurement, or protracted loss or impairment of the function of any bodily member or organ. The Court instructed the jury on various presumptions of impairment that existed under Florida law. In that regard, Judge Stacey first told the jury that, if the Defendant's blood-alcohol level was 0.05 or less at the time of the crash, it was presumed that the Defendant was not under the influence of alcoholic beverages to the extent that his normal faculties were impaired. But if at the time of the crash, the Defendant's blood-alcohol level was in excess of 0.05, but less than 0.08, that fact does not give rise to any presumptions of impairment, but may be considered with other competent evidence in determining whether the Defendant was under the influence of alcohol to the extent that his normal faculties were impaired. Judge Stacey further advised the jury that if the Defendant's blood-alcohol level was 0.08 or higher at the time of the crash, such a level would be evidence that the Defendant was under the influence of alcohol to the extent that his normal faculties would be impaired. Moreover, with a blood-alcohol level of 0.08 or more, the Defendant would be guilty of driving with an unlawful blood-alcohol level. Finally, the Court told the jury that these presumptions were to be considered along with all other evidence in the case in deciding whether the Defendant was under the influence of alcoholic beverages to the extent that his normal faculties were impaired.

After completing the rest of the instructions, Judge Stacey had the jury, other than the alternate juror, retire to the jury room to begin their deliberations. After the six primary jurors were in the jury room, Judge Stacey thanked the alternate juror, Maria Alvarez, for her service and excused her from the proceedings. John noticed that she didn't look very happy after just giving up three days of her life. Bailiff Simon brought the jury all the exhibits and other documents that had been received in evidence, as well as a copy of the jury instructions and verdict form to enter their verdict upon. Now it was a game of wait and see, a game that both John and Anna detested.

Chapter 13

As Anna walked to the elevator with John and Brisbane, her cell phone rang. Looking at her caller display, she saw that it was Tess Milan. "Hey, Tess. What's up?"

"I'm checking in to see what's happening with the trial."

"The jury got the case about five minutes ago and they're in the jury room deliberating. The Judge is having lunch brought into them, so we're hoping it won't be too long before we have a decision."

"I'd like to come to the courthouse and wait with you for their decision, if that's okay."

"I really appreciate that, but I don't want to take you away from work. You've got houses to sell."

"Don't worry. Two of my salespeople are here this afternoon and can cover for me. I'll see you there in about an hour."

"Okay, thanks so much. See you then." As she hung up, Anna thought to herself what a blessing Tess had been and was continuing to be to her. She was always there, through thick and thin.

Sitting down at a small café across the street from the courthouse, Brisbane ordered a cheeseburger with fries. Neither John nor Anna were very hungry, but they had to eat something, especially after they had both passed on breakfast. John decided to go with a chef salad, and Anna opted for a bowl of fresh fruit. As they waited for their order, the conversation turned back to the trial.

"Don, I want you to know how happy I am with the way you conducted the trial," John finally said to break the silence. "I couldn't have asked for any more from you. So, thank you *very* much for all your efforts. Now let's hope that the jury will see the light and come back with a good verdict for me."

"I agree with John," said Anna. Even though I'm not a lawyer, you did a wonderful job from my perspective."

"Believe me," said Brisbane, "I truly appreciate your comments. The best clients I ever represent are those that say similar things before the jury verdict. I got very good vibes from this jury during the trial, and I believe we'll get a favorable verdict." Brisbane then skillfully turned the conversation to a discussion about professional baseball, in order to get a respite from the pressures of waiting for the verdict.

As they slowly meandered back to the courtroom, John caught sight of Cassandra Brown heading back inside the building. "I just saw our friendly newspaper reporter returning to court. She reminds me of a vulture just circling around, waiting for its prey to expire. I sure hope she leaves court today feeling disappointed she didn't get the story she wanted."

"Actually John," replied Brisbane, "Cassandra isn't all that bad. I've dealt with many reporters who are much less objective than her. At least she normally tries to show both sides of a story."

John didn't respond, but he couldn't help thinking Cassandra Brown was out for a juicy story that would help her career. Never mind about the truth. That took a backseat to advancement up the corporate ladder. As Brisbane and the Taylors exited the elevator, there was Brown sitting outside the courtroom door, pounding away again on her laptop.

"Great closing, Don. Hopefully, the jury will come back for you," said Brown in a too-cheerful voice.

Brisbane smiled and nodded at her in response. Then he whispered into John's ear, "I told you she's not all bad."

"Let's just wait and see when the story comes out. Then we'll know."

Brisbane and John headed back into the courtroom. Anna told them she needed to wait for Tess and would come in after she arrived. As John and Brisbane entered the courtroom, they heard loud talking coming from the jury room. Although the door to the jury room was closed, and they couldn't make out what was being said, it sounded as though a heated argument was taking place. Brisbane noticed that no one else was in the courtroom and decided the two of them needed to go back outside. No matter what the jury was arguing about, there was nothing they could do about it, and no good could come from remaining in the courtroom. When they got back outside, John wanted to know what Brisbane thought the spirited dialogue was about.

"There's really no way of knowing. I don't view it as a bad sign. It probably means they're really into the case and are trying to flesh out any differences in opinions that may have come out. That's better than having a lackluster jury. Then you run the risk of having one juror control the show. I think the more they're mixing it up, the better it is for us."

"Sounds logical. I hope you're right."

Anna had walked down the corridor, waiting for Tess to arrive. It was now two o'clock, and the jury had been out for slightly more than two hours. Tess should have been here by now, Anna thought. She must have gotten delayed at work. Just then the elevator door opened and out walked Tess. She smiled warmly at Anna and embraced her. "Any word yet?" asked Tess.

"No, not yet. It's been a little over two hours. I really don't know how long it's supposed to take, but I'm starting to get concerned. You have no idea how glad I am you're here." Anna's game face was now off. The pressure of the trial over the last three days had been relentless. Now that the jury was not in front of her, her emotions were obvious. Tess could see how stressed she was.

"I wanted to be here for you, Anna. What you've been going through for the past year has been an incredible test of your faith. No one should have to suffer as much as you and John have, and your continued belief in a caring God is a true testament to your faith."

"It's only with the help of friends like you and Father Anderson that I've been able to hang on. The words of encouragement from you and Father have been a tremendous blessing. In fact, Father gave John a beautiful prayer card. It basically says that when we can't hear God speak directly to us in response to our calls for help, He often speaks to us through His children. That's how I feel about the two of you, that God is speaking through both of you to me."

"That sounds like a wonderful prayer, and I'm so thankful we've encouraged you. But what about John? You said Father gave the prayer to John. You've told me about his struggles with his faith after all that's happened over the past year. Has the prayer helped him at all to overcome his doubts?"

"Unfortunately, I don't believe it has. He keeps saying how he'll believe a good God exists if the jury decides in his favor. He continually conditions the existence of a benevolent God on whether he gets freed from these charges. In fact, just last night he refused to take a call from Father Anderson." Anna sighed and lowered her voice. "Tess, John yelled at me for asking him not to condition the existence of a good God on whether he's found innocent. He totally misconstrued my comments when I told him I struggle sometimes, too, and that I think Satan is planting seeds of doubt in us to try to alienate us from God. Things were so bad that he slept on the couch for the first time in our marriage. I'm so afraid something terrible will happen if he's convicted. That's why I keep praying that God will be with us and protect us, even if the jury finds him guilty."

Tears streamed down Anna's cheeks. Tess quickly took out some tissues and handed them to Anna.

"Well, don't stop praying for protection, and neither will I. I'm right here with you. We both know that John's a good man with a kind heart. Right now, he seems to be blinded with fear and anger. I have no doubt that with God's help, he'll return to the godly man of faith you fell in love with."

Suddenly, John appeared out of nowhere. "The jury's reached a verdict and Judge Stacey is about ready to call them into the courtroom. Let's go!"

The timing of John's announcement, during the emotional conversation with Tess, caught Anna totally off guard. Her heart was racing, and as John walked away, she struggled to catch her breath. She grabbed Tess's hand, and the two friends walked hand-in-hand down the corridor and into the courtroom. As they entered, the jury was coming in from the jury room. Everyone in the courtroom, other than Judge Stacey, was still standing as the jury arrived at their seats and took their places. Bailiff Simon then asked that all be seated.

John noticed that as the jurors came in, they were all solemn-faced. None of them would look at him. *My God, they're going to convict me!* he thought. He also observed that Jayne Hagan, the retired bank officer, held the jury verdict form in her hands. That meant she had been elected the foreperson as Brisbane had predicted. John was sweating profusely and felt like throwing up. Brisbane noticed John's reaction and placed his hand on John's knee in an effort to bolster him, but it wasn't working.

Judge Stacey asked the jury if they had reached a verdict. Hagan stood up and answered in the affirmative. The Court then asked the clerk to get the verdict and bring it to him. After the Judge received the verdict, he studied it closely. There was no show of emotion on his face. He handed the verdict back to the clerk and asked him to read it to everyone in the room.

The clerk silently read through the verdict form and then read it aloud.

"We, the jury, find as follows, as to the Defendant, John Taylor:

The Defendant, John Taylor, is guilty of driving under the influence of alcohol to the extent that his normal faculties were impaired or the Defendant, John Taylor, had a blood-alcohol level of 0.08 or higher, resulting in serious bodily injury to Anthony Luciano."

It was as though a lightning bolt had come down from the sky and struck both Taylors. Neither of them was able to hide or control their emotions. John sat at the table next to Brisbane with his head buried in his hands, tears rolling down his cheeks. He was breathing heavily and moaning as if he was in extreme pain. Behind him, Tess had her arms around Anna, who was now crying uncontrollably. Judgment day had come for the Taylors, and now began another test of their faith in God.

Some of the jurors also started to cry. The courtroom was beginning to degenerate into a sea of chaos, and it was time for Judge Stacey to regain control. And regain control he did. He began banging his gavel on the bench and shouted loudly several times for order in the courtroom. Slowly but surely, the room quieted down. Once he had reestablished the appropriate decorum, he addressed both counselors.

"Gentlemen, are there any matters we need to address before we discharge the jury?"

"The State has none," replied Del Garden.

"The Defendant requests that the jury be polled, your Honor," asserted Brisbane.

Judge Stacey addressed the jury and explained to them that

the Defendant had requested they each be asked whether the guilty verdict was, in fact, each of their decisions. If any of the jurors answered that it was not their verdict, then the Court would send them back to the jury room for further deliberations. If all jurors concurred that it was their verdict, the verdict would be entered into the Court records and the jury discharged. One by one Judge Stacey questioned each of the jurors. Foreperson Hagan and jurors Smith, Hartford, Bailey, and Perkins each affirmatively responded that it was their verdict, although Smith and Hartford were still teary eyed. The last juror to be questioned was Greg Chatsworth. He appeared visibly shaken and did not respond to the Court's question as to whether this was his verdict. Judge Stacey glared at him and repeated the question in a louder tone. Chatsworth finally responded that it was his verdict, although his body language was less than convincing. Stacey accepted the answer and proceeded to wrap up the proceedings with the jury. As the jury left the courtroom, none of them looked at John or Anna. They were all in a hurry to leave, and each of them rebuffed Cassandra Brown's attempts to speak with them.

After the jurors were gone, Judge Stacey announced that he wanted to schedule the sentencing hearing. Del Garden and Brisbane agreed with the Court that the hearing could take place in four weeks, and a date and time certain was set. The Court then asked Del Garden whether the State had any objections to John continuing to be free on the bond he'd previously posted. Del Garden advised the Judge that the State had no objections, and the Court allowed John to remain free pending the sentencing hearing. It was a small consolation to John, but right now he would take any reprieve from being jailed while he explored all his legal options with Brisbane. The Court then concluded the proceedings, pending the sentencing hearing.

Del Garden was the first to pack up his briefcase and leave. On the way out, he extended his hand to Brisbane and told him that he'd be in touch regarding sentencing issues. Although

Brisbane wanted to tell him where to go, he was much too smart and experienced for that. Grabbing Del Garden's hand, he firmly shook it and replied that he'd be available for a face-to-face meeting next week. Del Garden nodded his head in agreement and exited the courtroom. Only Brisbane, John, Anna, and Tess were left.

Tess still had her arms wrapped around Anna, even though Anna was no longer crying. John still struggled to regain his composure. Once he was able to speak, he began firing off a barrage of questions to Brisbane.

"How did this happen? How could they reach a guilty verdict? What about Chatsworth's response? He sure didn't look like it was his verdict. What do we do about that? What happens next with the sentencing? What are our post-trial motion rights and what about an appeal? Can I remain free if we file an appeal?"

"Hold on, John," asserted Brisbane. "Let's just stop right there. Right now you are way too emotional for us to discuss any of our options. We need to defer this discussion until you have a chance to calm down and think clearly. Tomorrow I have to be in Miami for a court hearing. Let's plan on you being at my office at nine on Friday morning. Then we can go through and sort out all our options, okay?"

"Not really, but I guess it will have to do."

"John, you've been a trial lawyer for twelve years, and you've been involved in a lot of fire fights. I know it's your butt on the line this time, but think back about the cases you tried that were lost at the trial court level. I'm sure you had some very upset clients when those big bucks were on the line. Didn't you get them to defer any questions of strategy until everyone had a chance to calm down and reflect on what happened?"

John sighed deeply and reluctantly acknowledged that Brisbane was right. Even though he wanted to sort it all out right now, the trial lawyer in him was still present enough to realize

Brisbane was making the correct call. The two of them agreed they'd meet Friday morning to try to figure out what had happened and what their next steps should be. Brisbane then left, leaving John, Tess, and Anna in the courtroom. Before anyone could speak, Bailiff Simon appeared through the side door reserved for court employees and asked them to leave as he needed to lock up the courtroom. On the way out of the courthouse, they saw Cassandra Brown talking with Brisbane. Even though John and Anna both desperately wanted to know what was going on, they decided they already had more than enough adversity to deal with for one day and left Brisbane and the reporter alone.

After they arrived home, both John and Anna were emotionally and physically exhausted, and neither wanted any dinner. They retreated to their bedroom with the hope that they could fall asleep and at least temporarily escape the depressing, life-shattering events of the past three days. A good night's sleep for the Taylors, however, was not to be. Both of them tossed and turned all night, and neither of them felt like talking about the verdict or what life might hold for them. They each needed time to digest the consequences of what had just occurred. Finally, around five in the morning, they both fell asleep for a temporary respite from the continuing nightmare.

Chapter 14

When John finally woke up, his thoughts turned to the newspaper lying in his driveway. He knew Brown's article about the trial would be center stage. Even though he wanted nothing to do with it, he couldn't help but wonder how badly the paper had portrayed him. Slowly rising from bed, he meandered through the house and out the garage in search of the dreaded report. As he lifted the paper from the ground, he saw a mug shot of himself on the front page. He thought the picture must be a copy of the one taken by the sheriff's office after he was charged with DUI. It was grainy, and he looked totally disheveled and overweight. He walked back into the house, slowly opening the newspaper, and was taken aback by the headline at the top of the front page.

"Prominent Palm Beach Attorney Guilty of DUI," screamed out the newspaper. The article took up about one-third of the front page and continued on page 6 for another half a page. It took every ounce of fortitude he possessed to read the story. As he read along, he realized his comment about Cassandra Brown being a vulture, circling around waiting for her prey to expire, couldn't have been more right on. John didn't see a shred of objective reporting in the story, other than a short comment about juror Chatsworth. The article contained Brown's observation that when Chatsworth was polled, he didn't really appear to agree that the guilty verdict was his, but very reluctantly told the Judge that it was. *At least Brown had gotten that one part right,* John thought.

The most distressing part of the story was that it mentioned the Smith & Patterson law firm on four occasions. John could just see the Old Man and Patterson fuming, particularly when Brown mentioned some of the high profile litigation clients the firm was representing. He expected his phone would ring at any moment with a call from the firm, summoning him to the office for a grand inquisition and proclamation of his fate with Smith & Patterson. At this point in his life, nothing surprised him, and he expected that he would be quickly banned from any further contact with anyone at the firm. Finishing the article, John was greatly annoyed with Brown's comment that his sentencing hearing would take place in four weeks before a judge who was known for handing out stiff sentences to convicted felons. The bad news just wouldn't stop, and John felt as though he was being sucked deeper into the bowels of hell.

Two minutes later, John's prediction about a phone call from the firm came true. It was nine fifteen, and he wondered what had taken them so long. Looking at his caller ID, he saw it was a call from Donna Hughes' direct line at work. He really didn't want to deal with this, but he would only be postponing the inevitable if he didn't take the call. "Hey, Red, it's me."

"John, I'm so sorry to be bothering you," said Red with more than a hint of nervousness in her voice.

"Don't worry about it. I knew this call was coming.

Obviously, everyone has seen the paper by now, and the Old Man delegated to you the unpleasant task of requiring my appearance at the office. That's why you're calling, isn't it?"

There was a prolonged period of silence on the other end of the phone. John could tell Red was struggling to regain her composure. When she finally spoke, there was no question as to how upset she was. "Actually John, the reason I'm calling is to see how you and Anna are doing. I did read the paper, and I know what happened. I feel so badly and couldn't wait to call and check on the two of you. I haven't spoken with George or Jim today and wasn't calling for anyone else but me."

Once again, John recognized what a big mistake he had made, just like the other night with Father Anderson and Anna. My God, how he hated himself!

"Red, I'm so sorry. I should have known better after all the years you've supported and helped me. I don't know what to say other than to please forgive me."

"It's okay, John. There's nothing to forgive. Please try to get some rest. Maybe you should try some surfing. That always seems to work for you. I just want you to know I'm here for Anna and you and will do whatever I can to help."

"Thanks, Red. Actually, there is one thing you can do right now, if you don't mind."

"Sure, anything."

"Would you go see Jayne this morning and see if she can arrange for a meeting with the Old Man, Jim, Steve, and me tomorrow? I know they're going to want to see me. They may also want you in the meeting as well. I'll leave that up to all of you. I have to see my lawyer in the morning, but I can be at the office at one o'clock for as long as necessary."

"I'll go take care of that right now. If I don't call you back, that means we're on for one."

"Thanks. And Red, thank you for caring about Anna and me. It really means a lot."

"You're welcome." Red was becoming more and more emotional and quickly hung up the phone.

Just then, Anna appeared from the bedroom. She had heard John talking on the phone and wanted to know whom it was. John told her about the conversation with Red and how he was trying to set up a meeting tomorrow at work.

"Speaking of work, I think I'm going to head over to school this afternoon and see how my substitute is doing with the children. I also want to stop in and see the principal. I'm sure that by now they've read or heard about the verdict." Looking over at the wrinkled newspaper, Anna wanted to know what the article said about the trial.

"Nothing good for me. The only thing that Brown wrote that was remotely in my favor was her reference to juror Chatsworth being polled and not looking like the guilty verdict was really his verdict. She referred to Smith & Patterson by name four times and also listed some of our high profile clients, which I'm sure is going to drive both the Old Man and Jim nuts."

"Did the article say anything about Brisbane? We saw her talking with him when we left the courthouse."

"There was one quote from Don. It was something to the effect that he felt the verdict was a travesty of justice and would be pursuing all legal avenues to overturn the jury decision. It sounded to me like standard lawyer bravado after a case is lost. I'll wait and see what he really thinks when we meet tomorrow. Right now, I'm starting to lose all hope that I'll avoid going to jail. Tell me, Anna, where is God in all this mess? I sure don't see Him anywhere."

Anna's biggest fears were coming true. Her beloved husband was continuing to lose his faith in the Almighty and any hope for the future. Rather than engage him right now in a discussion that would very likely turn ugly, she decided to skirt the question. "Let's not give up the ship, John. We both know that Don is very adept at handling these cases. I'm sure he'll have some better news for you tomorrow."

"I'd like to believe that. After all, I could be sentenced for up to five years in prison by a Judge who has a reputation for handing out tough sentences."

"I have a suggestion for you, John."

"What's that?"

"While I run over to school, please go surfing. That always seems to calm you down and help you refocus."

"Funny you should say that. Red also told me that's what I should do today. So I guess I will."

"Good. Just don't get bitten by any of those state's attorney sharks when you're in the water. You know how they're always after your caboose."

"Cute, really cute," answered John, with a hint of a smile on his lips.

Chapter 15

As Anna drove to the school, she recited in her mind the prayer given to her by Father Anderson. She now had it fully memorized, and it was becoming her fortress from the trials of life. How she wished John would embrace the petitions to God, but he would have nothing to do with the prayer. At one point after they had arrived home from the trial, he even flung the prayer card across their bedroom and then stomped on it before leaving the room. Anna was so fearful he'd destroy the card that she took it and hid it in a dresser drawer among her clothes. She was determined that the forces of darkness would not destroy either of them and prayed daily for strength to overcome the everlasting adversity they were experiencing.

Once she arrived at school, Anna went directly to Principal Alice Barnes' office. Principal Barnes had worked in education for her entire career, first, as an elementary school teacher at various schools for twenty-five years, then as the principal at St. Gregory's for the last fifteen years. She was well liked and respected by the faculty and staff. The principal and Anna had maintained a close working relationship, and Anna had confided in her on multiple occasions. Right now, Anna needed her sage advice on handling the negative publicity of the jury verdict with the children in her fifth grade class. As she entered the secretary's outer office, Anna saw that the door to the principal's office was closed, but she could hear the principal talking on her phone. The secretary was not at her desk, but Anna decided to wait and see if Alice was available to talk with her after the conclusion of the phone call. Five minutes later, the door opened and the principal walked out. When she saw Anna, she stepped back into her office and motioned for Anna to come in. After Anna entered, Alice pulled out a chair from the circular table in her office and asked Anna to have a seat. The principal then slid one of the other chairs next to Anna, and after being seated, grasped Anna's hands.

"Anna, I've read the newspaper article about the trial and know that John was found guilty. I cannot imagine what the two of you are going through. Please tell me what I can do to help. I'm here for you in any way I can be."

"You always have been. Thank you so much. Right now, I need your advice."

"Okay, that sounds easy enough."

"Maybe not. My concern has to do with my students. As you know, many of the students in my fifth grade class are avid readers, and I'm certain that most of them will have either read about the guilty verdict or heard about it from someone else. I'm struggling with how to deal with it when I go back to class. What do I tell them, and how do I tell them?"

"That's certainly not going to be an easy subject to deal with, but I have no doubt you'll get through it with your usual calm, well-reasoned approach. Your kids are always telling me how nice you are and how easy it is for them to talk to you."

A smile crossed Anna's lips. "Thanks," she quietly replied.

"Well, you know one of the things we're always preaching around here is about honesty in your dealings with others. Now I realize, of course, that you can't say or intimate anything that could hurt any appeal rights that John may have. That being said, I think you need to address it up front with the entire class when you return. You can certainly tell them how disappointed the two of you were in the jury verdict and that John and you still believe he wasn't driving under the influence of alcohol and was not at fault in the accident. You can also tell them how sorry you are that the other driver was hurt in the accident. Also, you should ask them to pray for John and you, and the other driver and his family as well, that all of you will be able to overcome this terrible tragedy."

Suddenly, Anna started to shake and began crying.

"What's wrong, Anna? What did I say to upset you?"

Through tear-stained eyes, Anna responded, "When you just talked about asking my students to pray for the other driver and his family, I realized I've never done that. I've been so wrapped up in what John and I have been dealing with that the thought of praying for them never even occurred to me. And you should have seen Mr. Luciano and his wife at the trial. If anyone needs prayers, it's the two of them and their children. How could I have been so insensitive and selfish?"

"Anna, please don't be so hard on yourself. It's understandable that you've been preoccupied with what you and John are going through, especially after losing Maria. With a heart as good as yours, it was only a matter of time before you would start praying for them. Forget about what you didn't do in the past and focus instead on doing what you know is the right thing to do now and in the future."

Anna silently thought to herself that this was another example of God speaking to her through another of His children in response to her cries for help. It helped her believe she was not alone in this battle to maintain her faith beyond the trials of life and hope for the future.

"Thank you so very much for your advice and kind words. I want to return to the classroom tomorrow, and I intend to speak to my students as you suggested."

"Sounds like a great plan. Welcome back."

After Anna left the office, she headed to her classroom. The students had already left for the day, but she knew that her substitute, Diana Jenkins, would still be there. As she entered the classroom, she saw Diana sitting at her desk grading papers for a quiz she had given the students earlier in the day.

"Hey, Diana, working hard again I see."

"Just trying to keep up with you. I've got big shoes to fill. I'm just finishing grading a quiz I gave the children today. I take it you're planning to return to work tomorrow?"

"Yes, if that's okay with you."

"No problem. Now you can hand back the quizzes, and they can blame you for any low grades." Jenkins starting laughing and then became serious. "I think you should know the children are already aware of the trial outcome. I saw that Amy George and Robbie Howard both had copies of today's paper. They were showing them to the other kids and discussing the article during recess. They didn't ask me any questions, and I didn't want to bring it up, but I think they'll want to talk with you about it tomorrow. I just thought you should know."

"I appreciate that Diana. As a matter of fact, I just got through talking with Alice Barnes about what I was going to say to them tomorrow. I feel that I'm as prepared as I can be, but I've come to expect the unexpected. So who knows what might happen."

"Anna, I can tell you that the children really missed you this week. We all got along great, and I truly enjoyed them, but they think the world of you. It seems to me that there might be some bumps in the road when you talk to them, but nothing major. Please let me know if there's anything I can do to help.

I'm available 24/7 for you."

"I appreciate your support. I'll let you know if I need anything."

...

Back in Palm Beach, John was doing his best to ride out some hard-breaking waves. Although five- to six-foot breakers would normally pose no real challenge, he was unable to clearly focus on the task before him and kept falling off his board. All he could think about was the likelihood that he would soon be in prison. The events of the trial kept running through his mind, and he was constantly wondering what could have been done differently to have avoided a guilty verdict. At this point, he didn't see an appeal as being successful and was scared to death of the upcoming sentencing hearing with Judge Stacey. Even Brisbane had told him that the rap on the Judge was that he was hard on defendants who had been convicted. In his case, that could mean five years in prison. How could he possibly survive in that kind of environment and be apart from Anna for so long? He also wondered how Anna would hold up for such a long period of time. If he received an extended jail sentence, would Anna leave him—or divorce him—while he was still imprisoned? Thoughts of the Luciano lawsuit and resulting financial ruin were also creeping into his head. All of these "parades of horribles" were beginning to lead him to one conclusion: A good and caring God simply did not exist. John's faith had been destroyed by the events of the past year, and hope for the future was nonexistent. Anticipating prison life, John started thinking in a survival-of-the-fittest mode.

Chapter 16

"Don, I've been running over the events of the trial in my mind incessantly since the jury verdict. Believe me, I'm not blaming you, but what could we have done differently so that the jury would have arrived at the right decision?"

"John, I don't believe we should have done anything differently. Even if we were able to do the entire trial over again, I'd still go at it in the same way. We had a very well-conceived strategy and game plan that we both agreed upon. Unfortunately, the old saying about never knowing what a jury's going to do rang true in this case."

John knew it was just a standard lawyer speech designed to cover the attorney's butt when the chips fell the wrong way. He also knew he'd given the same speech when his trials went south. It was part of protecting yourself against claims of ineptitude.

"Well, if that really is your opinion, then I want to focus right now on our post-trial motion and appellate strategy. Before you start to give me your thoughts, I want to say that I read the newspaper article written by Brown. She quoted you as saying that the jury decision was a "travesty of justice" and that you "would be pursuing all legal avenues" to set aside the verdict. When I read that, it reminded me of similar statements that I've made to reporters when a case was initially lost at the trial level, even though I really didn't believe we would ultimately prevail. So, I want you to give it to me straight. What are my chances of succeeding?"

"Okay, you asked for it, you got it. With Judge Stacey, I see your chances as nil. We've already given him our best shot with our motions and objections, and he hasn't agreed. I don't see him changing his mind at this point."

"Not surprising. What about our chances of winning on appeal?"

"My opinion is that we have a fifty-fifty chance of getting the verdict overturned based on the issues we raised at trial regarding the blood draw and the State's expert testimony."

"I don't like those odds when we tie them into first having to face Judge Stacey for sentencing. I vividly remember you telling me that the rap on Stacey was that he was tough on sentencing defendants who were found guilty by a jury. I know that the max I'm facing is five years. What's your opinion on what he does here?"

"I don't think he'll give you the maximum, based on all the circumstances of the case. But I do believe you're looking at a sentence of three years."

"As sick as that makes me, I can't even say that surprises me after all that's gone wrong for me over the past year. I can't take the risk of facing that much time in jail, even if by some huge stroke of luck I was allowed to remain free on bond while the appeal is pending. I simply couldn't live waiting for the results of the appeal. Also, I won't be allowed to practice law for who knows how long once the Bar gets formal notification about my conviction in the trial court. I'll be immediately suspended, and I know an appeal won't stop the suspension from practicing law. Besides that, no matter what I do about an appeal, my firm is not going to want anything to do with me. I'm headed over there this afternoon, and I know that it's the beginning of the end for me with Smith & Patterson."

"It sounds like you've got this all figured out already. Do you still need my advice?"

John could see that Brisbane was becoming irritated, and he realized Brisbane's frustration would only add more fuel to the slow-roasting furnace he was trapped in. It was time to calm down and let Brisbane run the show. "Yes, of course I want your advice. I didn't mean to upstage you. I was just trying to give you my thoughts and I got carried away. Sorry."

"Okay. In light of your comments, here's what I recommend. I go to Del Garden and work out a plea deal. As long as Luciano agrees to it, I believe Judge Stacey will be okay with it."

"Can you get them to agree to one year?"

"I'll do my best, but that's unlikely. I think the best I'll be able to work out is eighteen months."

"Do your absolute best for the year. Take the eighteen months if we've got no other choice. I've got to get this behind me before I totally flip out."

...

Over at St. Gregory's School, Anna had just finished reviewing a history assignment with the students. She decided now was the best time to bring up John's trial—before her class headed outdoors for a mid-morning recess. Taking a deep breath, she paused and silently asked the Lord for guidance and wisdom.

"Class, before we head outside for recess, there's something I want to discuss with you."

All twenty-five sets of eyes focused on Anna. It was so quiet you could hear a pin drop. "I know what avid readers all of you are, so you might have seen in the newspaper that my husband had to go to court for a trial. Sadly, the jury found him guilty. We were both very surprised and disappointed with the decision. We both think Mr. Taylor was innocent and that the evidence at the trial showed his innocence. Mr. Taylor is meeting today with his lawyer to figure out what he will do next. But unless something big happens and the decision changes, my husband will probably have to go to jail."

Several hands shot up. Anna knew the questions were coming.

"Yes, Amy. You have a question for me?"

"Yes, Mrs. Taylor," said Amy George. "The newspaper said Mr. Taylor might go to jail for five years, and the judge is really mean. Your husband's not going to jail for that long, is he?" Amy was shaking and looked like she was going to start crying any second.

Anna quickly walked over to Amy's desk and took Amy's hands into hers. "I hope and pray that Mr. Taylor will not go to jail for that long. That's why we need all your prayers. And we also need your prayers for the other driver, Mr. Luciano, and his family. Please pray that all of us will be able to get through this terrible tragedy."

Tears were streaming down Anna's face. She returned to her desk and sat down. Amy raised her hand again. "Mrs. Taylor, can we pray for you right now like we did when Jamal was in the hospital?" Anna agreed, and the students formed a circle around Anna's desk. One by one, each of them said a prayer. Some prayed for John, some for Anna, and others prayed for the Luciano family. Amy prayed for both the Taylors and Lucianos. Anna was overwhelmed by their wonderful show of support.

"I don't know what to say to all of you. This means so much to me. Thanks to all of you. I just looked at my watch and saw that we've already used up half of our recess time. You guys better hustle outside and burn off some energy." Anna managed to give them a big smile.

There was a mad dash for the door, and the children were all out in a flash. On the way out, Amy looked back and told Anna she'd be praying for both the Taylor and Luciano families every day. Anna felt as though a circle of light had surrounded her when the children gathered around her. A circle of light that had been sent to keep the forces of darkness at bay. Anna needed and would gladly accept all the help she could get. She wondered how John would get the psychological and emotional support he so desperately needed.

...

John's meeting with Brisbane ended earlier than he expected. He still had two hours to kill, and there was no way he was going to the office that far in advance of the scheduled meeting time, so he decided to go home and have some lunch. When he pulled into the driveway, he noticed the postal carrier had just put some mail in their mailbox. He walked over to the mailbox and pulled out a thick stack of envelopes and ads. After making a sandwich, he started going through the letters and bills, tossing the ones that were of no interest to the side. Suddenly, he came across a letter that was of keen interest to him. The letter was addressed to him and the return address indicated it was from Greg Chatsworth. He couldn't believe a juror was sending him mail. Tearing the envelope open, John began slowly and deliberately reading the correspondence from Chatsworth.

> *Dear Mr. Taylor,*
> *I really struggled with whether I should send this letter to you, but after not being able to sleep at all Wednesday night, I decided to mail it.*
> *I just wanted you to know what a very, very hard*

decision it was for me to find you guilty. Most of the jury also struggled greatly with the decision to hold you accountable for the collision. There was evidence supporting both sides of the case, but in the end we felt that the State had proven its case against you.

I am so sorry that you will now be going to jail, and God knows what else you and your wife have to face. This was a terrible tragedy for both your family and the Luciano family.

I wish both you and your wife the best of luck in the future in overcoming this horrible event.

—Greg Chatsworth

John couldn't believe it. Why would Chatsworth have written something like this? Was he just trying to get rid of a guilty conscience? John didn't see how this letter could help his case at all because Chatsworth had confirmed in it that the jury found that the State had proved its case. Nonetheless, he called Brisbane and read the letter to him over the phone. Although Brisbane initially agreed that the letter was not any help to their case, he asked John to bring it to his office. After he hung up with Brisbane, John went into the den and made a copy for his file. On the way over to Smith & Patterson, John stopped at Brisbane's office and left the original letter with his secretary. He couldn't wait to arrive at Smith & Patterson for more fun and games to begin.

Chapter 17

As he pulled his car into the parking lot at Smith & Patterson's law offices, John noticed that the reserved parking space with his name on it was still there. At least the firm hadn't given away the spot yet. His thought process was becoming more and more erratic, and paranoia was beginning to become the norm. As he walked into the building, he felt a tap on his shoulder. Spinning around, he saw that it was his secretary. Jayne grabbed hold of him and wouldn't let go. When she finally did, John could see she had tears in her eyes and was struggling to find the words to speak to him.

"John, I am so very sorry about the jury decision. I've been worried sick about you and Anna and wanted to call the house to check on the two of you, but I was afraid I'd be bothering you. Then Donna told me about her call and that you'd be coming in today, so I decided to wait until I saw you in person. I hope you're not mad at me for not contacting you sooner."

"Jayne, I could never be mad at you. Don't worry about it.

To address your concerns, Anna is doing as well as can be expected under the circumstances. She returned to school today, which should help keep her mind off this mess I got us into. Hopefully, she did well talking with her students about the trial. When she left this morning, it seemed she was as prepared as she could be for dealing with the kids."

"I'm really glad to hear that. What about you, Sweetheart? How are you doing?"

"Obviously I've been better. I'm trying to hang in there, but it's hard, especially after my meeting today with Don Brisbane."

"Why? What happened?"

"Well, to cut to the chase, as you know I like to do, I really don't have any hope at this point of avoiding jail time. Don thinks he can cut a deal with the State, but even under the best circumstances we're talking twelve months—and more likely eighteen months. So, it's really hard, Jayne. I just can't tell you otherwise."

Jayne started to cry again. She was having tremendous difficulty even responding to what John had told her. "This is so difficult for me to believe, John. For all these terrible tragedies to have happened to you over the past year is unthinkable."

"I couldn't agree more. We better get inside. I don't want to be late for this meeting, and knowing the Old Man, I'll bet they're all waiting for me in the conference room."

John was right. They were waiting for him in the conference room. The Old Man, Patterson, Archibald, and Red were all there. John noticed there was no sign of the new attorney they were bringing in to replace him. Maybe he hadn't been hired yet. The room was filled with tension. So much so that John thought no one was even going to speak. He decided to take the bull by the horns and get through this masquerade.

"Well, seeing as how I asked for this meeting, I guess I'll get started." All eyes were on John, and no one interrupted him, so he saw that as a positive sign to continue.

"I'm sure all of you have read the paper and know the outcome of the trial."

"It was hard to miss, John," injected the Old Man. "Our clients certainly didn't, because the phones have been ringing off the hook the past two days. They all want to know what's going on. Even the four corporate clients mentioned by name in the paper have called wanting to know why their companies' names appeared in the paper. It took quite some time for Jim and me to get them calmed down. We're hoping we don't lose any business as a result of the trial and the newspaper article."

John sighed. The meeting was getting off to a horrible start. He was trying his absolute best to control his temper. After all he had been through in the past week, John didn't want to make his life even worse by having an explosion take place in this room, so he decided to take a conciliatory approach with the Old Man.

"George, I'm extremely sorry for any embarrassment or problems I've caused to the firm. Certainly, I never intended to hurt the firm in any way. I'm here today to try and make my departure as amicable as possible. I met with Don Brisbane this morning. The upshot of that meeting is that Don is going to try to cut a deal with the State for twelve to eighteen months in prison. In light of the jury verdict and the inevitability of prison time, I'm here to tender my resignation effective immediately."

The Old Man and Patterson were both poker faced. Archibald was staring out the window and unable to make eye contact with John. Red was sitting there with a stunned look on her face. John knew she was deeply hurt and troubled by his resignation and impending conviction. She had always been the most loyal to him of any of the attorneys in the office. John viewed her as a true friend, even under these impossible circumstances. He also thought of the associate attorneys and office staff in a positive light. Unfortunately, the same didn't hold true for the Old Man, Patterson, or Archibald. Right now, John's impression of the three of them was that they were all totally unsympathetic to his plight and that their only concern was for their own financial prosperity.

Patterson took the lead in responding to John's resignation. "John, we're all very sorry that it's come to this, but under the circumstances we have no option other than to accept your resignation. Obviously we all wish you and Anna the best in dealing with these terrible events. I know you've already transitioned your cases to other lawyers here in the firm, in the event it ever came to this. So at least we won't have to bother you with any of those details. We'll have Katherine get in touch with you to wrap up the financial details. If there's anything else any of us can do to help, you know how to reach us."

Patterson then got up from his seat, walked around the table and shook John's hand. He was followed by Archibald and the Old Man, both of whom also engaged in a polite handshake. The three of them then left the conference room, leaving only Red behind with John. He took his office keys out of his pocket and gave them to her.

"I'd appreciate it if you would give these keys to Katherine White." Speaking of Katherine, John thought how unprofessional it was for the Old Man and Patterson to leave wrapping up the financial details to Katherine. She was the firm's office manager/certified public accountant and not a partner or lawyer in the firm. The financial details should have been handled by one of the senior partners, not a non-lawyer employee. Although he wanted to express his displeasure to Red, he didn't want to inject her any deeper into this tangled mess and decided not to bring it up. She had enough on her plate with her caseload and pursuit of a partnership.

"I'll be glad to give the keys to Katherine. John, please let me know if there is anything I can to do help you or Anna. I don't want you to think I'm ignoring you, but on the other hand, I don't want to call and disturb either of you. Please know that I'm here for both of you in any way possible."

"I do know that Red, believe me. I'll let you know what you can do. Maybe you can come and visit me in prison," John said with a phony smile on his face.

"I can do that, John." She was dead serious, and he knew it.

"Thanks. Anna will let you know the details. Right now, I've got to run. I'm going out the back door of the conference room. I'll be in touch."

With that, John left the office to return home. He fully expected it was the last time he would ever set foot in the law offices of Smith & Patterson. *What a wonderful way to end twelve years of legal practice,* he thought.

When he arrived home, he saw that Anna was already there. How he hoped that she had a much better day than he experienced. Anna was on the phone when he walked into the kitchen. Based on what he heard Anna saying, he could tell that she was talking to Tess. He was glad Anna had Tess as a friend and knew Tess would be of invaluable assistance to Anna while he was in prison. John couldn't believe that he was thinking of such scenarios. Anna got off the phone and came over to him with her arms outstretched. For several minutes the two of them embraced each other without speaking. How they both wished that such intimate moments could continue uninterrupted in the future.

"How was your day, Anna?"

"Actually, it went much better than I'd anticipated. The students were all very supportive of me, and there were no real bumps in the road." Anna decided not to tell John about the students' prayers, as she was concerned about his reaction. *Better to let this go for now,* she thought.

"I'm glad to hear that. Unfortunately, my day didn't go as smoothly as yours."

"Why, what happened?"

John told her in detail about the day's events with Brisbane, the letter from Chatsworth, and the meeting at Smith & Patterson.

142

Fifteen minutes later, when John was finished, he collapsed on the couch. He was mentally and physically exhausted. Anna knew she needed to provide him with an emotional lift.

"John, you need to understand how much I love you and will always be with you spiritually, even when I'm not physically with you." Taking his hands into hers, she continued speaking to him. "Please don't get angry with me, but I must tell you that I feel God is watching out for us, and that with His help, we'll be able to overcome these trials we're going through."

"I'm not angry with you, Anna. I've been making that mistake too much lately and don't want to repeat it. But I do have to tell you that I'm very upset with God. If God was really as good as the Bible and all the religious demagogues portray Him, then none of what has happened to us over the past year would ever have occurred. In fact, at this point in my life, I'm not sure God or Jesus even exist. But if they do, I sure don't see them as being benevolent in any way. I'm sorry to be talking like this to you, but it's the way I feel."

Anna could see that her husband's battle with his faith and hope for the future was at a critical breaking point. Rather than engaging him in any further discussion along these lines, she skillfully changed the topic. But she knew he needed help dealing with the adversities of life quickly—before his downward spiral became irreversible.

"Let's focus on something we both enjoy. I haven't made Italian sausage and peppers in a long time. How about if I go to the store and get some sausage and some fresh pole beans? Then I'll cook us an Italian feast. That delicious dinner ought to cheer us both up."

"Sounds like a great plan. And I'll help."

"It's a deal."

Chapter 18

"Father Anderson, I want to thank you so much for seeing me. By the way, I really enjoyed your homily, and I noticed that the other parishioners did, too. You really have the ability to move the congregation," said Anna, on Sunday after Mass.

"I appreciate your kind words, Anna. Now tell me what I can do to help."

"Father, I just don't know how to deal with John. Ever since the jury found him guilty, he's become more and more negative and unable to focus on reality. He's also lost his faith in the existence of a good God, and he's not sure God even exists," Anna replied.

As Father Anderson attentively listened, Anna took a deep breath and continued. "Last Friday John had a meeting with his attorney, and the reality is that he'll be going to prison. If a sentencing agreement can be reached, it looks like it will be anywhere from twelve to eighteen months. Things are deteriorating daily, and I'm afraid that John might have a mental breakdown. I've suggested he come talk to you, but he absolutely refuses. I also told him he really needs to see a counselor, but he also rejected that idea. At this point, I'm running out of ideas. Do you have any suggestions?"

"Did John ever read the prayer card I gave him?" Father Anderson asked.

"No, he didn't want anything to do with it. I read it to him in the car on the Sunday you gave it to him, but I don't think he even heard it. And then, after the jury verdict, he was so aggravated that I thought he might destroy it. So I hid it in one of my dressers."

Father Anderson thought for a moment and then said, "Anna, I have to say that based on everything John has had to endure over the past year, his anger and rejection of God and Jesus is not unusual. Unfortunately, I've seen this happen many times when disastrous events overwhelm people. But I also have to say that sometimes a subsequent event will occur that causes the person to regain his faith in even stronger ways."

Father Anderson paused again and then asked Anna, "Let me ask you this: You're not concerned that John may harm himself or you or anyone else, are you?"

"No, Father, I'm not," Anna quickly answered. "I have no basis to believe John would ever do that. My concern is for his spiritual, mental, and emotional well-being, not that he would physically hurt anyone."

"I'm relieved to hear you say that," said Father Anderson. "For the time being, in view of John's refusal to seek either psychological or religious counseling, our options for helping him are limited. Of course, we'll both be praying for him, but we can't force him to seek professional help. But when he gets into the prison system, he will most likely be required to undergo a psychological evaluation. I served as a chaplain for several years at a state facility, and I'm familiar with the way the system operates. So, although neither of us wants to see John go to jail, there may be some value that comes from it. We need to pray that some positives come from John's incarceration and that he receives the help he needs for all he's dealing with."

"I never thought of that, Father. I appreciate your encouragement. It gives me hope."

"Speaking of faith and hope, Anna, how are you doing in those areas?"

"Truthfully, I've been better. The events of the past year are starting to take their toll on me. One thing that's been very helpful is the prayer card you gave to John. I read it every day, and it helps me focus on where my thoughts should be. One of my favorite parts is where it says that God often speaks to us through others when we cry out for help. I believe that's what you've done in the past and are doing now with me."

Father Anderson smiled. "I'm so glad to hear you say that, Anna. Your continued faith in a benevolent God will be rewarded, I can assure you. With your faith, which is much larger than a mustard seed, nothing will be impossible. I also assure you that I will do everything in my power to assist both you and John in overcoming this mountain of trouble that stands before you."

"God bless you, Father, for everything you've done for us."

...

Back in Palm Beach, John was re-reading a letter he'd received the previous day from his insurance company. The letter acknowledged receipt of the civil lawsuit filed against John by attorney Mayberry on behalf of the Lucianos. John was advised that defense of his case had been assigned to Bruce Davidson, Esq., and that John should contact Davidson as soon as possible to go over the details of the litigation. The letter also contained a reservation of rights clause that put John on notice that the carrier was investigating the circumstances of the suit and might later decide coverage was not available for some or all of the claims against John. He was also advised that the carrier did not cover claims for punitive damages against him. Davidson and John had litigated against each other on multiple occasions, and they mutually respected and trusted each other. John had Davidson's cell phone number and called him right away. The two of them agreed they would meet Monday morning at nine o'clock at Davidson's office, and John wanted to make sure he was fully prepared for the meeting. He carefully studied the letter from the insurer and the terms of the underlying and umbrella policies, both of which were with the same insurance company. During the course of reading the policies, he became drowsy and fell asleep. Suddenly, he was awakened by the phone ringing. He jumped up to see who was calling and saw that the call was from Katherine White's direct line at Smith & Patterson's office. He decided to answer the phone.

"Good morning, Katherine. Why are you working on a Sunday?"

"What else is new? Actually, I met earlier today with Mr. Smith and Mr. Patterson about finalizing your financial arrangements with the firm and was calling to discuss it. Is now a good time?"

"As good a time as any. What did they want you to tell me?"

"Well, the firm decided to pay you for three months salary beginning from this last pay period, but there won't be any bonus paid since your billing and collections were below your budgeted amount," Katherine explained. "All of the funds in your retirement account will be rolled over into whatever qualified account you specify. You should check with your CPA about that. The firm did not provide you with health insurance because you were covered under Anna's school plan. The life insurance policy you had with the firm can be transferred over to you individually, if you would like; and you will be solely responsible for the payment of any insurance premiums. I think that covers it."

Katherine paused. "Oh, yes, and we'll also need you to sign a general release as part of the termination package."

Although John was disappointed in what he was being offered, he realized he had no choice in the matter. *This was really a take-it or leave-it proposition,* he thought. Other than the three months' salary, there was nothing he was being told that he was not already entitled to under the law. So much for the twelve years of blood, sweat, and tears he'd given to Smith & Patterson. He saw no point in expressing his displeasure with Katherine. She didn't make this decision. The Old Man and Patterson did. Now he understood why they didn't want to personally attend to the details of the termination with him. He assumed they were too embarrassed to do so, based on their paltry payout to the attorney who for the last five years had been the largest revenue producer in the firm. *So what else was new,* he thought.

"When can we finalize the paperwork, Katherine?"

"I can have everything ready tomorrow."

"Would you please have George sign for the firm first and then bring the papers to me at my house to sign? I have a copy machine, so we can copy a set for me, and you can take back the original. That would make everything much easier."

"That's fine with me, John. Just talk to your CPA in the morning to see how he wants to handle the rollover of your retirement fund monies, and call me to let me know so I can have the necessary papers ready for you to sign when I come over."

"Will do. I'll talk to you in the morning."

Anna returned home shortly after John's conversation with Katherine. He filled her in on the details without expressing his opinion as to the inadequacy of the amounts he was receiving. John was becoming more and more numb with each passing day of continued turmoil. He was beginning to resign himself to a life devoid of purpose and significance. He desperately needed and wanted a change from what he felt was his meaningless life, but he couldn't figure out how that could be accomplished. It would take something or someone much larger than himself to provide the answer.

Chapter 19

"Good morning, my name is John Taylor, and I have an appointment to see Bruce Davidson," John announced to the receptionist.

"Please take a seat, Mr. Taylor. Mr. Davidson will be right with you."

Five minutes later, Davidson appeared in the reception area, and after exchanging the usual courtesies with John, led him back to his office.

Looking around, John commented, "Nice digs, Bruce. I never saw your office before."

"Thanks. It's my home away from home," explained Davidson sheepishly, wanting to get to the point of the meeting.

"John, I read the paper and know about the jury verdict. Saying I'm sorry just doesn't convey how badly I feel for you and Anna. But I'm prepared to give Mr. Mayberry the fight of his life. I want you to know I'm behind you all the way."

"I appreciate it, Bruce." John thought to himself that he would be in for a lot more lawyer bravado, just as he went through with Brisbane. None of that mattered to him. He was only interested in the final result; the rest was meaningless. "I guess we have a lot to talk about, especially the carrier's reservation of rights letter that I received."

"We sure do. Let's start with my being retained on your behalf by the insurance company. As you know, the insurer is paying my fees and costs, but you are my client in the litigation, not the company. You mentioned the reservation of rights letter. I got a copy of it from them and want to explore that in detail with you. I've also read Mayberry's Complaint. Based on the allegations of the Complaint, two things are clear: The punitive damages claim is not covered by either of your policies. Also, the total amount of your coverage under both policies is six million, and the Complaint seeks damages in excess of ten million. So you will have no coverage with the carrier for any award or settlement in excess of six million."

"I'm with you so far, Bruce."

"The more complicated part comes in with the carrier potentially determining in the future that no coverage is available due to the issue of the DUI. I'm not saying it's going to happen, but that's part of the reservation of rights. As you're probably aware, the carrier would still be under a duty to provide you with a legal defense in the case, even if it ultimately took the position that no coverage at all was available to you. I just want to make sure you understand all these nuances."

"I've understood everything you told me, and nothing surprises me. I appreciate you being so upfront on all these issues."

"I'll also be putting all of this in a written letter to you, in conformance with Bar rules. You'll need to carefully review it, and if the representation terms are acceptable, then sign it and return the letter to me. Also, John, one more thing. The letter will address your right, and need, to obtain counsel of your own choosing to independently advise you regarding the issues involved in the case. Under the facts and circumstances of this matter, you would be wise to do so. Of course, any legal fees or costs incurred by any lawyer you select will have to be paid in full by you."

"Yeah, I've already considered the need for obtaining advice of independent counsel. In fact, I've spoken with Chris McConnell about representing me, and he's agreed to do so. Chris told me he knew you well and that I was in excellent hands."

"That's good to hear, especially from Chris. He's one of the top insurance defense lawyers in Florida. How do you know him?"

"We were best friends in law school and have stayed close since then. Although I'll pay him for his time, he's really doing this as a favor to me. I don't intend to unleash him to watch your every move. His role will be much more limited in scope, and he'll only get involved if needed regarding potential issues in coverage or the amount of damages claims. Fortunately, with his talent and experience, I didn't feel going about it in that way would be imprudent, and neither did he."

"I absolutely agree. I'm glad we got all that behind us. Now, let's talk about the accident and the trial."

For the next two hours, John and Davidson discussed in great detail all the circumstances of the accident, the sheriff's investigation and charges, and the trial. Although John was impressed with Davidson's probing questions and legal acumen, he felt a sense of deja vu, as though the trial was repeating itself. He refused to allow himself any optimism as to the ultimate outcome of this phase of the continued nightmare.

On his way home from the meeting with Davidson, John called his CPA and got his advice on how to most effectively accomplish the rollover of his retirement funds. After that, he phoned Katherine White and relayed the information to her. She told him all the paperwork would be completed by mid-afternoon, and that she would bring the documents to his home today for signature. True to her word, White arrived at 3:30, and fifteen minutes later, John completed the termination of his partnership with Smith & Patterson. *Twelve years as a lawyer straight down the toilet,* he thought to himself. Now that he had completed this phase of his new life, his thoughts turned to Brisbane and whether or not he had been able to schedule a meeting yet with Del Garden about the sentencing deal. Although he was chomping at the bit to call Brisbane, he decided it wouldn't be a good idea to push him. This was in Brisbane's hands now, and no good could come of John interfering with the process. He'd just have to wait for the call from his counselor.

Fifteen minutes later, Anna arrived home and John shared the day's events with her. In turn, Anna described what had happened at school. Nothing earthshaking had gone on, although one of Anna's students had made a comment to her, which was apparently a quote from his father regarding John's trial. The student's father had said something to the effect that we're all better off with one less shyster on the streets. Anna was taken aback by the statement, but before she could react, the boy sitting behind the offender cracked him on the back of the head with his hand. No one was hurt, and Anna did her best to control the situation and equally reprimand both boys, although she had a hard time not laughing up a storm. When John heard the story he laughed harder and longer than he had in many months and thought to himself that justice had prevailed at school.

Chapter 20

It was now mid-week and still no word from Brisbane regarding the sentencing deal. John was becoming more and more annoyed and couldn't believe he hadn't heard anything. Although it was only ten in the morning, he was already exhausted. He collapsed on the living room couch and fell into a deep sleep. Even in his dreams he was unable to find any peace, and he awoke several hours later in a cold sweat. Looking at the clock, John saw that it was now one thirty. Focusing on the dreams he'd just had, he began shuddering. John dreamt that while he was in prison, Anna decided to hit the singles scene and hooked up with a lawyer in town who was his archrival. To top it off, Anna divorced him—and took all their money. John was left alone and penniless in this latest episode of his ongoing nightmare series.

Returning to reality, John was still apprehensive about the future. He was particularly concerned about how Anna would get along while he was in jail. Although he knew Tess and some of the employees at St. Gregory's School and Church would watch out for her, Anna had no immediate family members to support her. Anna's parents had both been tragically killed in a car wreck some ten years ago. Anna was an only child, and the few aunts, uncles, and cousins she had did not stay in contact with her—nor had Anna attempted to keep track of any of them. Although Anna would consistently pray for the well-being of all her extended family members, there had been no communication between any of them since the death of Anna's mom and dad.

The Taylor side of the family was no better for Anna as a possible support network. John's mom and dad had both been incessant smokers beginning with their high school years, and they both had died from lung cancer. Mr. Taylor was the first to go, four years ago, followed six months later by his wife. John had only one sibling, a younger brother named Ed, who had joined the Merchant Marines seven years ago. No contact had been made between the brothers since their parents' passing, and John had no clue as to Ed's present whereabouts. Both of John's parents were only children, so there were no aunts, uncles, or cousins on his side of the family.

The total lack of family support—especially for Anna— added to the never-ending pressure being experienced by John. He felt as though he'd explode at any moment. As terrible as it had been for the two of them when Maria passed away, they still had each other to turn to for support. But if John went to prison, neither would be able to seek help from the other. His thought process continued to deteriorate into a nightmare of hellish proportions.

Before he could sink further into the abyss, the phone rang. Looking at his caller ID, he saw it was Brisbane's office. Taking a deep breath, he answered. "Don, I've been waiting all week to hear from you. What's happening with the sentencing deal?"

"I'm sorry it took this long to get back to you, but I didn't want to call until I had everything lined up. I met with Del Garden yesterday morning. Initially, he was adamant for two years. I couldn't even get close to him agreeing to one year. But after two hours, I got him to go with eighteen months, as the two of us agreed."

"What about Luciano? Did Del Garden get his okay?"

"Yes, he did. Del Garden actually went over to his home this morning to talk with the family. Apparently, now that a guilty verdict was obtained, they've both calmed down and agreed to an eighteen-month sentence. So, with Del Garden's and the Lucianos' agreement, I think Judge Stacey will approve it."

"Okay, you did what I asked. I wish it was the year, but it's what we discussed. It's certainly better than the hard-nosed judge putting me away for three years or more. Let me ask you this: We're still some three weeks away from the sentencing hearing, which had been scheduled for half a day. Now that the parties have agreed to the jail term, can we move the date up? It seems to me that we ought to be able to conclude the hearing in an hour, and with Stacey being on senior status, he should be available sooner."

"We can probably do that. Are you sure you want to? It means you'll go to jail that much sooner."

"I want to get this over as soon as we can. There's no way I want to be here in this house for the next three weeks thinking about going to prison. It's already driving me nuts, and I'll be no good to Anna or myself if I have to stay here that long. So please, see what you can do to expedite the proceedings. One more thing. I want to start my sentence at the conclusion of the hearing. Can you arrange that as well?"

"Yes, you can turn yourself in at the hearing. I'll start working on an expedited date when we get off the phone and should be able to let you know by tomorrow."

"I appreciate it. Talk to you then."

After John hung up the phone, he decided not to tell Anna

about his conversation with Brisbane until after he'd heard back from him. There was no point in forewarning her of his decision, he thought, as his mind was already made up and nothing she could say or do would change it. From his perspective, the sooner he began serving his sentence in Hades, the sooner he'd be released.

Chapter 21

It was Friday morning, and Anna had just left for school. Thursday had passed with no word from Brisbane. John was becoming extremely agitated and decided if Brisbane didn't phone by noon, he'd call and give Brisbane a piece of his mind. At eleven, the phone rang. It was Brisbane calling from his cell phone.

"Okay, Don, what's happening with the new sentencing date?"

"We've got it set for next Friday at four o'clock. The Court has set aside one hour for the hearing. The Lucianos will be there to tell the Judge they approve of the eighteen months. I've also told Del Garden that you want to turn yourself in at the conclusion of the hearing, and he's making the appropriate arrangements with the Sheriff's Office. So everything has been lined up like you wanted, John."

"Thanks for the information. I guess we'll talk sometime early next week about the hearing?"

"I'll call you Monday morning, and we'll go over all the details."

After he hung up the phone, John thought about what he was going to say to Anna. He knew she wouldn't be happy that the sentencing had been moved up two weeks, but she would just have to understand and deal with it. John spent the rest of the day sleeping on the couch. For a change, there were no nightmares, and he was able to get some much-needed rest. Around five p.m., he was awakened by the sound of the garage door going up. As Anna entered the house, he sprung off the couch and prepared for the anticipated battle.

Greeting Anna with a kiss, he asked how her day at school was. She replied that it was uneventful except for one of her students falling during recess. The child had to be taken to the emergency room for stitches in his elbow. The student's mother had called from the hospital to report that he was doing fine and would be back to class on Monday.

Then Anna asked John about his day, and John decided to tell her about his conversation with Brisbane.

"I spoke with Don today. He has everything lined up with Del Garden regarding the sentencing hearing. The Lucianos will be there to tell the Judge that they don't object to an eighteen-month sentence," John said. "Don thinks the Court will accept the deal. There's one more thing," John said with little emotion. "The hearing will take place next Friday at four p.m., instead of three weeks from now."

"How did that happen?" Anna nervously asked.

John wanted to tell her the Judge moved it forward, but instead he decided to be honest with her. "I asked for the hearing to be moved up, Anna." He faked a half-smile and continued. "I couldn't bear the thought of staying in this house for another three weeks, just waiting for the sentencing. It seemed to me that the faster I start serving my time, the faster I'm released." He paused and took her hand in his. "I know you won't be happy with that, but I hope you can understand."

Anna's mind raced back to her conversation with Father Anderson about John receiving psychological counseling in prison. He had refused to seek help of any type. Perhaps it was best for him to start his sentence sooner so he could begin dealing with the tragedies in his life. Anna knew better than to communicate those thoughts to John and instead expressed her feelings in a different way.

"You're right, John. I'm not happy with that, but I do understand everything you're saying, so I support you in your decision. Dealing with this is hard on both of us, so I want us united in how we handle it. I don't want to be divided. That would only make matters worse for us."

"Thanks, Anna. I was hoping you'd understand. The sooner I get this over with, the better."

Chapter 22

Anna had re-instituted her exercise regime and was out first thing Saturday morning for a six-mile run. She now had her time down to an eight-minute-per-mile pace and was looking forward to regaining her old form of clipping along at seven minutes per mile.

The next morning Anna met Tess for a tennis match at seven. She was playing better now than she had several weeks ago, and she gave Tess a run for her money. Tess was happy Anna was doing so well in spite of all the adversity she was facing.

Tess was adamant about doing everything possible to help Anna, especially when John would be incarcerated. Tess recognized that would be when the real test for Anna would come. So Tess had called a family conference a few days earlier, and it was unanimously agreed by all four Milans that Anna would be invited over every Sunday afternoon for some lively board games and dinner. Tess decided to wait to tell Anna anything about the invitation until after John began serving his sentence. After their match was over, Tess struck up a conversation with Anna about the sentencing hearing.

"Anna, when did you say the sentencing hearing was?"

"At four p.m. on Friday. I'm leaving school a little early to go home and get John for the hearing. He's going to surrender to the Sheriff's Office right after, so he won't be driving anywhere."

Tess could see how upset Anna was and put her arm around Anna's shoulders. "Anna, would you like me to meet you at the hearing? I'd really like to come, if it's okay with you."

"Believe me, I'd really like you to be there, but I'm worried about John's reaction. This is going to be very difficult and embarrassing for him. It would probably be better if you weren't there. Thanks, though. I really appreciate your offer."

"I understand. How about if I come over to your house that evening?"

"That'd be good. Thanks, Tess."

After Anna got home, she quickly showered, changed, and headed to Mass. John had fallen asleep in the den watching a tennis match on television, and she decided not to wake him. She knew that not only would he refuse to go to Mass, but he might even become aggravated with her for going. There was no sense running that risk, so she left without disturbing him.

When Anna arrived at St. Gregory's, she noticed that Father Anderson was not in his usual position before Mass, greeting the congregation as they walked in. Anna asked one of the ushers where he was. "He's enjoying a week of vacation visiting his family up North," the usher explained. "He'll be back for services next Sunday." Although Anna was glad Father Anderson was able to spend time with his family, she was disappointed she wouldn't see him.

After Mass, Anna headed to the cemetery to visit Maria's grave. As Anna knelt in front of the gravestone, she prayed, thanking God that her baby was in Heaven with Him. She asked for help for herself and for John in dealing with his prison sentence. Although she did not directly hear from the Almighty, the message of the prayer card came to mind. Anna recalled how Father Anderson, Principal Barnes, and Tess had spoken with her in such a way that she believed it was a response from Heaven. A sense of peace and well-being washed over her as she prayed. She knew deep in her heart that Maria was safe in Heaven and that she and John would overcome the mountain of trouble that stood before them.

While Anna was visiting their daughter's grave and praying, John was at home continuing his downward spiral. His negative thinking was becoming more and more pervasive, yet he still wouldn't admit he needed help. Since the jury verdict, his life had continued to go downhill. He was now sitting in front of the television watching some mindless program in order to escape the realities of his new life. Even his usual forms of stress relief—surfing, weightlifting, and pounding away on his punching bags—had fallen by the wayside. The world had become a dark and miserable place for John, devoid of justice and any hope for the future.

Monday came and went without any earth-shattering events. In the morning, John spoke with Brisbane by phone for nearly an hour regarding the sentencing hearing and the subsequent surrendering to the Sheriff's Office. Brisbane briefed him fully on what to expect. After that, John had an extended phone conversation with Davidson about the personal injury case. John explained how Davidson would need to contact Anna next week to find out the details of his imprisonment so the two of them could communicate about the case. Davidson also faxed John a copy of the "Answer and Affirmative Defenses" that was filed in response to the Complaint prepared by Mayberry. Speaking of Mayberry, Davidson advised John that Mayberry and his entire office were all wrapped up for the next thirty days with a jury trial that was just beginning at the West Palm Beach Courthouse. John was glad to hear that. It would help keep the wolves at bay in his case, even if just temporarily. The last business matter John had to wrap up concerned speaking with Chris McConnell. John let McConnell know about his surrender after the sentencing hearing, and that Anna would be able to tell him how to make contact with John. Now that John had attended to all of his business matters, he resigned himself to another four days of waiting for his hell on earth to become even hotter and more miserable.

...

On Thursday morning, John and Anna were extremely edgy. This was the last day and night they would have together for eighteen months. The very thought brought both of them to tears, but they were powerless to change the situation. Now the question was how they would handle the troubles that stood before them. When they went to bed, John held Anna in his arms for the entire night. Although they didn't speak, the physical intimacy of each other's touch provided them with a measure of peace and comfort, even if it was short-lived.

Chapter 23

John woke up before Anna and quietly got out of bed. Silently he made his way into the kitchen. He had decided to whip up one of Anna's favorite breakfasts—turkey sausage links and whole wheat pancakes. Just as he finished cooking and was putting breakfast on their plates, Anna appeared with a quizzical look on her face.

"What's all this, John?"

"I thought I'd prepare one of your favorite breakfasts this morning," John replied with a big smile on his face. Suddenly, his expression changed, and he added, "After all, I won't be able to do this again for a long time." Tears rolled down his face, and he opened his arms to embrace her. After several minutes of holding Anna close to him, he regained his composure and said, "Breakfast is getting cold, Sweetheart. Let's eat." He poured each of them a cup of coffee and a glass of orange juice. They sat down and ate what would be their last meal together for an extended period of time.

After Anna had showered and dressed, she reminded John she'd be back to pick him up at three p.m. to drive to the courthouse. He nodded but did not verbally respond. After she left for school, he sat in a hypnotic state in front of the television set in the den, unable and unwilling to focus on the events that would be transpiring later in the day.

Meanwhile, over at St. Gregory's School, Anna was having a difficult time focusing on her class. She decided to give the students a surprise test, which was met with a round of boos. After she announced that the test would be an open-book exam, and they would be allowed two hours to complete it, the class calmed down, and she was able to continue in the classroom without having to concentrate on any specific matter. While Anna was in class with her students, Tess was on the phone with Principal Barnes. The two of them knew each other through Anna. Tess had called Barnes to discuss the need for Anna to have a formal support group from the school once John was imprisoned. Although Tess told the principal that she would do everything she could to help Anna, Tess knew it would not be adequate and that Anna would also need help from some of the teachers and staff. Alice Barnes wholeheartedly agreed and told Tess she would recruit several employees at the school and get back to her the following week with a game plan.

Anna arrived home precisely at three. As John left their home, he looked around and realized this was the last time he'd be there for eighteen months. It hardly seemed true. He felt like lashing out at God for not helping him to be found innocent. Fortunately, he refrained because he knew it would upset Anna even more than she already was. On the way to the courthouse, neither of them spoke. When they arrived at the courthouse, John saw Cassandra Brown disappearing into the elevators. He thought to himself, *The vulture has returned for her last meal.*

As John and Anna entered the courtroom, they saw Del Garden and Brisbane as well as Cassandra Brown. There were

166

also two sheriff's deputies present. John assumed they were there to take him to jail once the hearing concluded. Anna took her seat in the same spot she had occupied during the trial, and John went to the counsel table and sat next to Brisbane. They talked quietly about the hearing until Bailiff Simon commanded everyone to rise. At the very same moment Judge Stacey entered the courtroom, Mrs. Luciano wheeled her husband into the room. After the judge sat down, Del Garden motioned for Mrs. Luciano to bring her husband up to the front where Del Garden was sitting. After positioning him next to Del Garden's chair with Bailiff Simon's help, Mrs. Luciano took a seat in the back of the courtroom.

"Gentlemen," Judge Stacey began, "I understand that a proposed sentence has been agreed to between the State and Mr. Taylor and that you are here today seeking my approval."

Both Del Garden and Brisbane simultaneously rose from their seats and responded in the affirmative. They each remained standing as Judge Stacey questioned them in detail regarding the sentence. Stacey appeared satisfied with their responses and turned his attention to Anthony Luciano.

"Mr. Luciano, I understand that you and your wife are in agreement as to the proposed sentence of incarceration for eighteen months, is that correct?"

"Yes, your Honor. We're in agreement."

"And do you both also understand the maximum sentence Mr. Taylor could receive is five years in prison?"

"Yes, we do, your Honor."

"I understand that you and Mrs. Luciano are pursuing monetary restitution from Mr. Taylor via a civil lawsuit."

"Yes, we are. Mr. Robert Mayberry is our attorney and has filed the case."

Judge Stacey looked impressed at the very mention of Mayberry's name. He then asked Mrs. Luciano if she had anything to say. After receiving a negative response, he proceeded to accept the agreed disposition and sentenced John to eighteen months in prison. The judge then remanded John into the custody of the Sheriff's Department for further transfer to the State prison authorities, declared that the proceedings were concluded, and left the courtroom. Anthony and Elizabeth Luciano were the next to exit. Then the two sheriff's deputies approached John to take him into custody. John asked if he could say goodbye to Anna, and they agreed.

John embraced Anna and kissed her on the lips. Both of them were in a state of shock and didn't know what to say to the other. The deputies led John away through a side door to be photographed and fingerprinted before they brought him to the main jail facility of Palm Beach County for further processing pending transfer to the State correctional officers. As Anna watched John being led away and then disappear into the recesses of the courthouse, the reality of her husband's incarceration struck at the fabric of her being. She sat down and wept. Brisbane was the only other person in the room. He came over, handed her some tissues, and sat down next to her.

"Anna, I know this is incredibly hard on you, and I am so sorry this happened. Would you like to know what's going to happen to John now?"

"Yes," she managed to reply.

"The first thing is that he'll be fingerprinted and photographed by the Sheriff's Office. Then he'll be transported to the main jail facility of Palm Beach County. After he arrives, he'll be put in a prison uniform and wait for transfer to the State officers. That probably won't happen until tomorrow. More than likely, because of his short duration in the Palm Beach County jail, he'll be placed in a cell by himself where he'll be able to sleep. Of course, he'll receive meals while he's there. When John is picked up by the State officers, they'll take him to what is known as a reception center for inmates, located in western Dade County. While he's there, he will undergo a barrage of tests and exams. The prison authorities will want to make sure he's not carrying any communicable diseases, and he will have his hair cut. His stay there is temporary. It could be several days or perhaps a couple of weeks, depending on the results of John's tests and exams, and where the State officials feel he'd best be relocated." Putting his hand on hers, he smiled gently. "I hope this helps you understand the process a little better."

"Yes, it does. Can I ask you a couple of questions?" Anna asked quietly.

"Sure, ask away," Brisbane replied.

"Will John receive psychological or spiritual counseling while in prison? Also, when will I know where he's being sent and when I can visit him?"

"I'm not an expert on the counseling matters, but it's my understanding psychological counseling may be mandatory depending upon the results of John's interviews with the medical staff. I believe the spiritual counseling is voluntary because the State really can't force religion on the inmates. As to your other question, when John knows where he is permanently going, he'll be allowed to call and tell you. After that, you can get in touch with the prison where John is being sent to determine how and when you can visit him. And please don't hesitate to contact me if I can help you in any way."

"Everything you told me is very helpful. I'll let you know if I have any more questions."

On the way out of the courthouse, Cassandra Brown approached Anna to speak with her. "Mrs. Taylor, I'm not here to ask you any questions or get a statement from you, I just want to tell you something."

"What's that?"

"I'm sorry about what's happened to your husband. I sat through most of the trial and thought the jury would find him innocent. I wish he had been. That may be hard for you to believe in light of my article, but it's the truth. I tried to be as objective as I could when I reported on the trial, and I'll do my best again with my article on the sentencing."

Anna looked intently at the young woman standing before her. She couldn't be more than twenty-five years old. With her svelte figure, long brown hair, and freckles, she was the epitome of the All-American girl. Anna didn't think she had a dishonest bone in her body.

"Thank you for your kind words, Ms. Brown. I realize you have a job to do. It's just extremely difficult for my husband and me to read these articles about him. You obviously don't know John, but let me assure you that he is one of the kindest, most gentle men I have ever known. Hopefully, he will be released from prison eighteen months from now and still have those attributes. Now, please excuse me. It's been a very long and trying day, and I need to go home."

"Of course. Thank you for your time."

On the way home, Anna called Tess on her cell phone. Between sobs, she asked, "Would it be possible for you to meet me at my house? The hearing is over, and John has been taken away. I really need to be with someone, Tess."

"I'll be there within thirty minutes."

Thirty minutes later Tess rang the front doorbell. Anna let her in, and then fell into her arms. They sat down on the sofa, quietly hugging each other. For several minutes no one spoke. Then Tess decided it might be good for Anna to talk about what had happened.

"How bad was it Anna, when John was taken away?"

"Next to the day Maria died, it was the worst moment of my life. I can't believe he's gone, and right now I don't even know where the State is going to send him. I would never say this to anyone except you, but right now I'm very angry and upset with God for not only what's happened to John, but also for what happened with Maria. I'm starting to think that maybe John is right about there not being a good God. Tess, please help me."

Anna started crying. Her body shook as all her stored-up emotions of the last year came out. All the while, Tess sat with her silently, holding Anna's hand while Anna broke down. Finally, when Anna stopped crying for a few minutes, Tess said, "Anna, I'm going to say a prayer for you and John right now. Just listen. You don't have to say a word. Okay?" Anna nodded her head in agreement.

"Dear God, we respectfully come before You and ask for Your help for John and Anna. Please help John deal in a Christian manner with everything he's facing while in prison, and please help him return to the godly man of faith he's always been. He needs You right now more than ever. Please let him hear You speak to him through other of your children here on earth. And please, God, continue to stay with Anna during these dark times. Please help her to remember and believe all the petitions in the prayer given by Father Anderson to John. I also ask, dear God, that You help Anna realize that it's not wrong to be angry for what has befallen the two of them. Please listen to her cries for help, and comfort her. Just as with John, let Anna know of Your concern and Your goodness by the words and actions of other of Your children here on earth. And please remind Anna that when she has doubts as to Your existence or Your goodness, those doubts are the result of Satan trying to separate her from You. And we thank You, God, for all the blessings You have bestowed upon John and Anna over the years, and in particular, the blessing of bringing them together to live out their years with each other here on earth and in the eternal life You've given them. Thank You for all the blessings John and Anna have received. They are many, abundant, and varied. In Jesus' name we pray. Amen."

"Amen," replied Anna. "Thank you, Tess. I don't know what I'd do without you."

"Probably a lot better. You know what a pain I can be." Big smiles erupted on both ladies' faces.

"Speaking of my being a pain, Anna, I hope that I won't

poison you, but all the Milans would like you to be our guest at dinner this Sunday. Why don't you come over around three, and we'll play some games with the kids first. Of course, that's if you're even speaking to me after I kick your behind at our tennis match Sunday morning!"

"We'll just see who kicks whose behind!" Anna chuckled. "I can't wait to put you in your place! Oh, and I'll bring dessert for our dinner soiree."

Chapter 24

On Saturday morning at six thirty, Anna was already out and cruising along on an eight-mile run. Her goal was to head down the beach road to where it connected to North County Road and then run on North County until she reached Royal Palm Way. That would be the four-mile mark. She would then turn around and return home for a total workout of eight miles. The first two miles had passed easily enough and, looking at her watch, she saw she was moving at a seven-and-half-minute-per-mile pace. Anna was determined to push herself even harder as she really wanted to crack the seven-minute-mile barrier.

She picked up her pace and by the four-mile turnaround, she had reduced her speed to an average of 7:15 per mile. The fifth and sixth miles were equally as quick, but then she hit a brick wall and had to stop running. Anna felt exhausted. She had pushed herself too hard for too long. Next time out, she would be careful to pace herself. As she walked home the last two miles, her thoughts turned to John. She wondered how he was doing. She couldn't believe he was gone and wouldn't be at home when she returned. Suddenly, thoughts of reporter Brown's newspaper article about John's sentencing came to mind. She knew the paper would be in the driveway, and she dreaded reading it. Still, she felt she had no choice because she wanted to know how Brown had publicly portrayed her husband.

When she arrived home, she snatched the paper from the driveway and brought it inside. After pouring herself a glass of orange juice, she went outside onto their screened-in patio and looked for the article. This time it was not on the front page. She finally found the story—a small one—on page six. The headline read, "Palm Beach lawyer agrees to eighteen-month sentence." Thankfully, there was no picture of John this time. As Anna read the report, she realized Brown had been as objective as she could be in presenting the story. John was not made out to be a monster, and, in fact, the article portrayed him as accepting the punishment for his crime. Although she wasn't pleased there was even mention of the sentencing in the paper, at least there wasn't a public flogging of John.

While Anna read the paper at home, John was eating breakfast in his cell at the Palm Beach County jail facility. Brisbane's discussion with Anna had been accurate. John had spent the night in the cell by himself and actually slept fairly well under the circumstances. So far, he really hadn't experienced much contact with the other inmates, and breakfast had been brought to his cell. The officer who delivered breakfast advised him that the State correctional officers were on their way to transport him to the State reception center in western Dade County. About thirty minutes later, two officers arrived, signed the necessary paperwork, and transported John in a small prison van down to the reception center. When he arrived at the center, the intake procedures immediately proceeded. Over the next several days, John was given a series of physical, mental, and emotional exams. His head was shaved, and he was checked for communicable diseases. Life under the very watchful eyes of the State prison authorities had begun. Where John was headed next to serve out his prison sentence was an open question at the moment. Waiting for that answer was driving John crazy, but there was nothing he could do about it, as control over his life was presently nonexistent.

...

On Sunday morning, Anna met Tess at precisely seven o'clock at the tennis courts. For the next ninety minutes, the two of them engaged in the most spirited and competitive games they had ever played. Finally, at eight thirty, Anna looked at her watch and told Tess she had to stop in order to have enough time to go home, shower, change, and arrive at Mass by nine thirty. They decided to call today's contest a draw, and Anna quickly made her way off the court. Before she left, Tess told Anna she looked forward to seeing her at three o'clock.

Anna hustled home and prepared for church in record time. She arrived at St. Gregory's with time to spare. As she entered the back door of the church, she saw Father Anderson at his normal station greeting the church members and visitors as they walked in. She was hoping to speak to him after Mass ended, and it worked out perfectly when the priest asked her if she could stay to talk after services had concluded. Father Anderson gave another of his stirring homilies, and Anna was happy that he was back at his parish. At the conclusion of the service, and after he'd said his good-byes to the congregation, he asked Anna to come into the small office located at the rear of the building.

"How was your vacation with your family, Father Anderson?"

"Outstanding, Anna. I must say I can never get enough of my nieces and nephews, let alone the grandnieces and grandnephews. We had quite a time in Old Forge, N.Y., and the

Adirondack Mountains. I don't know if you've ever been there, but it really is God's country."

"I've never been there, but it sounds great. Maybe someday John and I can make it up there," Anna said wistfully. Father Anderson could see the disturbed look on Anna's face.

"I read the paper yesterday, Anna, and I know about the eighteen months. Where is John now?"

"I don't know yet. Initially, he was taken to the Palm Beach County jail. According to his attorney, from there they were going to take him to what's known as the reception center in western Dade County. After that, it's anybody's guess."

I'm familiar with the reception center. While I was a prison chaplain, I made numerous visits there. It's not all bad. They really do work with the prisoners to try to get them assigned to the correctional facility that will be in the best interests of the State and the inmate. I know some staff at the center. If it's okay with you, I'll make some calls tomorrow and see what I can find out about where John is in the process and what possible alternative sites there may be for him."

"Father, you have no idea how relieved I am to hear you say that. Would you please call me as soon as you know something?"

"The moment I know, I'll call you. I've got your cell, and I'll call you at that number."

After saying good-bye to Father Anderson, Anna went to the cemetery to visit Maria's grave and then traveled back to Palm Beach. By three thirty that afternoon, she was engaged in a lively board game with the Milan family. In addition to Tess, her husband, Bob, and their two children were there. Alex, age twelve, was her oldest child. Her daughter, Meaghan, was ten.

As the game progressed, Anna reflected on what a wonderful family the four of them were. At 5'11" and 150 pounds, Bob wasn't much bigger than Tess. Bob had blonde hair and blue eyes and looked like a male fashion model. Not that

Tess was any slouch. With her long dark hair and dark eyes, coupled with her athletic body, Tess also stood out in a crowd. Their children were cute, with facial characteristics resembling both parents. More important than any of their physical attributes, Anna thought, was this family's heart and soul. They were all faithful churchgoers at West Palm Lutheran Church, and all four were involved in various charitable activities. But right now, Anna was most impressed by the love they showed for each other. Anna felt good being there, sharing this time with them. She needed some relief from the constant emotional turmoil she was experiencing. Today their home provided a much needed escape, even if temporary.

"Okay, kids," exclaimed Tess after about an hour. "Both of you have taken the three old people to the cleaners! It's time to pick up and start dinner."

"What are we having, Mom?" asked Alex.

"Dad's going to cook some lobster and steaks on the grill, and I'm making salt potatoes and pole beans," Tess told him.

"Anna, we never eat this good around here!" Alex exclaimed. You've got to come every Sunday so we get more of these great dinners." Both Meaghan and Alex started laughing, followed soon by Anna and Bob.

"Oh, yeah?" responded Tess. "Just for that, none of you get a piece of the homemade chocolate cake Anna brought for dessert. I'll just have to let all of you know how good it was!"

A round of boos and hisses enveloped the room. Now it was time for Tess to laugh, and laugh she did.

"Okay, okay," Tess finally said. "I give up. All of you can have some chocolate cake."

Now cheers filled the air. Tess had gone from villain to heroine in the span of a few moments. Dinner was delicious, and the Milans enjoyed Anna's company as much as she did theirs. Good friends like the Milans were invaluable to Anna, and she hoped for many more positive and enjoyable experiences in the

Chapter 25

On Monday morning, Father Anderson had several discussions with his contacts at the State reception center. Based on the conversations, he learned John was undergoing various tests and that no decision had yet been made as to which correctional facility he would be assigned. During the course of these talks, Father Anderson was told that Newtown Correctional Institution, located in the western fringes of Palm Beach County, had recently become a Faith and Character-Based prison under a program the State had established several years prior. According to the State officials Father spoke with, the mission of Faith and Character-Based facilities such as Newtown was to assist inmates in building moral character, developing spiritual resources, and obtaining life skills that would lead to positive behavior both in prison and after release.

Father Anderson was also told that an inmate's faith, or lack thereof, was not considered in determining eligibility for placement into a Faith and Character-Based prison. The facility did not attempt to convert prisoners toward a particular faith or religious preference. Rather, the ultimate goal was to prepare inmates for a successful reentry into society and reduce the recidivism rate so ex-offenders could become productive members of society and remain ex-offenders.

Inmates were allowed to choose among such courses as life-skills training, religious education, substance abuse recovery, family-life training, mentoring, and academic or vocational subjects. In order to gain entry into the program, a prisoner must have received no disciplinary reports that resulted in disciplinary confinement during the previous ninety days, be in a general population status, fit the institutional profile parameters, and volunteer to be placed in the program. Statistics showed that inmates who were placed in the program had fewer fights and less disciplinary reports. Father Anderson was also told that Captain Peter Maxwell was the officer at the reception center who would ultimately make the decision on where John would be assigned. Father Anderson knew Captain Maxwell and called him to discuss John.

Captain Maxwell and Father Anderson had a lengthy conversation about John and the circumstances of the DUI charge and conviction. The pastor also spoke in detail with the Captain about the circumstances of Maria's death and how all the events of the past year had led John to a crisis of faith. Father Anderson expressed his opinion that, if John were allowed into Newtown, both John and his fellow inmates would benefit from being together at the facility. Father Anderson made it crystal clear that he was not asking Captain Maxwell to take any action that was inappropriate, and that if John did not qualify for the program or a legitimate exception could not be made, that Father fully understood.

Captain Maxwell made no promises, but indicated that because the Newtown program was new and not yet at full capacity, he would look into the possible placement of John at the facility, especially in light of what Father Anderson had explained. Captain Maxwell also told Father Anderson that even if John could be transferred to Newtown, his assignment there was still contingent upon John's voluntary agreement. Father Anderson asked Captain Maxwell not to let John know they had talked, as Father did not believe that John would appreciate such discussions. The Captain assured Father Anderson their conversation would be confidential and that he would call Father after looking further into the matter.

Glancing at his watch, Father Anderson saw that it was around noon. He had promised Anna he'd call her after his discussions with the State officials, but, in view of the lunch hour presently going on at school, he decided instead to walk over to the cafeteria to see Anna in person. When he arrived, Father saw that she was sitting by herself at a table reading a book. He walked over and took a seat across from Anna.

"Sorry to disturb you, Anna, but I want to let you know I spoke with several officials at the reception center this morning."

"You're not disturbing me, Father, believe me. What did they say?"

Father Anderson relayed to Anna all the information he had received so far about John. He then explained to her in detail what he had been told about the Newtown facility and the initiation there of the Faith and Character-Based program. He told her about his discussion with Captain Maxwell regarding John possibly being assigned there.

"Well, Father, that certainly sounds encouraging. But even if the State allows John to go there, I'm concerned that he will reject it because of the faith-based connotation. I feel as though he has a long way to go before his faith is restored and his anger at God is released, if it ever is."

"You're probably right about that, Anna. But consider this: John is a smart, sophisticated man. As long as the program doesn't force religion on him, which is what I was advised, he may very well think that type of prison may be easier to exist in, as opposed to a more conventional one. Plus, the location of the facility would be only about an hour or so from your home, which would make it easier to visit him than if he was located somewhere else in the State. So those factors just may make him reach the conclusion that Newtown is his best bet."

"That makes sense, Father. I hope you're correct. I guess we first need to see whether the State will even allow him into the program." Just then, Anna's cell phone rang. She didn't recognize the number but decided to answer the call anyway. "Excuse me for a minute, Father, while I see who this is calling."

"Hello, this is Anna Taylor."

"Anna, it's me. I finally got to call you. I haven't been able to stop thinking of you. Are you okay?" John sounded as though he was in panic mode, which caused Anna to take a deep breath and relax for a moment before she responded.

"Yes, John, I'm okay. I've been concerned about you. What's going on down there?"

"Outside of being poked and prodded the past two days, nothing terrible has been going on. I just can't believe all the physical and mental tests I've been subjected to, and they're still not finished. I have to go to see a psychologist next for some more fun and games. Then tomorrow afternoon, I'm supposed to meet with a Captain Maxwell to discuss where the State will send me. I was told that after it was determined where I was going, I'll be allowed to call you again to let you know. There's not much more time right now for me to talk, but as soon as I know where I'm headed, I'll let you know. I love you, Anna."

"I love you, too. I'll talk to you soon," Anna replied. The call was over, but at least she had heard from her husband. Anna told Father Anderson what John had said.

"Well, Anna, in light of what John told you, I may be hearing from Captain Maxwell tomorrow. I'll let you know as soon as I hear anything. Keep your chin up, and rest assured I'll be praying that John is sent to the facility where he will receive the most help."

"Thank you for everything you've done for us, Father. I can't even begin to tell you how much it means." Father Anderson nodded and smiled.

Anna returned to her classroom, and Father went back to the rectory. While Anna was teaching her class, the principal was on the telephone with Tess once again.

"Tess, thanks again for calling me last week about Anna. I was able to talk with a number of teachers and staff. We're prepared to help Anna in any way we can."

"That's wonderful. Who agreed to help?"

"Well, besides myself, my secretary, Julie Vance, has volunteered to check on Anna and to invite her out for lunch, dinner, or a movie. Also, Diana Jenkins, one of our substitute teachers who has worked extensively with Anna, is on board and will also spend time with Anna. The fourth lady is Nicole Cassatly, one of our teachers and a dear friend of Anna's. Between the four of us, I believe we'll be able to help you in keeping her spirits up."

"That's more than I could ask for, Alice. Thank you for jumping on this."

"You're more than welcome. Before we hang up, there is one last thing that I want to mention. I plan to tell Anna that the four school employees I mentioned have talked, and it's our intention to get together with her for various social events and help in any way possible while John is away. However, I don't want to tell Anna anything about our conversation, nor have I told the other three ladies. It seemed best to me to keep that to ourselves."

"I absolutely agree."

Chapter 26

"Good morning, Father Anderson. It's Peter Maxwell calling."

"Hi, Peter. How are you on this lovely day?"

"Couldn't be better, Father. I wanted to let you know that I've thoroughly reviewed all the files and reports on John Taylor and talked with my superiors about sending John to Newtown. They are in agreement with my recommendation that we allow John to be assigned there for the reasons you have given me. I have a meeting today with John at two p.m. and will be talking with him at that time about going to Newtown. Now, please don't forget, Father, that the decision to be placed in Newtown is totally voluntary on John's part, and if he decides not to go there, that's the end of the matter."

"I understand, Peter. Tell me, if John should decide not to go to Newtown, do you know where you would assign him?"

"Yes, it's one of two different facilities. One is in the

northern part of the State and the other is on the west coast. After I meet with him today and a decision is made, he'll be allowed to call his wife and tell her where he's going to be located."

"I can't thank you enough for all your help, Peter."

"Actually, Father, you're the one who has been extremely helpful regarding John's possible placement. We're trying to make an assignment that we believe is in the best interests of the State and John, and Newtown seems to be the best alternative for everyone. So thank you for your input, Father."

Father Anderson looked out the rectory window and saw that the students were out for their mid-morning recess. He decided to walk over to tell Anna the news that he had just received. Anna was in the schoolyard—and when she noticed Father approaching, she practically sprinted over to him.

"Anna, slow down. All your students are watching. If they see you running that fast, they'll be challenging you to a race," said Father, with a hearty laugh.

Anna was nearly out of breath. "You're right, Father. I'm too old for that. It's just that when I saw you, I thought you must have heard from the prison officials about John."

"I did. Captain Maxwell just called me. The bottom line is that the Captain and his superiors believe it would be in the best interests of both the State and John if he were allowed to go to Newtown. So now the decision is in John's hands. Based on what I was told, you should be hearing from John sometime today about where he'll be assigned. Please remember, Anna, not to tell John that you or I knew anything about his alternatives."

"I won't. As soon as I hear from John, I'll let you know."

Father waved good-bye and returned to the rectory. Anna rejoined her class at recess and began counting down the minutes until John called.

At two p.m., John was brought to Captain Maxwell's office to discuss the results of his tests and exams and the decision on the prison facility where he would be sent. As he entered the office, he noticed a plaque on the wall with a quotation, but he couldn't make out all the words. Captain Maxwell eyed John trying to read the inscription, and after asking John to have a seat, the Captain took the plaque off the wall and set it in front of John.

"I noticed you trying to read the inscription, John. It's a quote from the Russian novelist, Fyodor Dostoevsky, who lived in the nineteenth century. It reads, "The degree of civilization in a society can be judged by entering its prisons." I keep that up there because it serves as a reminder of our responsibility here to do our best to see that the State's prison system is maintained in a civilized manner. When I use the term "our" that means that it's the responsibility of both the prison employees and the inmates."

"Interesting concept," replied John. He wondered to himself how such a lofty ideal would be carried out in the real world of prison life.

"It's more than just a concept. In order for our prison system to be effective and reduce the recidivism rate among the inmates that are released, it's a motto that must be acted upon. I try to do my best to follow it every day, and I hope you will also."

There was no reply from John. The Captain decided to move on with the conversation.

"John, I've thoroughly reviewed your entire file and discussed it with most of our medical staff that examined you. Based on that, it appears from a physical standpoint, you have no issues. Your mental and emotional state, however, is another matter."

John thought that pronouncement was a brilliant deduction. He did not respond and waited for what was coming next.

"As a result of the medical staff's recommendations, while you are in prison, you will receive psychological counseling. It has also been suggested that spiritual counseling be provided to you, but I understand from these reports that you are not interested and would refuse to attend."

"That's correct, which I guess is the beauty of separation of church and state."

"You're right. The State will not force you to seek spiritual assistance, although from everything I see here, it would be in your best interest to do so. That leaves us with the issue of which correctional facility you will be sent to for your prison term. There are three options. The first two are traditional facilities. The first is in northern Florida, outside Jacksonville. The second is on the west coast, near Tampa."

"And the third facility?"

"The third facility is located close to the western boundary of Palm Beach County and is known as the Newtown Correctional Institution. This particular prison was recently converted from a traditional institution to one that is known as a Faith and Character-Based Facility."

John wanted to know what that meant. Captain Maxwell explained the program in detail to John, along the same lines that Father Anderson had been told about Newtown. John didn't miss a word of the Captain's statement and was thinking about what his best option would be. He didn't like the idea of the other two jails being so far away from Anna, but John also refused to let anyone cram religion down his throat. He seemed to be caught between a rock and a hard place. Clarification was needed from Maxwell.

"Can you assure me that if I volunteer to go to Newtown, no one will try at any time to force me to go to religious services or counseling?"

"Yes, I can. Just as you mentioned earlier, due to the separation of church and state in our country, no one can or will require you to attend religious services or counseling against your will. The decision to do so is totally voluntary on your part."

"In that case, I volunteer for Newtown. It will certainly make it easier for my wife to visit."

"I'll make the necessary arrangements for you to be sent there. You'll be taken to Newtown tomorrow. I know you want to advise your wife on where you are being sent, so you can call her from my phone. Also, tell her that after you arrive at Newtown and they brief you on visitation privileges, you'll be allowed to phone her with the details."

John called Anna on her cell from the Captain's office and told her about his assignment to Newtown and how he would be in further touch after he had been advised about visitation privileges. Anna was greatly relieved that John had agreed to be assigned to Newtown, and after they concluded their call, she phoned Father Anderson and told him the news. From the sound of his voice, Anna thought that Father seemed as relieved as she was.

Chapter 27

The next afternoon, two correctional officers from the reception center brought John to Newtown. As the car he was riding in passed through the barbed wire fence into the facility, John looked around and saw four large, one-story buildings. Adjacent to them were two smaller buildings. After that, they passed a basketball court and an expansive open area that looked like it was some kind of a park. The boundaries of this area were demarcated by barbed-wire fencing. As the vehicle continued moving along this long, winding road, John could see a two-story structure in front of him that looked like it contained administrative offices. Beyond that edifice were a series of smaller buildings. As the driver pulled into a parking space, John wondered what was next on the agenda.

There wasn't much time to be concerned about that, because a uniformed officer came marching out of the building and up to the car. After introductions were made, they all went inside to complete the paperwork regarding John's transfer to Newtown.

Thirty minutes later the process was done, and the reception center officers left John with the Newtown official for the remaining segment of John's eighteen-month prison term.

"John, as I mentioned outside, my name is Captain Ed Thomas. I'm in charge of processing all new inmates at Newtown. I understand that you've already been advised that Newtown is a Faith and Character-Based Institution and that you volunteered to be assigned here."

"Yes," replied John. He wanted to say he was also assured that he would not be forced to attend religious services or counseling, but thought better of it and remained silent.

For the next fifteen minutes, Captain Thomas explained to John where he would sleep, what his daily agenda would be, and the types of programs Newtown offered the inmates. After that, the Captain advised John what Newtown expected from him and what John could expect from Newtown. A discussion then ensued as to visitation.

"John, I know that you are probably concerned about visitation rights."

"Yes. I'd like to see my wife as soon as possible."

"I have no doubt you would. Unfortunately, the process is going to take longer than you would like before your wife can actually get here to see you."

"What do you mean?" John was starting to get upset, and Captain Thomas could see it.

"Take a deep breath, John. I see your blood pressure is starting to rise, but you have to remember where you are. Because this is a prison facility, there are numerous details that must be attended to before anyone is allowed to visit an inmate. First, any potential visitors must complete an application that you send to them. I have the applications and will provide them to you. So you'll send the applications to your family and friends that you want to be considered for placement on your visiting list."

"And how do I mail them out when I'm in here?"

"Don't worry about that. We'll provide the envelopes and postage. The mail is picked up from this facility every day except Sundays and holidays, so they'll go out quickly. How many applications do you think you'll need?"

"I definitely need one for my wife, and there are two attorneys who may need to see me about a civil lawsuit. Besides them, there are a few other people who may come to see me. So I guess a half dozen would be okay."

"I'll get you those today. The sooner you get them out and our office receives the completed applications, the sooner we can start processing them."

"And how long will the processing take, once you receive the completed applications?"

"Approximately thirty days from the date an application is received."

"You've got to be kidding!" John was incredulous. "You mean I can't see my wife for more than thirty days?"

"John, what did I just finish telling you about remembering where you are? There are numerous background checks and other matters that must be investigated before anyone is allowed to visit an inmate at Newtown. In your wife's case it may go a little quicker, as I'm assuming she has a clean record."

"Anna has no record of any kind. She's a schoolteacher in West Palm. I miss her so much. I can't believe it will be more than a month before I get to see her again." John looked like he was going to explode.

"Listen, John. I'll see if I can't expedite the process, but it won't be by much. We're constrained by the investigation that must be completed. I'll let you phone your wife today to tell her you're here and about the visitation process. Tell her to get the completed application back to me as soon as possible by overnight mail, and I'll see what I can do. I just don't want you to get your hopes up."

"Okay. Thanks for trying to help. Let me ask you this: When Anna is able to start visiting me, when and where do the visits take place?"

"Visitation takes place between nine and three on Saturdays and Sundays and on certain holidays. There is a visiting park here at the facility where visitors are allowed to meet with the inmates. You may have noticed it when you were driven in today."

"Yes, I did. I thought it looked like some kind of park setting."

"That's it. Do you have any more questions about visitation or anything else at Newtown?"

"Not right now. May I call my wife now to let her know I'm here and about the visitation application?"

"Go ahead and use my phone."

John called Anna's cell. She was in class, but hoping that it was John, she excused herself and stepped out of the room. After a brief greeting, John explained everything about visitation. Although Anna was upset about the wait time until she could see John, she managed to hide her disappointment. She assured him that the application would be completed as soon as she received it and then sent to Newtown via overnight mail.

At the conclusion of the school day, Anna walked to the rectory to see if Father Anderson was available. She rang the doorbell and Father opened the door and asked her to come in.

"Thanks for seeing me, Father. I wanted to let you know that John called me this morning from Newtown. Fortunately he arrived there without any incidents, but there's one problem." Anna's voice trailed off, and she struggled to speak.

"What's wrong, Anna?"

"It's about visitation. From what John told me, I have to fill out a visitation form, and then it has to be processed before I can see him. Unfortunately, it takes about thirty days before everything is completed and I'm approved. The officer John was with today told him he'd try to obtain the approval sooner but for

John not to get his hopes up. Father, I just can't believe it's going to take that long. It seems like every time things start looking up, something negative happens to erase the good."

Father Anderson could see how discouraged Anna was. He knew he needed to choose his words carefully. "Anna, I was afraid that this time lag might happen. When I was a prison chaplain, it took around thirty days for the approval process on visitations. I didn't want to say anything to you because I was hoping the system might have been streamlined, but obviously it's not. I know you're disappointed right now about having to wait so long to see John, but let's focus on the positive. John is at Newtown where a Faith and Character-Based program is in operation. Although John will likely reject any meaningful participation in any faith-related programs right now, let's pray that in the long run he embraces the positive and spiritual nature of Newtown and returns to the man of faith and hope that he was. So, do your best to hang in there during the next month, and please come to see me whenever you want to talk about anything. I am always here for you."

Anna said nothing in response. She was still in disbelief about the day's events. Instead, she warmly embraced Father, and after letting him go, waved good-bye and left the rectory. Anna headed home and tried to imagine how she would deal with not seeing her husband for the next thirty days, knowing he was fifty-some miles from her in a State prison. Bedtime came early for Anna as she attempted to escape the realities of her life.

Chapter 28

The next morning, John woke up at five a.m. and temporarily could not fathom where he was. At first, he thought he was in the midst of a nightmare. Then he realized he was awake and in a huge room with many strangers in other beds, some of whom were snoring loudly. He also noticed an aroma of flatulence in the air. Where was he, and why was he here? Gradually his memory returned, and he realized he was in an open bay housing dorm at Newtown Correctional Institution. Shivers went down his spine at the thought. His memory flashed back to yesterday afternoon, after he had finished talking with Anna. Initially, Captain Thomas kept John in his office for another hour detailing all the nuances of prison life at Newtown. After that, the Captain turned John over to Sergeant Robert Gaetano who was in charge of the housing dorm John had been assigned to live in.

Sergeant Gaetano, referred to as "Sarge" by all the inmates

and staff at Newtown, gave John a detailed tour of the facility. The four one-story buildings that John had noticed when entering Newtown were all open-bay housing dorms. Each building could house up to one hundred fifty inmates. The physical configuration of each of the dorms was identical. The buildings consisted of one large room with bunk beds on one side of the room and single beds on the other. There were also lavatories and showers contained on one side of each dorm. At the present time, three of the buildings were fully occupied. The dorm John was assigned to currently had only 50 residents. The prison was not at full capacity due to Newtown recently having been converted to a Faith and Character-Based Institution. Some inmates wanted nothing to do with the project and were transferred elsewhere, creating a temporary surplus in available housing for inmates.

During the tour with Sarge, John also viewed the two smaller buildings next to the dorms. Each of these buildings was referred to as cell housing units. The first building contained thirty individual cellblock units, with one bed and a lavatory. The second structure contained twenty cellblock units, with two beds and a lavatory. Both buildings were used to temporarily house inmates with disciplinary problems. Being sent to the cellblocks would result in the loss of athletic activity privileges and the opportunity to participate in any programs offered at Newtown. Once the offender had corrected his behavior, he would be allowed back into the dorm and could again participate in physical conditioning and the other Newtown programs.

Sarge also showed John the inmates' dining hall. It could seat up to one hundred seventy-five inmates at one time. Sarge explained that the inmates were on a rotating system for eating their meals. Each dorm would separately go to the dining room for breakfast, with the first dorm sitting down at five thirty a.m. The inmates were allowed a total of thirty minutes for breakfast. Once the first dorm left the dining room, the next dorm would be brought in and allowed thirty minutes. The same procedure applied to the last two buildings. Lunch and dinner were set up in the same fashion, with the first lunch segment beginning at eleven a.m. and the first dinner seating at five p.m. Each week the starting times for daily meals were rotated among the dorms, so that no one dorm always began the process. Except in cases of health reasons approved by the prison doctor, all inmates ate the same meals with no food choices allowed. Only plastic silverware was used, and the plates were plastic with compartments separating the items of food. Beverages consisted of water, iced tea, lemonade, and coffee.

Next John was shown the athletic facilities, which consisted of a basketball court, a baseball field, and an oval, one-eighth mile circular track. There were no weight lifting machines or weights available. The last stop yesterday with Sarge was the visiting park. The park was in a large, open area with different types of trees. It was surrounded on its perimeter by a 10-foot barbed-wire fence. Inside the park were a series of pavilions containing wooden tables and benches that were shielded from the sun and rain by roof overhangs. Vending machines were also located at each of the pavilions so that snacks, candy, and cold drinks could be purchased during visitation.

As John rested in his bed, reflecting on what he had seen and heard yesterday, the reality of where he was and the personal liberties he had lost resonated in his head. No longer was he free to come and go as he pleased. For the present time, and for the next eighteen months, he would be told when he would go to bed, when he would wake up, when he would eat, what he would eat, and what he would do during the course of each day. He could not drive a car, go surfing, go to a restaurant, or for that matter go anywhere—except within the confines of Newtown Correctional Institution. Even then, it would only be when he was given permission to do so.

His opulent home and lifestyle had been stripped from him, and he was now reduced to sleeping in a room with multiple strangers, under the worst possible conditions. Privacy was nonexistent, even for such personal matters as showering and using the toilet. All of that paled in comparison to the greatest loss he had suffered. The inability to be with his wife on a daily basis and to share life with her was driving him to the brink of a nervous breakdown. He had no faith to support him in his struggles, as any thought of a good God had been wiped out by the tragedies he'd experienced. If there were any chance for his life to be salvaged, that process needed to be implemented immediately or John faced the very real and omnipresent danger of losing everything that mattered to him, including Anna, on a permanent basis.

Suddenly, John was distracted from his thoughts by a menacing figure rising out of the bed adjacent to him. The two of them were located on the side of the dorm with single beds, and John's view of this man's bulk was totally unimpeded. As the giant stood up, John thought that he must be 6'7" or more and weigh close to 300 pounds. Brisbane looked like a sissy compared to this bruiser. John wondered where he came from, as no one was in the bed on either side of him last night when he fell asleep. Right now, John was afraid to move a muscle.

Noticing that John was awake, the hulk spoke to him in a muffled voice. "Good morning, Sir. Excuse my whispering, but a lot of the men in this room are sleeping right now and won't wake up until the bell starts ringing." He extended his hand to John and declared, "My name is Robert Williams. What's yours?"

John gingerly shook Robert's hand, which was twice the size of his, and meekly responded, "John Taylor. Nice to meet you."

Robert flashed a big smile at John and motioned for him to get out of bed. John quickly complied.

"John Taylor," said Robert. "That's a very strong, noble sounding name. What nationality are you, John?"

John wondered why Robert was asking for all this information, but standing next to him and observing his height and girth up close, John wasn't about to question his motives. "On my father's side, I'm English and Scottish. My mom was Italian."

"And I'll bet you were raised as a Catholic. Most Italians are."

"Yes, I was raised Catholic."

John hesitated to ask Robert any personal questions, but he didn't need to as Robert quickly volunteered the information. "Well, as you can see, John, I'm African-American. I was born and raised in Athens, Georgia, and I'm a Baptist." Robert smiled at John again. He was starting to become much less intimidating to John, who now decided to ask him why he wanted to know these personal details.

"Robert, if you don't mind me asking, I'm wondering why you want to know all this information. After all, we just met each other less than five minutes ago."

"I apologize if it seems that I'm coming on too strong, John. It's just that you and I are now roommates, and this is a Faith and Character-Based Institution. So I thought asking those questions was a good way to start to get to know each other."

Before John could respond, a loud bell sounded for about twenty seconds, followed by a bellowing voice. "All right, gentlemen. Rise and shine, the time for breakfast is upon us. Stragglers will go hungry."

Who in the world is screaming like that at five thirty in the morning? John thought. The answer to his question came ten seconds later. Directly in front of his bed appeared a strapping figure, not nearly as large as Robert but still big enough to command John's attention.

"You must be our new inmate, John Taylor. Sarge told me about you before he left his shift last night. I'm Corporal Sean Alexander, and I'm in charge of this dorm when Sarge isn't here. Now that you're up, get a move on to the showers and toilet. You've got thirty minutes until we leave for breakfast, and what

I said earlier is true. Stragglers will go hungry." With that, Alexander left to stir other inmates, without allowing John any opportunity to respond.

"Corporal Alexander has a tendency to be loud and sometimes very difficult. He wants to make sure all the inmates know he's in total control," declared Robert. "But if you play your cards right with him, you should be okay. But there's one thing you need to be very careful about."

"What's that?" asked John.

"Do not, under any circumstances, ever let him hear you call him by his unofficial nickname, 'Pretty Boy.' Carlos Delgado, one of the inmates, used that nickname on Alexander and paid the price."

"What happened?" John asked, anxious to learn the unofficial prison-survival rules.

"Delgado was cleaning the officers' restroom in the administrative building one day. Alexander didn't know he was in there, and Delgado could hear him talking to himself in front of the mirror, saying what a 'pretty boy' he was. When Delgado came out from the toilet area, he asked Alexander, 'How's it going, Pretty Boy?' The Corporal flipped out and busted Delgado on the spot for insubordination. He ended up serving two days in solitary. A lot of the inmates still call him 'Pretty Boy' behind his back, but none of them are foolish enough to say it to his face. So just be careful with that."

"I will. Thanks for the warning."

Both John and Robert noticed Alexander coming back in their direction and hustled the other way toward the showers. Twenty minutes later they were on the way to the dining hall for breakfast. After going through the food line, they sat down at the same table. Robert asked John what job he had before being sent to prison. John told him he'd been a lawyer, and Robert told John that he'd been a high school English teacher. Before they could continue with their conversation, several other inmates joined them. The first inmate who sat down looked John up and down and started to speak.

"Well, I see we got a new face here, and I don't mean your old, ugly one, Robert." Speaking to John, he said, "My name's Carlos Delgado. What's yours?"

"John Taylor, and I don't think Robert's all that old or ugly." A round of laughter and hisses came from the table. Delgado looked annoyed.

"First of all, John Taylor," came Delgado's response, "Mr. Goliath here can take care of himself and doesn't need a sissy boy like you coming to rescue him." Another round of laughter and hisses ensued from everyone at the table except Robert. He was waiting to see how John would respond. Delgado continued. "The more important thing is that I didn't ask for your opinion. If I want your opinion on something, I'll ask for your opinion. Otherwise, you just keep your mouth shut, you got that?" No laughter or hisses this time. All eyes were on John waiting for his response to Delgado.

"Although we're all here in jail," John said calmly but confidently, "the Constitution still reigns, and I've got freedom of speech. If you don't like what I've got to say, walk away and don't listen."

All eyes shifted to Delgado. "Constitution? You're talking about the Constitution? What are you, a lawyer or something?"

"As a matter of fact, I am."

"I should have known. You look like a lawyer. But now you're dressed right. Instead of your pin stripe suit, you've got your prison suit. This is where crooks like you belong." This time there was banging on the table and high-fives all around. The commotion drew the attention of Corporal Alexander. He hurried to the table and demanded to know what was going on.

"Nothing, Corporal Alexander," responded Delgado. "We're just having some fun with the new guy. Everything's cool."

"Well, just keep it down and stop banging on the table. You

know the rules."

"Yes, sir," replied Delgado. Alexander appeared satisfied and slowly walked away from the table. After he was out of earshot, Delgado started back up.

"So tell me, what did a big, bad lawyer like you do to get sent to jail? You must have stolen money from your clients. How much did you steal? Where is it now?" Muffled snickers ensued, as Alexander was still in the vicinity.

For a moment John weighed whether he should answer and how much information he should give. Finally he said, "DUI with bodily injury. But I wasn't drunk. What about you? I bet you beat up little kids and sent them to the hospital." There was now total silence as all the guys waited for Delgado's reply.

"Let me tell you something, sissy boy." Delgado was steaming, and Robert put his hand on Delgado's arm to restrain him. Delgado shook it off. "I did get sent here for assault and battery, but not on little kids. I put the hurt on two guys who thought they were real tough dudes. They had it coming, and I see that you need to learn some respect, too. So be prepared to be put in your place." Just then the bell rang, and the inmates filed out and returned to their dorm.

John's first full day at Newtown had gotten off to a rousing start. What further misadventures lay ahead?

Chapter 29

One week after John arrived at Newtown, Anna received the visitation application package. She immediately completed it and sent it back the next morning via overnight mail. Anna was praying for a quick response. She desperately missed her husband. Although she kept busy with school, the nights at home were very lonely. Tess had been faithfully checking in on Anna and was good about keeping her busy on Sundays with tennis in the mornings and dinners with the Milan family in the afternoons. On this particular mid-week day, class had finished, and Anna was on her way to a faculty meeting. After Principal Barnes excused the teachers, she asked to see Anna in her office.

"Anna, I've been so busy over the past week that I haven't been able to speak with you, but you've been on my mind. How are you doing?"

"Well, to be honest with you, it's been difficult. I haven't been able to visit John because there's a lot of red tape involved in visitation privileges, even for spouses. In fact, I just sent out an application for approval yesterday. It may be as long as a month before I'm allowed to see him." Alice could see how dejected Anna looked.

"I'm sorry things have to be so complicated and time consuming. I take it that telephone calls aren't allowed?"

"Only in the event of an emergency."

"What about writing letters? You must be able to do that, can't you?"

"Yes, that's allowed. But all outgoing and incoming mail is read by prison staff for security reasons."

"Okay, so that may put a bit of a damper on what you write to each other, but it's still a way of keeping in contact with him. Isn't that something you want to do, Anna?"

"Yes, I know you're right. I need to write him. I'll sit down tonight and do it."

The principal smiled. "That's what I wanted to hear from you," she said. "By the way, Anna, there's something else I wanted to discuss."

"What's that?"

"Last week I spoke with some of our staff, and there are four of us who would like to spend some time with you outside of school. We don't want to overwhelm you or make you feel as though you're obligated to spend time with us, but we thought it might help some of your long evenings pass more quickly and pleasantly."

Anna was quick to reply, "You wouldn't be overwhelming me, and I'd appreciate the company, believe me. Who are we talking about?"

"Julie Vance, Diana Jenkins, Nicole Cassatly, and me."

Anna put her hands partially over her face in response to this news. There were tears rolling down her cheeks. She stood up and hugged the principal. "This means so much to me. I don't think I can even begin to express how much."

"I know it does, Sweetheart. We all love you and just want to help you in any way we can. I still vividly remember losing my husband. He went to be with the Lord seven years ago, before you came here. The staff was just wonderful in helping me through some difficult days. We hope we can do the same for you."

Anna looked at Principal Barnes and thought about what a good, kind person she was. Alice was 63 years old and had previously told Anna that in two years, when she reached 65, she would be retiring to spend more time with her children and grandchildren. Anna knew she'd miss her a lot, as would the rest of the school. Anna silently thanked the Lord for sending this wise woman into her life as she hugged her again.

After Anna arrived home, she immediately wrote a letter to John. She felt constrained by the thought of some stranger reading her personal message to her husband, and she struggled to find the right words. After about thirty minutes, she completed the letter and read it from top to bottom to make certain she felt comfortable with it and that John would be okay with someone else reading it, too. The letter read:

> Dear John,
>
> I wanted to let you know I received the visitation application and sent it back Tuesday, by overnight mail. By the time you receive this letter, the Newtown staff should be processing the application. Hopefully we will receive good news soon that I can visit you. As you know, you're in my thoughts every day, and I can't wait to see you.
>
> I sent copies of the application to both of your attorneys so they'll be able to visit you to discuss the personal injury lawsuit. Also, I sent three copies of the application to Donna Hughes and gave a copy to Tess. So hopefully, you'll have other visitors in the near future.
>
> I also wanted to let you know how supportive

*the Milan family has been to me. They are paying
close attention to me and have been very helpful.
They truly are wonderful friends.*

*Today, we had a faculty meeting after school.
Alice Barnes asked me to come to her office
afterwards, and we had a nice discussion. Much to
my surprise, she arranged for some of the school
staff to periodically take turns going places with me.
So I am being well cared for and don't want you to
worry about me.*

*Everything is fine with the house, too, and I'm
continuing to stay on track with my running and
tennis. In fact, I'm planning on taking Tess to the
cleaners when we play again this Sunday!*

*I hope you're doing okay. As soon as you hear
about the application and when I can come to see
you, please let me know or have someone at the
facility contact me.*

You have my undying love and support.

Love,
Anna

Anna thought the letter was written as well as she could do
under the circumstances. Besides being concerned with a staff
member reading the letter, she had also tried her best to not upset
or offend John. She purposely left out any religious references
and tried as best she could to let him know she was okay, while
still conveying how much she missed him. Anna hoped and
prayed the letter would be well received by John. Looking at her
watch and seeing that it was only five p.m., she decided to drive
to the post office and mail the letter so it would go out for delivery
this evening.

On the way home, Anna stopped by the Milans to see what
they were doing. When she pulled into their driveway, both Milan

children were outside in the front yard tossing a football. When they saw Anna, the two of them sprinted over to her. As Anna got out of her car, Meaghan literally jumped into her arms and squeezed her with as much force as a ten-year-old girl could.

"Okay, Meaghan, I give up. Please! Let me go before you break my back!" said Anna, her laughter letting Meaghan know she was teasing her.

After Meaghan released Anna, she replied, "Anna, you know I would never hurt you because you're one of my best friends." A huge smile crossed Anna's face.

"Besides that," piped in Alex, "if Meaghan hurt you and you couldn't come for dinner on Sundays, we'd have to eat that slop Mom usually makes us." Before any of them could react to his comment, Tess bellowed out her response. She had come out the side garage door, and unbeknownst to any of them, had overheard the entire conversation.

"Just for that, Alex Milan, while the rest of us are enjoying an Italian feast this Sunday, you'll be dining on liver and onions. And to top it off, you're in charge of all the cleanup! Maybe then you'll learn a lesson about insulting my cooking!"

"Mom," protested Alex, "I was only kidding. You don't feed us slop. At least you haven't in the past several months." Alex smiled meekly at his mother and waited for her response. Tess let out a big belly laugh and laughed hard, along with all the others.

"Okay, Alex," Tess finally responded. "I take your statement as being your way of apologizing. So you don't have to eat any liver and onions. But you are in charge of clean-up, agreed?"

"Okay," Alex conceded. "Boy, next time I really better keep my eyes open. You're like a ghost or something, the way you can appear without anyone knowing it and hear everything we say."

"That's a very good thing for you to remember, my son."

"Well," said Anna, "I certainly am glad I stopped by to see how you guys were doing. Good laughs like these are hard to come by. I hope there are many more in the future."

"Don't worry, Anna," replied Alex. "I can take care of that, but next time I'll make sure Mom is nowhere around. I don't think she'll give me another break."

"You got that right, my boy! This was the second time, and that's it," said Tess.

After another five minutes of more serious conversation, Anna said good-bye and headed home to grade the tests her students had completed today. She tried to focus but kept wondering how John was doing at Newtown. It was going to be a lengthy and difficult time while the two of them were separated. She continued her prayers to the Lord, asking for faith, hope, and strength during the trials.

Chapter 30

"Thanks for seeing me, Captain Thomas," said John. "You probably already know why I'm here."

"I sure do," replied the Captain. "You're here to check on the status of your wife's visitation application. Well, I've got good news and bad news. Which do you want first?"

"Let's get the bad news out of the way."

"The bad news is that her application has not yet been fully approved. It's only been two weeks since we received the document, and all the necessary background checks have not yet been completed."

"What's the good news?"

"I anticipate having the application process finalized next week, and she should be able to start visiting you the first weekend after that. So at least we'll have cut a week out of the normal time frame."

"Thank you for your help, Captain Thomas. When you have

a definite answer, may I call Anna to let her know? I don't want to do that yet, just in case something happens."

"Yes, as soon as we know for sure, I'll have you come in and make the call."

Although John was disappointed he wouldn't be seeing Anna sooner, he was glad for the reduction in wait time. He had now been at Newtown for over three weeks, and the only communication with Anna since the phone call the first day was the letter she'd sent him—and his reply in return. When John received Anna's letter, he was greatly relieved to hear about the support network surrounding her. He quickly replied, letting her know how glad he was that she was doing well. John thought she may have sugarcoated the letter, but he didn't let on in his correspondence back to her. He also left out some significant details of prison life because he didn't want her to stress at what he was going through. It was bad enough that he was enduring a constrained and regimented life in jail. He was not about to make matters worse for her by revealing the daily grind he faced. Nor did he want any prison staff knowing what he thought about life at Newtown.

After he left the Captain's office, John returned to his job at the prison library. The library consisted of almost ten thousand books, all of which had been approved by the State prison authorities. Included were several thousand legal digests, periodicals, and case reports. John had been assigned to work at the library due to his background in law. He was allowed to help inmates find different legal materials, but he couldn't do any research for them or prepare any documents they might file in the court system. John was always under the very watchful eyes of at least one correctional officer, and he wasn't about to break any of the rules and risk being punished. The library was open seven days a week, and he asked to be assigned there every day.

There were a number of different voluntary programs he could participate in, but so far he elected not to be a part of any of them. The library was open from eight a.m. until five p.m., so John spent much of his time in the confines of the library walls. Although he was bored silly, he preferred this existence to anything else being offered to him. The only exceptions to his library time were his participation in athletic programs, which usually took an hour or so, and his required weekly visit to the prison psychologist for an hour's discussion. Exercise and athletic competition were the highlight of his days, while the counseling visit was normally a source of irritation and aggravation. In fact, he was on his way right now to his counseling appointment, and his blood pressure was already starting to rise.

"Good afternoon, John. How are you doing on this beautiful South Florida day?" asked Dr. Philip Mayne.

"Better. It looks like my wife will be allowed to visit next weekend. That is definitely an upswing to my existence here."

"That's good to hear. I'm sure it will positively affect your outlook on life. But let's talk a bit about your use of the phrase 'upswing to my existence here.'"

John knew he had made a big mistake with his choice of words. Now he would be subjected to a long discussion and analysis of his "existence" at the prison. He determined to be more careful in the future. This psycho-babble was bad enough without making it harder on himself by being loose with his word choices.

Dr. Mayne continued analyzing John's word choice. "John, I know that a sophisticated lawyer like you is very conscious of the words used in a conversation. Your use of the word "existence" implies you don't believe you have purpose or significance. In fact, your words convey a pessimistic attitude with little or no hope for the future. And I'm not just getting those signals from that one sentence today but also as a consistent message during our past two sessions. Do you disagree with what I'm saying?"

John grimaced and struggled to find the right words to speak before this meeting got even more out of hand. "Dr. Mayne, as you know, I'm obviously not happy here. I've been incarcerated against my will, and in my opinion, for no legitimate reason. I still don't believe I was at fault for the automobile collision. Everything I worked so hard for has been taken from me. Most importantly, I still can't see my wife, let alone be with her. So when I used the word "existence," the reference point was more to my involuntarily being here than anything else. Please don't read too much into my wording."

"Do you disagree with my observation that you feel as though your life has no significance or purpose and that you have no hope for the future?"

Boy, this guy just won't give up, John thought. He needed to figure out a way to curtail this line of interrogation. "Dr. Mayne, the questions you're asking me seem to have religious overtones. I thought that our discussions were to be completely secular and not geared toward any religious beliefs. Am I incorrect in my understanding?"

Mayne knew exactly what John was doing and was determined not to let him get the upper hand. "John, your question reflects a misunderstanding of the process here at Newtown. It's true that none of the programs at this facility, including our counseling sessions, will attempt to convert any prisoner here toward a particular faith or religious preference. But, it's also true that part of the mission of a Faith and Character-Based prison such as this is to assist inmates in building moral character and developing spiritual resources in the hope of reducing recidivism and preparing them for a successful re-entry. So, none of my questions to you are inappropriate, and I'm still waiting for an answer to my last question. Do you need me to repeat it?"

"No, I don't need you to repeat it." John really wanted to put an end to this part of the session. He decided the only way to do so was to answer the question. "Let me answer your question by asking you some questions. How would you feel if your infant daughter was taken from you in the middle of the night, and no one was ever able to explain why? On top of that, how would you feel if you were wrongly convicted of a crime you didn't commit and were sent to jail, resulting in the loss of seeing your wife and the loss of your career?" John's face was getting red, and his volume was increasing as he continued. "I suspect you'd be hard-pressed, Dr. Mayne, to see any legitimate purpose in your life—or that you would have any hope for the future. And that's exactly how I feel about my stinking, rotten life." John was out of breath and sweating profusely.

Dr. Mayne knew this was a huge step forward for John. Any chance of getting John refocused and on the right path was a process that would take a long time, if it ever were to be accomplished. There was no point in trying to accelerate the process, so Mayne decided to appease John with the answer to his questions and then move on to another topic. "I would feel the same way you do, John. There's no doubt about that."

Dr. Mayne then steered the remainder of their discussion onto much less controversial issues, fully cognizant of the formidable task that lay ahead. He was an intelligent man and had enough experience to know any chance of success with John would take more than just their sessions. Help would be needed from other sources as well.

Later that same day, as John was making his way from the food line in the dining room, he looked around and saw that Robert Williams was sitting by himself at one of the tables. So far, the two of them had been getting along pretty well with each other, and John decided to sit next to him. "Hey Robert. Do you mind if I sit here?"

"Please do. I hate eating alone and talking to myself. It makes the guards think I'm whacked," Robert replied, smiling.

"You're always good for a laugh, Robert," responded John, although he wasn't laughing. John had spotted Carlos Delgado walking in their direction, and he was hoping Delgado wouldn't sit near them. Since their initial encounter, John and Delgado hadn't had any real contact with each other, and John wanted to keep it that way. He got his wish. Delgado strode by, glaring at John, but fortunately moved on to another table.

"I sure am glad he kept going," said John. "That guy is a real nut job."

"You got that right," replied Robert. "I've been meaning to tell you about him. Bro, you need to be real careful around him and watch your back. He's a martial arts expert and really knows how to put the hurt on someone. He's still ticked about your little incident at breakfast a few weeks ago. I think he's waiting for the right time and place."

"Thanks for letting me know, but I'm not afraid of him," John told Robert. "I've got at least four inches in height and thirty pounds on him, and I know how to handle myself. In college, I was a boxing champ and kept up with it over the years. So thanks for the warning, but I'll be okay."

"Man, I hope nothin' happens," Robert said, "but if it does, he's smart enough to make it look like an accident. So keep your guard up."

"I will," John assured him. The two men sat quietly for a moment, eating their food. Then John spoke. "Robert, there's something I've been meaning to ask you. If you tell me it's none of my business, that's fine and we can move on to other topics."

"That's cool. What's up?"

"I was just wondering why you were sent here. You heard me tell Delgado why I'm here, but I don't know why you are."

"Well, like you, I was charged with a DUI. But in my case, the other guy died. He was a seventy-five-year-old widower, no kids. Rather than go to trial, I pled out and got sentenced to ten years. I've been in prison for eight years now. Got two more to serve."

John couldn't imagine spending ten years behind prison

Chapter 31

Ten days later, Anna was on her way to Newtown. Her visitation application had been approved, and she was sent an identification card that allowed her access to the visitation park. It was Saturday morning, and visiting hours were between nine and three. Registration began at eight thirty, so Anna was on the road at seven fifteen. She anticipated that it might take her a little more than an hour to get there. She had woken up at five thirty, was on the running trail by six, and completed a six-mile-course in forty-five minutes. The exercise helped reduce her stress level, but she was still edgy. Anna hadn't seen John in a month and had absolutely no idea what to expect. The last time she saw him was when he vanished behind the interior courthouse doors, being led away by two sheriff's deputies. That terrible memory was now compounded by her driving to a prison where he was incarcerated by the State. As she pulled into the visitors' parking lot, her heart was racing and she was sweating. She silently asked God to help John and her through this day.

As Anna left her car, she was taken aback by the scene unfolding before her. There appeared to be a hundred or more people waiting in line to access the visitation park. All around her were menacing twelve-feet-tall barbed wire fences. Beyond the fences she could see a series of plain looking buildings that were also surrounded by barbed wire. It looked like visitors were being funneled down a narrow pathway where correctional officers were checking identification cards and giving instructions. As she waited in line, a heavy-set, middle-aged woman intently eyed Anna and finally spoke to her.

"You look really nervous, Sweetie. Is this your first time here?"

"Yes. My husband was just sent here a month ago."

"Well, Sweetie, try to relax. You'll get used to it. I was pretty uptight my first time here. But, after that, it was okay. My husband's been here three years, and he's got two more to go. How long is your husband in for?"

"Seventeen more months."

"That's not so bad. Before you know it, he'll be out and you two will be back together." Anna nodded as the woman continued. "I've just got one piece of advice for you."

"What's that?" Anna asked curiously.

"Just make sure you don't get caught hugging or kissing your husband during your visits. The officers will tell you that the only physical contact the two of you are allowed is holding hands. I've seen people here get caught kissing and hugging. The visitor ends up getting thrown out, and the inmate is sent back to his housing dorm. So, if you're going to try to do more than hold hands, be careful not to let the guards see you."

"Thanks for the advice." Anna was disappointed about this physical contact rule but had anticipated something along those lines. Speaking of lines, this one had moved along very quickly and she was about to be addressed by one of the officers.

"Ma'am, my name is Officer Henry Longo. Welcome to

Newtown. May I see your visitors' identification, please?"

"Yes, Sir." Anna handed him her card, and he carefully examined it. He handed it back to her and explained the visitation rules. When finished, he asked Anna what items she had with her.

Reaching into her pockets, she pulled out her car key and several dollar bills. "I don't have anything other than my car key and some money. I was hoping we could buy some sodas and snacks."

"Yes, Mrs. Taylor, you can. I'll go find your husband now and bring him into the visitation park. Please follow me." Anna was led to a hallway where several other visitors were waiting. Longo motioned for her to stay and then opened a locked door and vanished behind it. Five minutes later, he was back and asked Anna to follow him. They walked about a hundred feet down a corridor where Longo unlocked another door leading into the visitation park. When the door opened, John was there waiting for her.

Anna's gaze met her husband's tear-filled eyes. She desperately wanted to run and jump into his arms but managed to restrain herself. Instead, she walked over to John and grabbed his hand. Then they strolled, hand-in-hand, into the park and proceeded toward an empty table shielded from the sun by a roof overhang. Neither of them said a word. Their eyes were still totally transfixed upon each other. After they sat down, John began to speak. "Anna, you have no idea how badly I want to kiss you right now."

"Oh, yes I do!" Anna answered with passion. It's taking every ounce of self-restraint I have not to jump over this table and lay a big kiss on you . . . but I'm afraid of getting thrown out of here. So we'd better behave if we want to keep seeing each other."

"You're right. Speaking of seeing each other, I've missed you so much, Anna. I can't believe it's been a month since we last saw each other at the courthouse. I want to hear about everything that's been going on in your life, every single detail."

For the next hour, Anna tried to comply with John's request. She filled him in on everything that had happened at work, at home, and with the Milans. They talked about her running program and how she had to get her car fixed. The only thing Anna omitted from the discussion was her church attendance, talks with Father Anderson, and visits to Maria's grave. She was leery of John's reaction to these subjects and didn't want their reunion to be spoiled. She first needed to gauge where he was in his faith journey.

After she finished talking, they got up to get some diet sodas and snacks. When they returned to their table, Anna asked John about his life at Newtown. She waited with mixed emotions to see what he would tell her.

John took a deep breath and reflected momentarily on how much to tell Anna. Although he wanted to share his prison experiences with his wife, he didn't want to alarm her or cause any more concern than she already had. He quickly decided there would be no mention of Carlos Delgado. No good could come of that discussion. Robert, on the other hand, was a different story. He began his dialogue with how the two of them had first come into contact with each other.

"Well, believe it or not, my first night here I thought I had met Goliath."

"What are you talking about?" asked Anna, laughing.

"I'm serious. It was like five in the morning, and all of a sudden I see this guy in one of the beds next to me rising like some gargantuan. It was the first time I had laid eyes on him, and he was enormous! At first, I was so scared, I couldn't move a muscle."

A concerned look appeared on Anna's face. John thought he better quickly move on with the story. "Don't worry Anna, it's not bad. I soon found out that despite his size, he's really softhearted. In fact, he's one of the nicest people I've ever met."

"Well, that's great, John." Anna was thrilled that John had made such a positive contact. Her enthusiasm was short-lived, however, as John continued on.

"Yeah, one of the things I've really come to appreciate about Robert is that he's not trying to cram religion down my throat. It seems that because this place is a Faith and Character-Based Institution, there are a lot of inmates running around here trying to outdo each other with the "who's the holiest of them all" routine. Apparently, they're trying to atone for what landed them in here—or running some kind of a con game with the guards and staff to make their lives easier. Either way, I don't buy into it. That's what I really admire about Robert. Even though he's a Bible study leader and assists the chaplain's office, he never throws God in my face or tries to solve my problems with some faith analysis and reflection."

John could tell by the look on Anna's face that he had gotten carried away. He knew he needed to retreat a bit from what he'd just said or she would leave the prison upset and discouraged. He certainly didn't want that to happen because he loved her, and despite his careless words, he desperately wanted to spare her from further turmoil. "Anna, I didn't mean to go overboard with what I just said. You know how I'm feeling about God and faith, and I didn't need to bring it up right now."

"That's okay, John. I understand."

"Well, I also want to tell you that I'm getting psychological counseling once a week for an hour. The guy's name is Dr. Mayne, and I've seen him three times now."

"How's that going?" There was a glimmer of hope in Anna's voice.

John was adamant that he wouldn't screw up this response. "It's going okay. I think we have a difference in philosophy over what our discussions should center on, but he's a smart, experienced guy and means well. I know he's trying to help me, so I'm doing my best to work with him." Looking at Anna, John could tell she felt a sense of relief.

"You have no idea how happy I am to hear you say that, John." Suddenly, a loud clap of thunder erupted, followed by a lightning bolt and strong wind gusts.

"You better hit the road, Anna. Our lovely South Florida weather is acting up. I'll see you tomorrow, right?"

"Of course you will. I've got a 7:00 a.m. match with Tess. Then I'll go home, shower, change, and be here by ten."

"Go to church first, Anna. I know how important it is to you. You'll still be here before noon, and we'll have several hours together."

"Okay, Honey. I will."

The weather was deteriorating, and the guards started asking everyone to leave. They said the visitation park needed to be cleared because a bad storm was developing. Dark clouds filled the sky. Anna scampered out and waved good-bye to John. Then she disappeared from his sight. How glad he was that she'd be returning tomorrow. At least he didn't have to wait another month to see his wife.

The next morning Anna was at the top of her game. She had Tess scrambling all over the court, to no avail. Finally, Tess decided to call a halt to the trouncing. She wanted to stay and talk, but Anna was in a hurry. She was a woman on a mission, and her first goal was to be at Mass on time. Anna extended her apologies to Tess, explaining her rush and assuring her loyal friend she'd catch up with her that afternoon. Then, in whirlwind fashion, she rushed home, showered, dressed, and managed to arrive at church ten minutes early. Anna saw Father Anderson before the Mass started. She told him what a busy day it was and let him know she'd speak with him sometime the following week. After Mass, she decided to head directly to Newtown and stop at the cemetery on her way home. At eleven forty-five, she pulled into the prison parking lot, relieved to see there was no one in line waiting to enter the park. She needed that break after the hectic morning. Ten minutes later she was in the park with John, sitting at the same table they had occupied the day before.

"John, we never got to finish our conversation yesterday. You told me about Robert. Who sleeps in the bed on the other side of you?"

"John Vitiglio. Everyone calls him 'Johnny Boy.' He's all Italian and a real wise guy—but not vindictive. I guess I'm pretty lucky to have two decent guys next to me."

"That's encouraging. Tell me more about your job in the library."

John decided to sugarcoat the description of his work in the library. As was the case yesterday, he didn't want to distress Anna with any stories of his bleak existence. Later, John filled her in on other details of his life at Newtown, but again he didn't mention Delgado. The two of them talked nonstop until Officer Longo came by to tell them visiting hours were over.

Before she left, John carefully looked around and saw that no one was watching. He quickly kissed Anna on the lips and then headed back to his dorm. On the way out, Anna turned around, saw John looking at her, and gave him a thumbs-up. They both wished the kiss could have lasted longer, but they were happy.

On the way home, Anna stopped to visit Maria's grave and then went on to the Milan's home. They had another wonderful dinner, and afterwards Tess sent the kids upstairs to do homework while Anna filled Tess and Bob in on her two visits to Newton. Anna told them she thought John still needed a great deal of help to overcome his mental and emotional scars, but she was optimistic that he was headed in the right direction. Only time would tell if Anna was correct.

Chapter 32

"Step it up, Sissy Boy! You've got to be quicker than that! My grandma moves faster than you," screamed Delgado to John. Their housing dorm was in the middle of a basketball game, and Delgado and John were on opposite teams. Delgado and his teammate Derrick Mays had been harassing John throughout the game. John reached his boiling point and decided to show them up. He dribbled furiously down the court, getting by both Delgado and Mays with ease. He then lobbed the ball high into the air toward Robert, who was on his team. Robert responded by catching the ball in midair with one hand and slammed the ball through the hoop for a thunderous dunk. Hooting and hollering erupted from both teams. John smiled smugly at Delgado and Mays.

The next time down the court, Delgado had the ball, and John was closely guarding him. Delgado took a fifteen-foot jump shot, which was partially blocked by John, and the ball started to roll off the rim. Both of them went for the rebound. Delgado managed to get a better position than John for the rebound and soared high in the air to grab the ball. John was directly under him, and on the way down, Delgado's left elbow viciously slammed straight into the left cheekbone of John's face. John went flying out of control, smashing the back of his head onto the pavement. Everyone froze. They looked to see if John was okay, but he remained motionless. He was unconscious.

Thirty minutes later, John woke up in the prison infirmary. Dr. Harry Scott, one of Newtown's physicians, was attending to him. Corporal Alexander was also in the room. John was groggy and temporarily could not remember where he was or how long he'd been here. Alexander told him, "Just relax, John. You're at Newtown Correctional Institution. You've been here for the past five months. Right now you're in the infirmary because of an incident on the basketball court. When you're ready, I have some questions to ask you."

Slowly but surely, John's memory was returning. He let out a groan, more from the recognition of where he was than from the pain he was experiencing.

"Are you okay?" asked Dr. Scott.

"Well, my head feels like it got run over by a truck and my face is numb, but other than that, I'm okay."

"You had a nasty collision with the ground, John. Your head is going to hurt for a couple of days at least. I've got some pain meds to give you now, and then every eight hours for the next few days you'll need to come back for more," Dr. Scott explained. "As far as your facial numbness, I gave you a shot to protect against infection from the gash you received. The effects will wear off in the next hour or so, and then the numbness will disappear. I already put a medicated bandage on your face. That will need to be changed daily. Keep wearing it until the cut is healed. You also have quite a shiner, but that will go away over the next week or so. You don't appear to have a concussion or any other serious injury other than the large bump on the back of your head."

"Although I really don't like the pain I'm feeling," John said, "the worst thing about all this is that it's Friday, and my wife will be here tomorrow to visit. When she sees me, she'll think that I was beat up by a bunch of inmates and start freaking out."

"Speaking of being beat up," injected Corporal Alexander, "I'd like to talk with you about how this incident happened. Are you feeling up to it?"

"Yes, go ahead."

"I've already spoken with Carlos Delgado, and he tells me that it was an accident when he fell down on you. He claims the two of you were both going for a rebound. Then he told me that he was in the air above you, lost his balance while airborne, and came falling down and landed on top of you. None of the guards saw the incident, and the inmates who did corroborate Delgado's version of the events. What do you believe happened?"

John thought back to how Robert warned him that Delgado was out to get him and how Delgado had the ability to purposely hurt someone while making it look like an accident. *Robert was right,* John thought. John believed Delgado had intentionally fallen on him and smashed his elbow into John's face to repay him for their verbal feud. Rather than express his feelings to Alexander, however, John decided to agree that it was an accident and not seek to have Delgado punished. Instead, John determined to repay Delgado—at the appropriate time and place.

"It appeared to be an accident to me. I can't say Delgado purposely hit me," John said.

"If that's the case," responded Alexander, "then my investigation is concluded and the incident is deemed to be an accident, with no disciplinary action to be taken."

. . .

The next day, when Anna saw John at the visitation park, she nearly started crying. After John repeatedly told her that he was involved in a basketball accident, not beaten up by inmates, Anna calmed down and they moved on to more pleasant topics. She could not, however, take her eyes off his bruised and battered face. She suspected there was more to the story than John was telling. Her hope and prayer was that there would be no such incidents in the future, whether accidental or not.

Chapter 33

One month later, John was ready to get his revenge on Delgado. All his scars from the incident with Delgado had fully healed, and he was once again in top physical condition. John thought Delgado needed to learn a lesson, and he was more than happy to teach it. He wanted to show Delgado that he couldn't be intimidated—and hopefully deter Delgado from any future harassment. Taking his cue from Delgado, John knew that proper execution of "the lesson" required it to look accidental. John certainly didn't want to risk disciplinary action. And although John didn't intend to inflict any serious injuries on Delgado, the message needed to be strong enough to put an end to future misconduct. No one, including Anna nor Robert, knew of John's strategy. The battleground was once again the basketball court, and the battle was ready to begin.

As the ball game heated up, John taunted Delgado, telling him he was the slowest man on the court and couldn't make a basket to save his life. Delgado was becoming enraged from the trash-talking, and John knew it. He decided his moment for revenge had arrived. The next time John got the ball he sprinted down the court with Delgado in hot pursuit. Then he slowed up enough for Delgado to catch up to him, without anyone noticing his reduction in speed. Delgado wasn't prepared for the slow down and went crashing into John, who ducked, causing Delgado to flip over John's back and up into the air. Delgado landed squarely on his back. He wasn't seriously hurt, but the wind was knocked out of him, and Mr. Tough Guy couldn't get up. John, on the other hand, acted as though nothing had happened.

Officer Peter Deem saw the entire incident and ran over to Delgado. Dr. Scott was summoned to see if Delgado should be moved, and it was a good ten minutes before he could stand. Delgado had to be assisted by two of his teammates for the slow crawl to the infirmary. Delgado had sustained some serious bruises to his back, which resulted in the use of pain medication for several days. He was also unable to participate in sports for the same period of time. The most severe injury, however, was to his ego. John had won the battle.

Everyone who witnessed the collision, including Delgado, thought Delgado had run head-on into John. The best part was that John had not felt any effects, while Delgado went down for the count. Some of the inmates were now referring to John as Superman, which added to Delgado's chagrin.

A week later at dinner, John and Robert were sitting next to each other. No one else was in the vicinity. Robert was unusually quiet and had a disturbed look on his face. John couldn't help but notice and asked what the problem was. Robert was slow in responding, and his voice was sullen.

"I'll tell you what's wrong, John. I'm getting bad vibes that you set Delgado up for his fall last week, the same as I think he did to you. I should have said this to you sooner, but at first I was uncertain. But now, the more I think about it and remember how you were talking smack just before the collision, I'm thinking you were out to get him." Robert looked John squarely in the eyes. "Am I wrong?" he asked.

"So what if I did? He had it coming. Maybe now he's learned his lesson and will leave me alone. Since then there's been no harassment, and I hope it stays that way for his sake."

Robert let out a big sigh and shook his head from side to side. "John, this revenge-seeking and uncontrolled anger and hostility has got to stop. I haven't talked to you about your attitude and lack of faith in anything or anyone because I was hoping the counseling would help. But you've been here for more than six months and those meetings don't seem to be working. I'm starting to worry about your future."

John was taken aback. "Why do you care? What business is it of yours?" he said with indignation in his voice.

"The first reason is because you're one of God's children, and we all have a responsibility to look out for each other and love each other like the Bible tells us. The second reason is because I know you're a decent man and good husband who lost his faith because of your child's passing and the DUI. Those kinds of tragedies could shake anyone's foundation."

"Putting aside your religious mumbo-jumbo, I told you those things so I could get them off my chest while I'm here in jail. I know you had a DUI, too, but don't even try to understand what it feels like to lose a child," John retorted.

Robert took a deep breath. "John, I lost a child, too. It happened suddenly, and I still don't understand why God let it happen. So actually, I do understand."

John looked incredulous. "What are you talking about? You've never mentioned this to me before!"

"You're right. I haven't. I find my son's death extremely painful to deal with, even after all these years."

"What happened?" John asked, his voice softening.

Robert stopped for a moment to reflect on what he would

say. He rarely spoke about his son's passing. Slowly, however, he explained his own tragedy of losing a child.

"It was ten years ago that my son, Mark, was taken from my wife and me. He was seventeen and a senior at the high school where I taught English. I was also the assistant defensive line football coach, and Mark was our star running back. He was a good kid, a straight-A student. Mark had been offered a half dozen college scholarships and was trying to decide where to go," Robert said, swallowing hard. "One night, he went to a church dance with a bunch of his friends. When they were leaving, three guys in a van drove by and randomly started firing shots. Mark was struck by a bullet in the head and killed instantly. Weeks later, the three shooters were found, convicted, and sentenced to life imprisonment. They had no motive for the shooting—other than a desire to kill someone."

John took a moment to digest this new information. Finally he said, "I'm so sorry, Robert."

The two men sat side by side, realizing the similarities of their pain. After a few minutes, John broke the silence. "You mentioned your wife. You've never talked about her before. Where is she now?"

"We divorced a year after Mark's murder. I was unable to deal with losing him. I hated God. I turned my back on Christ, my wife, and everyone else on the planet. I anesthetized my pain with alcohol, and I got hooked. I was a drunk, John. I lost my job. I lost everything."

Robert took a deep breath. He was glad to finally share his secret with John, but it wasn't easy. "The night I killed Mr. Stevenson," Robert quietly explained, "I had a liter of whiskey and was totally smashed. At the time, I didn't even care that I had taken a life. There was no point in having a trial, and I ended up pleading out in exchange for ten years."

John stared at Robert. He didn't know what to say. The man John had once thought of as Goliath looked like he was going to break down and cry. "So, John," Robert continued, "that's how I know about losing a child. Like you, I know tragedy in an up-close and personal way. Now you'll have to excuse me. I need to get out of here." Robert got up and quickly left the building.

John was astounded. He sat there, unable to eat. He couldn't believe the utter agony and despair Robert had been through. John was determined to find out how Robert dealt with such devastation—and how he could live his life with such gentleness and kindness. It didn't matter how long it took, John knew that the answer must be found.

Chapter 34

"Jayne! Red! It's so good to see both of you," exclaimed John to his former coworkers. "I wish it were under better circumstances, but at least I've got eight months done. Now if I can just get through the next ten months."

The women looked at each other. It was difficult for them to be here, but it was something they had wanted to do for a long time. Red and Jayne both felt an obligation to John, especially because he had been so kind and thoughtful to them while at Smith & Patterson. On this particular Saturday in November, they were visiting in place of Anna. The fifth through eighth grade classes at St. Gregory's had departed yesterday, via train, for a five-day field trip to Washington, D.C. Anna was one of the chaperones. Anna had contacted Red to see whether she could visit John that weekend, and Red immediately agreed. When Jayne found out about the plans, she arranged to go as well. Now that the three of them were together at Newtown, it felt strange.

The atmosphere was the polar opposite of Smith & Patterson's law office.

Red was the first to speak in response to John's comment. "You'll get through the next ten months, John. I'm just so sorry that this is the first time I'm seeing you in eight months. I should have been here much sooner."

"Me, too," piped in Jayne.

"Don't worry about it, ladies," John responded. "I'm glad you're here now. So don't keep me in suspense, Red. Has the partnership decision been made yet for next year?"

Red and Jayne exchanged glances again. A smile appeared on each woman's lips, as Red replied. "The decision was made just last week. I'm in as of the first of January!" John could tell that Red felt like screaming in triumph.

"You have no idea how happy I am to hear that," John replied. "After all the years of blood, sweat, and tears you invested, nobody deserves it more than you. Congratulations! If I thought I could get away with it, I'd jump over this table and give you a big hug. But of course if I do that, the officer standing over there will throw both of you out and send me back inside. So my best wishes to you will have to suffice, at least for now."

Although John was truly pleased at Red's success, he thought she'd better watch her back with the Old Man, Patterson, and Archibald. He was still having a hard time dealing with his perception of abuse by the three current partners. Or was there already a fourth partner? John was certain he'd find out shortly.

"John, I would never have made it this far without your guidance, training, and patience. I'm forever grateful to you. I hope someday I can repay you for all you've done for me."

"Don't think twice about it. I always enjoyed working with you, and seeing how far you've come in your career is payment enough. Jayne, tell me, who are you working for these days?" John thought the answer to this question might reveal who had been hired to replace him, and he wouldn't have to directly ask.

"My gosh, John. The firm has me working as hard as when it was just you and me. Except now, I'm under the gun with two six-year lawyers. They don't have your experience or knowledge, but they sure work long and hard. They're like you in that way. But I have to say, Sweetie, that nobody will ever replace you. I sure do miss working with you." A big smile was on Jayne's face. John smiled, too, knowing she was flattering him, but right now he was enjoying it.

"I miss working with you, too, Jayne. How many new lawyers has the firm hired since I left?"

"Just the two associates Jayne is working with," replied Red. "After you left, I understand there was some discussion about an experienced partner coming in to replace you, but apparently the Old Man and Jim couldn't agree with him on all the financial terms, and the acquisition never happened. I don't know the specific details because I wasn't involved in the discussions, but that's my understanding."

John silently gloated to himself over the failure of the proposed deal. *At least there was some justice in this world,* he thought. The conversation then turned to John's life in prison. As with Anna, he shared selective details. After another half hour of wide-ranging discussions, the women said their goodbyes. John enjoyed the visit and asked both of them to return. They each said they would, and John felt certain they meant it.

The next day another visitor greeted John. This time it was Bruce Davidson, his personal injury defense attorney. Davidson had called Anna because he wanted to see John to discuss the status of the case brought by Attorney Mayberry as well as their strategy in defending the lawsuit. Anna suggested Bruce visit John on the Sunday she was in Washington, and Bruce agreed. After they exchanged pleasantries and John spoke briefly about prison life, Davidson began filling John in on the status of the litigation.

"John, the reason you haven't heard anything from me about the case these last eight months is because nothing significant has transpired. Because we're in a defense posture, I haven't been pushing the case." John nodded his head in agreement. "I believe Mayberry hasn't been aggressive with the case so far for two reasons. One is his trial schedule, which I know from personal experience has been very time consuming over the last year. Secondly, he's been waiting for Luciano's doctors to confirm that Luciano has reached maximum medical improvement before he noticed the case for trial. Mayberry called last Monday to say the doctors advised him that Luciano has reached that point. As a result of the doctors' advice, Mayberry will have his expert witnesses calculate damages. I've requested all Anthony Luciano's medical records, as well as the expert reports, and should be receiving them in the near future."

"Did Mayberry notice the case for trial yet?"

"Yes. That was one of the other reasons he was calling me. The notice arrived by fax last Monday, and this past Friday the Order scheduling the trial was received by my office from the Court."

"When's the case set for trial?"

"It's on a three-week trial docket next year, beginning in mid-October. That's after you're released from here, isn't it?"

"Yes, I'm scheduled for release in early September. That gives me a whole month to enjoy my life away from prison walls before I go back to being imprisoned in a courtroom. Wonderful!" John was extremely annoyed at the news.

"Well, hopefully, we can get this case settled on financial terms that make sense so you don't have to go to trial."

"That would be great," John said wistfully.

"Also, when Mayberry called me, he told me he wanted to take your deposition here at Newtown early next year. So, I'll need to coordinate with the prison authorities to set that up."

"It doesn't make any difference to me when it is. I'm here every day for the next ten months."

Chapter 35

"Happy Thanksgiving, John," said Anna warmly as she walked into the visitation park. Hearing her greeting, John wanted to scream out, "What's so happy about it when you're coming to see me in this stinking prison?" But he decided the better course of action would be to return his wife's statement in kind.

"Happy Thanksgiving, Anna," John managed to blurt out. Anna could tell he was in a negative state of mind, so she braced herself.

As they sat down at one of the tables in the park, neither of them knew how to begin their conversation. Being in a jail on Thanksgiving Day, rather than enjoying a traditional holiday dinner at home, was more than strange. It was absolutely depressing. They were both feeling the strain of John's continued incarceration, especially now at the beginning of the holiday season. Finally, Anna managed to start a discussion.

"Later this afternoon, Alice Barnes and Diana Jenkins are coming over to the house for Thanksgiving dinner. I've already placed an order with the grocer for a turkey dinner to be prepared. All I have to do is to pick it up on the way home and then heat everything up after they arrive. Alice is bringing two side dishes, and Diana is baking pies for dessert."

"Where are their families today?" John was more than a little surprised at the news, and Anna knew it. She had struggled with whether or not to tell him, but she didn't want to lie so she had decided to bring the topic up first.

"Well, the principal is a widow. All her children and grandchildren live out of state, and she would have been alone today. Diana is single, and her parents and siblings all went to Orlando for the weekend. She decided to stay in West Palm and suggested the three of us get together today. I mentioned to you several months ago how several of the faculty and staff were planning on getting together with me periodically, and they've been really good about doing that. The three of us thought it'd be a great idea to have dinner together rather than be alone."

Thinking back to when Anna had shared the news with him about the St. Gregory's support network and how relieved he was, John felt embarrassed by his question and was struggling with how to recover from putting Anna on the defensive. Suddenly, thoughts of the Milan family came to mind. "Well, I'm glad to hear you'll be sharing dinner with your friends. I guess I was just a little surprised you weren't going to the Milans."

"Oh, they went to the Bahamas, and they were concerned about what I would be doing after visiting you. When they heard about my work friends coming over, they were relieved," Anna explained. Trying to change the subject, she asked, "So is anything special going on here for Thanksgiving?"

"Sarge told us there would be a turkey dinner today, complete with all the trimmings. There's also a religious service this evening, but I don't intend to go. I'll just spend some time reading a few books I checked out of the library."

Anna was deeply disappointed over his decision but decided

not to make an issue of it. After another hour of conversation, Anna left to attend to the dinner details. About forty-five minutes after she reached home, the doorbell rang. Alice and Diana had arrived at the same time. After commenting on the apparent coincidence, they told Anna they'd driven together because they lived in the same apartment complex. As Anna's two guests entered her home, Diana appeared awestruck at what she saw.

"Wow, Anna, your home is huge . . . and gorgeous. I've never seen anything like it," Diana blurted out.

"I told you it was beautiful," replied the principal. "When I was here for a dinner party several years ago, I couldn't believe it either."

The three ladies proceeded to the kitchen. Alice suggested Anna give Diana a tour of her house while she checked on the food in the oven. As Anna led Diana around the house, they walked past Maria's room without stopping. Diana could see the crib. She knew what the room was and didn't ask any questions. Anna then led Diana into the master bedroom area.

"My gosh, Anna. I can't believe how large your bedroom and bath area is. It must be as big as my entire apartment."

Anna felt uncomfortable at the statement and decided not to respond. She skillfully changed the subject by suggesting they help Alice get dinner on the table. The three women enjoyed a lovely holiday meal together, although Anna's mind kept wandering to thoughts of John and his absence. This was the first time in their marriage they hadn't been together on Thanksgiving, and Anna profoundly felt his absence. How she absolutely dreaded the thought of John not being around at Christmas.

. . .

Back at Newtown, John hadn't fared any better. Although the prison staff whipped up a first-rate turkey dinner, not being with his wife was causing a mountain of anger and bitterness inside of him. John desperately wanted to move this mountain of trouble but couldn't bring himself to pray for help to do so. The thought of giving thanks for anything on this Thanksgiving Day never even occurred to him.

...

On the Monday after Thanksgiving, Anna headed over to see Father Anderson after school. She was feeling very sad about John's absence, particularly during the holiday season, and she knew she needed to talk to someone. She hoped Father Anderson would have some words of wisdom to help her overcome this ever-present state of aloneness.

At the rectory, Anna spilled her heart out to the priest. "Father, I feel so lonely. I miss John so much, especially now that the holidays are here. I know it's supposed to be a time of reflection and appreciation for our blessings, but right now I don't feel grateful for anything." Father Anderson remained quiet, knowing Anna needed to talk.

Anna continued, hardly taking a breath between thoughts. "On Thanksgiving evening, Alice Barnes and Diana Jenkins came over for dinner. I should've been thankful they cared enough to spend the holiday with me, but I wasn't. Alice said a prayer of thanks before we ate dinner, and I should have appreciated its truth and beauty, but I didn't. Although I had been faithfully reading the prayer card you gave to John, I stopped last week, just before Thanksgiving. I haven't been able to read it again. I'm afraid I'm losing my faith, Father. What can I do to regain it, especially now as Christmas approaches?"

Anna had done her best to control her emotions as she spoke, but she could no longer do so. Father handed her some tissues and waited for Anna to regain her composure.

"I'm sorry to be coming to you again," Anna said, "but I don't know where else to turn."

"First Anna, let me say that you should never be sorry about coming to talk with me. That's why I'm here. I also want to tell you that the crisis of faith you're going through is not unusual. Everyone on this planet, including me, has gone through such a crisis at one time or another." Anna wanted to stop and ask him what his crisis was but decided to let him continue.

"And Anna, you shouldn't feel guilty for feeling the way you do, because God fully understands and wants to help you through the problems you're experiencing."

"But how do I deal with everything that's happened and still trust in God—and maintain my thankfulness to Him?" Anna questioned.

"One thing in particular comes to mind right now, but I must warn you, it won't be easy."

"What's that?" Although Anna felt uneasy about his warning, she recognized she was in the battle of her life and badly in need of assistance.

"Well, sometimes when we go through trials, it's best to get our mind off our own troubles. As you know, Anna, there is always a need to feed and clothe the people in our community who are struggling, and that need has become even greater by our country's current economic problems. I know of a food pantry and clothing store just a few miles from here where they're assisting our brothers and sisters and helping them overcome adverse circumstances, especially during this holiday season. Many of these families have little or no money to cover the essentials in life, let alone such luxuries as Christmas gifts. In several weeks, the pantry is going to have a Christmas party where they will have pizza, sodas, and gifts for the children.

I know there's a shortage of volunteers, especially for the Saturday morning shift. As I said, it wouldn't be easy, but I think it may be helpful to you in your own struggle. If you want to volunteer, I can make the appropriate arrangements with my contacts at the pantry."

Anna thought about what Father Anderson had told her. Although volunteering on Saturday morning would cut into her visitation time with John, Anna recognized her need for spiritual help. The young couple's weekly visits were not sufficient for either of them to battle the crisis of faith they were both experiencing. Anna was determined to get help, not only for herself, but also for John. She thought that perhaps John could use the time the two of them would not see each other on Saturday mornings volunteering for a program at Newtown, while she was at the food pantry. Then they would still be able to visit with each other for a couple of hours on Saturday afternoon, as well as on Sunday.

After letting Father Anderson know that she would discuss the idea with John, Anna asked Father to tentatively arrange for her to start volunteering in two weeks.

Chapter 36

Two weeks later, at eight forty-five on a Saturday morning, Anna arrived at the food pantry. The pantry was open from nine until noon, and there was already quite a crowd gathered outside waiting for the doors to open. Today marked Anna's first time volunteering there, although she had attended a two-hour training session earlier in the week. There were two other volunteers working with her, Brian McHenry and Jill Britton, both of whom had volunteered at the pantry for several years. Although Anna had been advised in detail at the training session about what to expect, she was unprepared for the emotional and psychological toll that was about to face her. At nine o'clock, Anna was given the task of opening the door to let the families in—and was greeted by a sea of faces—some smiling and laughing, others sullen or stoic.

"Good morning," Anna welcomed one family after another.

"Good morning," came the responses, some in English and some in Spanish.

The people receiving aid from the pantry were referred to as clients. As they entered the building, they first checked in at the reception desk, where Jill was stationed. All the clients had been pre-qualified by the office administration regarding their eligibility and need for assistance. Once the office determined that a potential client's need was legitimate, the person was issued a "client card" and was allowed to participate in the program. As part of that process, unemployed clients agreed to attend a job counseling and placement center located near the pantry. The two organizations operated in tandem with each other, so that clients of the pantry would hopefully become self-sufficient through new employment.

This morning, Jill had her hands full checking in the multitude waiting in line. Once the clients were checked in, they went to the window where Anna and Brian were distributing bread, pastries, canned goods, pasta, sauce, cereal, and other food items. Used clothing was also provided when needed—and when available.

Taking the card from her first client of the day, Anna read the name and saw the family consisted of two adults and four children. "Good morning, Mrs. Anderson. My name is Anna, and I'll be helping you today. Other than the normal food items we provide, is there anything else I can check the availability on for you?"

"Do you have any candy bars?" Mrs. Anderson asked. "You know how kids love candy, and mine are always asking for some. Unfortunately, my husband and I both lost our jobs due to the recession, and right now candy is a luxury we can't afford."

"Let me see what we've got in the back." Anna walked to the back room where the food items were stored and nervously searched for candy bars. She couldn't believe there were people in her community who couldn't afford a candy bar! Worse yet, there wasn't a single candy bar to be found in the storage area. The closest she could come was a few packages of cookies.

Although disappointed, she kept her game face on and went back to the window to deliver the entire food package to Mrs. Anderson and her family.

"I'm sorry, Mrs. Anderson, but we don't have any candy today. I did find some cookies that I've put in your food box. Anna glanced at the four children and could see the disappointment on their faces.

"Don't worry about it, Sweetheart. The cookies are great," replied Mrs. Anderson. "Kids, what do we say?"

"Thank you, Anna," the four children shouted out obediently.

"And God bless you, Anna," said Mrs. Anderson. "Thank you for what you're doing for us and for all the other people here. You're truly a gift from God for all of us."

As the Andersons headed out the door, Anna excused herself and ran to the back room. She didn't want Brian or anyone else to see her tears. It didn't work; Brian soon appeared.

"Hey, Anna. I know that what you just went through was very difficult. But what you're experiencing now is what we all went through our first time here," Brian consoled with a sincere smile. "You'll get through this, but I can't say you'll get use to it. I still haven't after three years. But God has given me both the desire and strength to help our brothers and sisters in need, and He'll do the same for you. After you've been here for awhile, you'll come to realize that not only are you a blessing from God to our clients, as Mrs. Anderson just told you, but our clients are also a blessing to you from God."

"Thanks, Brian. I needed to hear that. I guess we should get back out there. We've got a lot of hungry people to feed."

The rest of the day wasn't any easier for Anna. So many people in Palm Beach County had tremendous needs for the basics, and she had been totally ignorant of their plight. Now reality was slapping her in the face. As she continued through her day, she became more and more determined not to run from the need but to be part of the solution.

Anna's last client of the day was Mrs. Martinez, accompanied by her five-year-old son. The little boy quietly asked Anna if he might get a bike next week at the Christmas party the pantry was hosting. Reluctantly, Anna told him that no bikes were available this year. The pantry administration had warned the volunteers about such special requests and had also informed them that there wasn't enough money to purchase the fifty bikes already requested by clients.

· · ·

Meanwhile, back at Newtown, John was mentoring Derrick Mays, one of the inmates who had harassed him on the basketball court. Anna had strongly encouraged John to volunteer, as she was planning to do, when she spoke with him just after Thanksgiving. Even though they couldn't volunteer together per se, she knew it was an experience that would draw them closer together. As a result of her persistence, John became a mentor for a few inmates each week. Although he wasn't allowed to provide them with any legal advice or opinions, John served as a fountain of knowledge in regards to understanding and complying with the vast and complex legal system.

In some cases, John was providing an even more basic service, as he did with Mays today. Many men like Mays couldn't read nor write very well, and some of the inmates were completely illiterate. John was doing an excellent job teaching them these basic life skills, and although not everyone was enthusiastic, the majority of inmates expressed deep gratitude for his efforts. That sense of appreciation, coupled with something new in his otherwise boring routine, was starting to have a positive effect on John's attitude. However, he still had a long and bumpy road to travel.

· · ·

The following Saturday was Christmas Eve, and after a morning of working at the food pantry, Anna headed over to a local church hall for the food pantry's annual Christmas celebration. As she drove to the party, she thought about her last visit with John. Anna had not been able to go to Newtown on Saturday, but she made up for it by spending six hours with him on Sunday. During their visit, Anna had told John in great detail about her experience at the pantry and how she felt God tugging at her heartstrings to help the clients in any way she could. Anna convinced John that they should make a donation to cover the costs of the fifty bikes the clients had requested. Although John really didn't want to spend the money, he knew there was no point in arguing with Anna on this issue, and he reluctantly agreed. Anna arranged for fifty new bikes to be delivered to the church, all fully assembled. Anna also spoke to the food pantry and requested that the donation remain anonymous.

As Anna pulled into the church parking lot, she couldn't wait to see if the bikes had arrived. The party was scheduled to start in one hour, and she hoped the bikes were already there. She got her wish. As soon as Anna walked in, she was greeted by the sight of fifty brand new, shiny bicycles—and the very happy faces of the pantry staff.

"Look, Anna. Isn't this wonderful?" hollered out Jill Britton. "Some anonymous person donated fifty bikes for the children. I'm so happy I could cry."

Anna looked at Susan Smith, the director of the food pantry, the only one there who knew the source of the donation. They smiled at each other, and Susan exclaimed, "Yes, God has blessed not only our clients, but all of us with a kind and generous benefactor. The person is so humble that he or she doesn't want any recognition for this wonderful gift." Susan smiled again at Anna, who now blushed in embarrassment.

Suddenly, the outside doors opened, and the families started to arrive. When the children saw the bicycles, there was a roar of excitement. The hall was filled with joy, although some of the parents were crying. Mrs. Anderson saw Anna and came running over to her. Although she was one of the parents crying, she nonetheless managed to express her appreciation for what the food pantry had done. Her husband soon joined her, and Anna was warmly embraced by each of them. The Anderson family then went around the entire room thanking the staff for the wonderful gifts. The same scene of gratitude and happiness was replayed throughout the entire afternoon, and Anna left the party uplifted and refreshed, something she had not experienced in a very, very long time. She was now headed home to change, then on to the Milan's house for Christmas Eve dinner, followed by midnight church services. Christmas Day would be spent with John at Newtown. While she made her way home, Anna gave thanks to God for the wonderful day she and all the pantry staff and clients experienced, and she prayed that John would also be similarly blessed.

...

While Anna was on her way to a late Christmas Eve dinner with the Milans, John was walking into a large room at the administrative building at Newtown. Approaching the room, John could hear music and singing. They were having a Christmas concert, and the room was packed with inmates and prison staff. John had not planned on being here, but after Robert asked him to attend, he decided he might as well go. The musical group performing consisted of twelve inmates of various racial and ethnic backgrounds, and Robert led the group. Some of the musicians played instruments, while others sang and danced. Robert was center stage, playing lead guitar and singing. The music was all Christmas related, some secular, some religious. The crowd loved each song, and there was a feeling of electricity in the air. Even John was touched by this magnificent display of musical giftedness. He couldn't believe he was in a prison with convicts playing and singing like they belonged in some renowned concert hall. After about two hours, Robert announced that the next song would be their last. A round of boos arose, but the crowd quickly quieted down. Robert put his guitar down and began singing "Silent Night," accompanied by one of the inmates playing the piano. His voice was so melodious that it sounded as though the heavens had opened and God's angels were giving praise to their Lord.

As Robert was singing, John's mind went back in time to when he had been an altar boy at St. Peter's Church in Downers Grove. He had served in that role for six years and truly enjoyed every moment of that time. The wonderful memories of Christmas Eves from long ago came flashing back. Where had those times gone, and why were they no longer a part of his life? Or were they? Here he was, having one of his most moving and spiritual moments ever, and it was taking place in a prison. How could this be? What—or Who—was causing this? As the song ended and John looked around, he saw Carlos Delgado on the other side of the room. John could swear Delgado was wiping tears from his face. What was going on here tonight?

Later that night as John lay in bed, he reflected on the night's activities. It was now officially Christmas Day, and he wondered if Robert was still awake. A second later, Robert sat up in his bed and whispered, "John, what did you think of the concert?"

John thought for several moments and then quietly responded, "Robert, it was the most enlightening and refreshing time I've had in several years. Right now, I don't know what it's all about, but I feel a peace I haven't felt in a long time." John paused, and Robert didn't say anything. "To top matters off," John continued, "I think I saw Delgado crying when you were singing! Can you believe that?"

"Yes, I can, John. Merry Christmas."

"Merry Christmas to you, too, Robert."

Later that morning at breakfast, John was sitting next to "Johnny Boy" Vitiglio. They were talking about how their mothers had cooked such wonderful feasts on Christmas and how much they missed those occasions. Suddenly, Delgado walked up to the table.

"Johnny Boy," Delgado said, "how about giving me some alone time with Taylor? I need to say something to him."

"No problem," responded Vitiglio, as he got up and left the table.

John couldn't imagine what Delgado wanted to say to him. He braced himself for whatever was coming.

"Taylor, my man Derrick tells me you've been teaching him to read and write. He feels real good about that and about you."

"I'm glad to hear that."

"Let me finish, Taylor. What I'm trying to say ain't easy, and I don't want to take too long to say it."

"Okay, sorry."

"What I say to you now is between you and me only. Deal?"

"Deal."

"I'm coming to tell you that I'm sorry for putting the hurt on you on the basketball court. I took you down on purpose because I needed to teach you a lesson. But I'm sorry that I did. You've helped out a lot of brothers around here, and now I know you're okay. That's what I came to say."

"Okay, now it's my turn to tell you something that's only between you and me. Deal?"

"Deal."

"I knew you took me down on purpose, Carlos."

"So, why didn't you tell Alexander?"

"Because I decided to teach you a lesson and set you up for the fall."

"You're saying that you set up the whole crash, that you didn't just take it like Superman, like they're calling you around here?"

"You got it."

A huge grin spread across Delgado's face. He started clapping his hands like his basketball team had just won a championship game. "Well, don't that beat all! Taylor, you have no idea how happy you just made me. Knowing you're not Superman and I'm no wimp is about the best thing that's happened to me since I got here!"

"Just remember, Carlos. It's our secret, just like what you told me."

"No worries."

"Okay."

"One more thing. If I decide I need some help with my reading and writing, can I get it from you?"

"I'll be glad to help, if you need it."

"Okay, I'll keep that in mind." With that, Delgado got up and left, leaving John in a state of amazement at what just happened.

. . .

As Anna made her way to Newtown that Christmas Day, she reflected on what a wonderful dinner she'd shared with the Milan family the night before. After dinner, they exchanged Christmas gifts and sang Christmas carols. Then she attended Midnight Mass at St. Gregory's, where Father Anderson gave a beautiful sermon on the meaning of Christmas. She wondered how John's Christmas Eve had been. She would know soon enough.

As Anna walked into the visitation area, she saw John standing there with a big smile on his face. "Merry Christmas, Anna," he called out across the park.

"Merry Christmas, John." Anna was relieved he had greeted her first—and with such enthusiasm—and was wondering if that attitude would continue.

"Anna, let's go sit down. I've got a lot to talk to you about." For the next hour, John talked nonstop about all that had happened on Christmas Eve. Anna was absolutely delighted to hear John speak in such an uplifting manner. After awhile, Robert interrupted their conversation. He was carrying plastic utensils and two plates of food. Anna had no idea who he was or what this was about.

"Anna, this is my friend, Robert, the guy I told you about. The lasagna is a surprise dinner for you. The staff arranged to make a special dinner for Christmas, and several inmates volunteered to serve it to visitors," John said as he reached out to take a plate of food and handed it to Anna. "Boy, this smells delicious!" he said to Robert.

"Anna, I'm Robert Williams, and it's my pleasure to meet you. After everything John has told me about you, which is all good, of course, I feel as though we already know each other." He set the other plate of food on the table.

"Likewise, Robert. John has told me what a good man you are and how much you've helped him. I also understand you're quite the singer."

"Thank you. It's been a lifelong passion," said Robert. "Now, I don't mean to be rude, but I've got to get a move on. There are other visitors to serve, and I see some of them looking at me with hungry eyes. So you two enjoy the meal—and Merry Christmas!"

Anna wished Robert a Merry Christmas and then, after commenting to John about Robert's size and charisma, gave John a Christmas card her class had made for him. John opened it and saw that it contained the well wishes and signatures of her students. Many of them said they were praying for him. Some of the students said they wanted him to come to their Christmas party next year. John smiled as he read all the good wishes, and he had a few chuckles at some of the kids' messages.

"I thought the comments about me coming to the Christmas party next year were funny. They probably want to ask me a million questions about life in prison, but that's okay," John said with a laugh. "More importantly, Anna, are the comments about the students praying for me. Be sure to tell them how much I appreciate it, and I hope they keep the prayers coming every day. Tell them I still have a ways to go, but with their prayers, I just might make it."

Anna hadn't heard John speak like this in ages. It sounded as though his faith was being restored. She silently asked the Lord for His continued help in bringing back to her a godly man of faith, as Tess had described John. A man whose faith would be able to sustain him beyond the trials of life they'd recently experienced and unexpected ones that would surely come.

Chapter 37

"State your name for the record," came the command.

"John Taylor."

"And tell us where you reside," sneered attorney Robert Mayberry.

John knew Mayberry's game and was well prepared to deal with this lawyer's pugnaciousness. It was now mid-March, and John had six more months to serve at Newtown before he was released. For today, however, the focus was not on how long it was before his release. Rather, the focus was on performing well at this deposition. The only other people present in the administrative building conference room, besides John and Mayberry, were Davidson, the court reporter, and a correctional officer. John and Davidson had met a week earlier to prepare for the deposition, and Davidson had been extremely thorough so John would be ready to meet this challenge. Mayberry's tenaciousness and bravado was on display from the get go. John knew he was in for a long and painful afternoon but was determined not to let Mayberry get to him. He was not about to blow the deposition, which was exactly Mayberry's goal.

"Mr. Mayberry, right now and for the next six months, I reside at Newtown Correctional Institution. After that, I will return to my home at 280 Reef Road, Palm Beach, Florida."

"And what is the reason you presently call this lovely jail your home?" inquired Mayberry, with a huge smile on his face.

"Object to the form of the question," asserted Davidson. "You can go ahead and answer it, Mr. Taylor."

"A jury found me guilty of driving under the influence of alcohol, causing serious bodily injury to your client, Mr. Luciano." John was totally calm and deliberate in his response, and Davidson was very pleased.

For the next several hours, Mayberry's abrasive questioning and rude behavior continued. John performed very well in response to the interrogation and theatrics, and the only real interruptions in the flow of the deposition were Davidson's occasional objections. Mayberry was now getting down to his last area of inquiry, which he had purposely saved for the end.

"Mr. Taylor, my last subject of questioning for today is going to center upon your financial status. The first thing I want to know is, what is your net worth?"

"Don't answer the question, Mr. Taylor," roared out Davidson. Turning his attention to Mayberry, Davidson said, "I'm sorry Mr. Mayberry, but you're not entitled to know that information at this time. You don't have a judgment against Mr. Taylor, and discovery into his finances is not allowed pending any judgment you may obtain."

"Of course it is," bellowed back Mayberry. "As you know, I have a claim for punitive damages against your client and am fully entitled to seek discovery regarding his financial condition."

"Oh no you're not," fired back Davidson. "The punitive damages claim only allows you to pursue financial worth discovery after the trial court makes a determination that there is a reasonable evidentiary basis for the recovery of punitive damages. In this case, you've not sought such a determination, and therefore, you're not entitled to discovery regarding Mr. Taylor's financial worth."

"And how hard do you think it will be for me to convince the judge of that under the circumstances of your client's shameful and egregious acts, which have devastated my client and his family?" retorted Mayberry.

"Look, Mr. Mayberry, I've had enough of your self-serving innuendo. Take up your position with the Court, and I'll respond accordingly. Right now, please tell me if you have any other areas of inquiry. If not, I have no questions, and this deposition is over."

"I have no other questions at this time other than those pertaining to financial worth discovery. But you're wrong, Mr. Davidson. This deposition isn't over by a long shot. I will take my position up with the Judge, and then I'll resume the deposition. Normally, when the opposing side refuses to answer questions at a deposition, and I have to obtain a Court order requiring them to answer questions, I also have the Judge require them to come to my office to complete the deposition. But seeing as your client is incarcerated in a state penitentiary and can't travel anywhere, I guess I'll be back to this beautiful establishment one more time." Mayberry was flashing his trademark obnoxious grin at both Davidson and John. John felt like telling Mayberry not to be so certain he might not be here himself for an extended stay in the future, but refrained from making those comments.

After Mayberry and the court reporter left, Davidson and John had an long conversation about the deposition and their strategy going forward in the case. The correctional officer stepped outside of the room to provide privacy for their attorney-client discussion, but kept tabs on them by looking through the window on the door.

"John, we both know it's only a matter of time before the Court allows Mayberry to proceed with financial worth discovery. I also think that before Mayberry returns to resume your deposition, he'll send a document production requesting you provide him with all your financial documents. That being said, what will he find out about your financial worth?"

"A couple years ago, my net worth was in excess of $5 million. But since I haven't had any income while in prison, coupled with the hit my retirement plan and stock market investments have taken due to the recession, it's probably somewhere around $4 million now. Most of that is tied up in our home in Palm Beach, which is titled in both my name and Anna's. It seems to me, Bruce, that if Mayberry ever does get a judgment in excess of my coverage limits, there are a myriad of legal hurdles he would have to overcome in collecting on the judgment. The homestead exemption on our residence immediately comes to mind as a huge obstacle for him."

"You're absolutely right, John. All of those issues would have to be carefully analyzed when we get to that point. For now, I just wanted to have a general overview so I know the parameters we're talking about. It's also why I recommended you obtain independent counsel, and I'm very glad you have Chris McConnell to assist you in that regard."

"So am I. Well, I guess we'll wait and see what happens next." The old wait-and-see game had returned to haunt John once more.

That evening, John became more and more upset thinking about the way Mayberry had treated him during the deposition. He was also frustrated with the very real prospect of losing most, if not all, of his wealth on a permanent—and not just temporary— basis. The "one step forward" he had taken over the past few months in his faith journey now seemed to be replaced by two steps backward. His state of mind scared him, and he knew he needed to talk to someone. His first thought was of Robert. At the moment Robert was leading a Bible study, but John knew he'd be back at the dorm shortly. So he waited.

An hour later, Robert appeared. Seeing the concerned look on John's face, he immediately asked what was wrong.

"I underwent several hours of a terrible deposition today. The attorney is a prime example of why the legal profession has such a sterling reputation. Not only was he rude, he was downright spiteful. I know his tactics; he was trying to break me." John took a deep breath and continued.

"Robert, he nearly did break me. I think I remained calm on the outside, but inside I despised him. The worst part is that I'm starting to hate myself for feeling this way, especially after trying to do better the past few months."

Robert quietly listened. This was the most John had ever shared, and he knew better than to interrupt.

John looked at the floor and put his head in his hands. His body shuddered, as though he were trying to shake off the bad feelings that clung to him. "Tell me, Robert, with all the adversity you've dealt with, how have you managed to stay positive and, and . . ." John struggled to find the right word. Finally he said, " . . . and loving?"

The last thing Robert wanted to see was his friend spiral downward into the abyss. He silently prayed, asking Jesus for the right words. "John, as I mentioned to you the last time we talked about my son, I was a mean, spiteful person for years following his death. It took me a very long time to return to the person of faith that my mama raised me to be. There were many different people who guided me slowly but surely back to the right path. But ultimately it was my relationship with Jesus Christ that restored my faith. I stopped being angry at people who were rude, and I stopped trying to control situations that weren't going the way I wanted."

"But how did you do that, Robert? That's the answer I'm

looking for."

"I'm afraid there's no simple answer to your question, John. But the most important thing is for you to develop a personal relationship with Jesus. Accept Him as your Lord and Savior, and truly believe that He died on the cross for your sins and the sins of all mankind. After I did that, I continued to build a personal relationship with Jesus by asking Him each day for strength to love others—especially those who aren't easy to love. That certainly wasn't easy. It's still not easy. And there are plenty of times when I falter and become upset over actions that people take or what they say. One of the things I've gotten into the habit of doing is praying daily for Jesus to bless me with a heavenly view of others and not a worldly view."

"What does that mean, Robert?"

"I ask Jesus to provide me with His view of others instead of my human perspective of what they are like. In other words, I try to see the good in people, as Jesus does, rather than just the bad, as the world does. Believe me, I know it's a terribly difficult thing for any of us on this planet to do, but give it your best shot. Maybe you'll eventually see some good in Mr. Mayberry, with the Lord's help and guidance."

"Right now that sounds like an impossible task, but you've given me a lot to think about. I really appreciate it. There's one more thing I'd like your advice on."

"Sure, shoot."

"Because of the lawsuit the Lucianos filed against me, I'm looking at the very real possibility of losing almost everything my wife and I have worked so hard for over the years—if not everything. I'm having a hard time dealing with that. It's making it hard to believe in a good God. What are your thoughts?"

"John, the best thing I can tell you right now is to remember that you should not be concerned with storing up riches here on earth. Money will never bring true happiness and cannot be brought to eternity. If you keep those concepts in mind, hopefully you'll be at peace with whatever happens in the future regarding the lawsuit."

Those words sounded familiar to John, as though he had heard them before, but he couldn't recall where or when he may have heard what Robert said. Perhaps in the future he might remember. For now, Robert had provided John with a lot to reflect upon.

Chapter 38

"Good afternoon, Mrs. Taylor. I'm Bruce Davidson, and it's good to meet you. Chris McConnell is on his way and should be here in about ten minutes. I'd like to hold off starting the video until he arrives. Is that okay?"

"No problem," replied Anna. "Perhaps while we're waiting you can fill me in on the status of the lawsuit. John told me he had authorized you to speak with me regarding the case, so if it's okay with you, I'd like to know where we stand."

"Sure. The trial is set to begin in mid-October, some three months from now. As I understand from John, he's scheduled to be released in two months," said Davidson

"Yes, that's correct."

"When I met with John at Newtown last week, I told him that Mr. Mayberry had called me to say that his office had finished reviewing all the financial records pertaining to John's net worth, which the Court ordered us to produce. Those are the documents that you gathered and brought to my office for me to turn over to

Mayberry."

"Yes, I recall," Anna replied.

"I also told John that Mayberry said he was sending a settlement demand letter to me, along with a video which depicts a day in the life of Mr. Luciano and his family. Both the letter and the video have been received, and the purpose of our meeting today is for you to watch the video and then let John know your impressions. I asked Chris McConnell to be here to see it because he's John's independent counsel and needs to be fully apprised of what's happening in the lawsuit."

"That was a good idea. Thank you."

McConnell entered the room and after greeting Anna, the three of them viewed the recording. As the video played, Anna became more and more unnerved at what she was seeing. Lasting nearly thirty minutes, the video depicted a day in Luciano's life. Luciano was unable to get out of bed and into his wheelchair without assistance. The time it took to complete the transfer from the bed to the wheelchair was lengthy. The videographer gracefully and unobtrusively depicted Luciano needing assistance in basic elements of his life such as bathing, managing his bladder, and bowel movements. Getting him in and out of a specially equipped van to sit as a passenger was a slow and cumbersome process. On the positive side, the video also portrayed Luciano grooming, feeding himself, and brushing his own teeth. His voice was strong and clear, and he was shown laughing and enjoying time with his family, including card and board games. As the video ended, Anna stood up and began pacing around the room.

"Well," said Anna, "the start of that video was extremely depressing. Thank God that toward the end there appeared to be some things Mr. Luciano could do, especially being able to laugh and joke around with his children."

"Mayberry is very experienced with these types of videos and how to portray them to a jury. He knows better than to depict the video as all gloom and doom when his client has a great attitude and fully intends to resume working in some non-physical field in the near future," Davidson explained.

"What does that mean?" asked Anna with a glimmer of hope in her voice.

"Well, based on what all the doctors have told us, and Luciano's testimony at deposition, he is both capable of—and intends—to pursue a career in the computer industry," replied Davidson.

"At John's criminal trial, Luciano had a neck brace on; but he didn't have the brace on in the video. Why is that?"

"Because he no longer needs one," answered Davidson. "Since the time of John's trial, he's done remarkably well with the help of occupational and physical therapists. But the reality of the matter is that he'll never be able to walk, get out of bed by himself, drive a car, shower, or use the bathroom without some assistance. So, although things are much better for him and his family than they were two years ago, there are and always will be serious restrictions on his abilities to live a fully independent life."

"I'm very sorry to hear that, believe me," replied Anna. "What's our next step?"

"Chris and I are going to Newtown this Sunday to meet with you and John to discuss the settlement offer and the case. I arranged with the prison administration to use one of the conference rooms for several hours so that we'll have some privacy."

"One last thing. How much is the settlement demand, and what will insurance cover?" Anna asked.

"The demand is for $10 million, and the insurer will pay $6 million, which is the total amount available under both of John's policies."

"That's what I needed to know. Thanks to both of you for your help."

...

Two days later, John was in Dr. Mayne's office for his weekly counseling session. During the months since he had first started seeing Mayne, John had developed an appreciation for this man's intelligence, sophistication, and integrity. They had developed a cordial relationship with each other, and he no longer dreaded the time they spent together. On this particular day, John was in a very reflective mood and decided to ask Mayne a question John had never been able to answer.

"Dr. Mayne, I was wondering if I could ask you a question that I have never found an answer to. It has bothered me for the longest time, particularly during the past several years."

"You can ask, John, but I can't promise that I'll have the answer."

"Fair enough. Here's my question," John replied. "Assuming the existence of a good and caring God, which I am trying my best to believe and trust in, why do you think good people experience pain and suffering in this world?"

"Talk about a loaded question, John! That's one that the greatest minds in the history of mankind have pondered—and you expect me to give you the answer?"

"I'm not asking you for a definitive answer. But I know that in your line of work, over the course of the last thirty years, the issue must have come up in your practice on more than one occasion."

"Of course it has, and I can tell you what I believe, without having any empirical proof."

"Please do."

"I actually think about the answer to this question in a very simple way. To me, in order to have an understanding and appreciation for what we perceive via our physical and mental senses, we need a relative and not an absolute standard. What I mean is that in order to appreciate and comprehend the light, we must also know what the darkness is. Without one, the other could not exist. I believe the same holds true to your question about good people being allowed by a good God to experience pain and suffering in this world. Without pain and suffering, how would they know what joy, peace, and contentment are? There would be no basis for comparison and no way to know the difference," Mayne explained.

John pondered Mayne's answer for a moment and then asked, "But why couldn't God just show His children that, without letting us suffer through the process?"

"That's a question God will have to answer, so you'll have to wait and ask Him when you get to heaven. But it's my belief that good people are allowed to experience pain and suffering in this world for this reason: When they go on to their eternal reward as God's children, they'll have an appreciation for the beauty, joy, and peace of their eternal life with their Heavenly Father and His Son."

"That's an interesting concept. I need to think about it, but I appreciate you sharing your thoughts with me. Also, I want to thank you for you putting up with me over all these months. I know I haven't been easy to work with, but your sage advice and your kindness has been very helpful."

"I'm glad to hear that, John. It's what makes my job worthwhile."

...

On the following Sunday, John, Anna, Bruce Davidson, and Chris McConnell were all seated in a conference room at Newtown, discussing Luciano's day-in-the-life video and Mayberry's settlement demand for $10 million. Officer Peter Deem was stationed directly outside the door and kept peering through the window to check on them, although he couldn't hear a word of their conversation.

"Well," said John, "from everything you tell me, the video is a problem we need to carefully consider. Bruce, we've been talking now for well over an hour. I'd like to cut to the chase and get your recommendation regarding the settlement. After that, I'd like to excuse you so Anna and I can speak privately with Chris."

"I understand and agree," replied Davidson. "As you know, I've talked with the carrier, and they are prepared to offer the entire $6 million in coverage to settle the case. That leaves a shortfall of $4 million that you would have to cover, which I know would require you to liquidate almost all your assets, if not all. Mayberry is adamant that nothing under $10 million will be accepted, and I don't believe he's bluffing. We've already discussed the issue of your major asset being your Palm Beach residence, and the homestead exemption on your house, which would not allow Mayberry to force a sale of the residence. On the other hand, if you do go to trial, you run the risk of having a judgment issued against you in excess of $10 million, which as you know will last up to twenty years, assuming all the recording and rerecording requirements are met. If that happens, Mayberry will be relentless in pursuing you for years to recover any funds he can. So, for all those reasons, I recommend you strongly consider doing your best to raise the $4 million. The ultimate decision on what course of action you take should be made in conjunction with whatever advice Chris gives you, as your independent counsel."

"Okay, Bruce. Thanks for your hard work on the case. Anna will let you know later this week what we decide, and then if you need to see me, you can make the arrangements."

Davidson left the room, and John looked McConnell dead on in the eyes. "Chris, you and I have been close friends for many years. I trust and respect your opinion, which is why I hired you to help me. So, give it to me straight. What should I do?"

"Do your best to liquidate your assets and come up with the

$4 million. We've already talked about all your defenses, and they are significant. But just as significant is the risk you face if you proceed to trial. Plus, if you voluntarily settle now with Luciano, and avoid a trial, you can make a good case with the Bar that you have served your time and made full restitution—so your license to practice law should be reinstated."

"I appreciate the advice. Anna will call you this week."

McConnell then left the room, and Officer Deem agreed to let Anna stay for a few more minutes. John looked at Anna and shook his head.

"Anna, I just can't believe this is happening. But before I say anything, I want to hear what you think we should do."

"Sell the house, liquidate our assets, and pay the $4 million."

"I knew you would tell me that. What makes you think we can get $4 million?"

"I already made an analysis of all our accounts and talked to Tess about selling the house."

"I figured that as well. Okay, give me the details."

"Tess says that she has a cash buyer for our house at a price that will net us $3 million. The present cash value of our other assets totals about $1 million, which would be enough money to settle the case.

"Where would we live?"

"One of the teachers at work is moving out of state and has her home up for sale. It's been on the market for a while. She's willing to enter into a two-year lease, with an option to buy. The purchase price would be locked in at $250,000, with all the lease payments being applied toward the purchase price. Rent would be $2,000 per month, which would make it a little tight until you started working again, but we'll be able to do it. At least we'd have a roof over our heads and food on the table. Both our cars are paid for, and we've got health insurance through my work, so there's nothing we'd be lacking for." Anna was on a mission and John knew it.

"Working at the food pantry, along with everything else that's happened over the last few years, has really changed your perspective on things, hasn't it?" John asked.

"Yes, it has."

"Well, mine has changed as well, for a lot of reasons. So let's go ahead with your plan and pay the $4 million. It's time for me to accept responsibility for drinking and driving, and I want the Lucianos to get the money they need to help them get through what they're dealing with every day."

"John, I'm so relieved to hear you talk this way. You're a changed man from what you were just a few months ago. To be honest, I didn't think you'd be so willing to give up all your assets like this."

"Well, one of the things Robert said to me when I talked to him about this decision was that we shouldn't be concerned with storing up riches here on earth because money will never bring true happiness, and it can't be brought with us into eternity. I've been thinking about that since he said it, and I've come to agree with him. The funny thing is that I think I've heard that before, but I just can't place it."

"You have heard that before. It was part of the petitions in the prayer card that Father Anderson gave you at Mass when you went with me just before your trial."

"You're kidding?"

"Nope."

"That's strange. I need to ask Robert where he heard that."

"Please do. I'd like to know."

"I'll do that, Anna. Speaking of Father Anderson and the prayer card, Sweetheart, there's something else I need to talk with you about."

"What's that?"

"I just told you that my perspective on things has changed for a lot of reasons."

"Yes." Anna said hopefully.

"Well, the most important reason," John explained slowly, "is that I have finally returned to the beliefs I'd held since I was an altar boy at St. Peter's—until the day our baby was taken from us."

Tears streamed down John's cheeks. Anna grabbed his hands and waited anxiously for him to resume speaking.

"I had always viewed God as caring, and I believed in Jesus Christ as my Lord and Savior. Even when all our parents passed away, I knew each of them were in heaven and much better off than here. But when Maria died at such a young age, for no apparent reason, I started to lose my faith in a good God. The loss of Maria seemed especially cruel after we had tried for so long to have a child, and then she was taken from us at just six months. Then on top of that, the car accident happened, I get sent to jail, and I'm sued for all our money.

"Anna, although I never admitted this to you before, you were absolutely right when you said Satan was trying to separate us from God. But with your help and guidance, and that of Dr. Mayne, Robert, and other men here, I have returned to God. Jesus is my Lord and Savior, and I'm going to start living like it. I know that even though I left God, He never left me." John's eyes filled up with tears once more, and Anna started to cry, too. John continued, "Anna, I can't tell you how blessed I feel to have you as my soul mate. I can't wait to go home and share my life with you again."

Anna whispered, "Thank you, Lord. Thank you." Then, looking at John, she said, "John, hearing you say this is the answer to my prayers. This is a new day, filled with hope and joy for the future. I really believe everything's going to be okay."

As Anna drove home that day, one phrase kept coming from her lips: "Thank you, Lord. Thank you!"

Chapter 39

"John, this is your last dinner at Newtown," exclaimed Robert as the two of them sat down with their plates in the inmate dining room. "I bet you can't wait to get home tomorrow to Anna's cooking."

"You've got that right. But I do have to admit that the food here was pretty decent. Don't you agree?"

"Just look at my plate, and you know my answer. I'm sure not going hungry." Robert flashed his famous grin and let out a huge belly laugh.

Soon the two of them were joined at their table by a number of other inmates. John couldn't believe he would be a free man tomorrow, on his way home. Of course, this wouldn't be the home in Palm Beach that he left, nor was it a building he had ever seen or set foot in. But still, it was going to be John and Anna's home to share together. Anna had been able to successfully liquidate all their assets, and the lawsuit had been settled for the $10 million payment. Anna was even able to buy new furniture with the few thousand dollars they had left after the settlement, since the furniture in their other home was sold with the house.

John's thought process was suddenly interrupted by someone tapping on his shoulder. Turning around, he saw that it was "Johnny Boy" Vitiglio.

"John, I know that I sleep right next to you and will see you later tonight. But while I'm thinking about it, I want to make sure I don't forget to thank you for all you've done for me. Because of you, I can now read and write really well! In fact, I'm doing so good that in two months when I leave Newtown, I'm going to take the GED. So, thanks a lot, man, and I hope everything turns out okay for you after you leave." He gripped John's hand and shook it so hard John thought it would break.

During the course of dinner, several other inmates, including Derrick Mays, also came over and thanked John for his assistance. Although not every person John had mentored came to thank him, he was grateful for those who did and felt a deep sense of satisfaction for what he had been able to accomplish at Newtown. The last person to approach him was Sergeant Gaetano.

"Well, Taylor. I've got to hand it to you. For the longest time, I didn't think we'd get your sorry butt to do anything meaningful around here. But you really came through for the men you mentored over the last several months, and I'm here to thank you for that. I know you want out of here really bad, and I wouldn't blame you in the least if we never saw you again. But I hope you'll seriously think about coming back here as a volunteer mentor to some of these men. Our program could really use you."

"Just give me some time, Sarge, and I'll be back to help."

"Glad to hear that. You be careful out there and don't go drinking and driving. The only way I want to see you back here is as a volunteer, not an inmate."

"That's one thing you don't need to worry about."

"Good."

· · ·

The next morning after breakfast, John was in the housing dorm waiting for Anna to arrive. It was early on a Wednesday morning in mid-September, and Anna had arranged to take the day off from school. John was standing on the side of his bed, deep in thought, when Robert sneaked up behind him and gave him a huge bear hug. Robert then started effortlessly flopping John up and down, while incessantly laughing.

"Robert," stammered John, "stop it, you big lug, you're gonna break my back!"

Robert let him go and continued laughing. Then he became serious and extended his hand to John.

"John, I want you to know how proud I am of you—not only for helping all the men you did here, but more importantly for turning your heart and trust over to Jesus Christ. You truly are a man of God, and I'm honored to know you and call you a friend."

After shaking Robert's hand and exchanging a similar sentiment, a light suddenly went off in John's head. He realized he had never asked Robert about the petition in the prayer card regarding not being concerned about storing up riches on earth.

"Robert, there's something I've been meaning to ask you. I told Anna about your advice that I shouldn't be concerned about storing up riches on earth. She reminded me that a prayer card our priest gave us contained the same exact wording as what you told me, along with other petitions. We were wondering if you knew of any connection between what you said to me and the card our priest gave us. He told us he'd been given the prayer by a friend."

"By any chance, are you talking about Father Anderson?"

"Yes, I am! How do you know him?"

"About five or six years ago, when I was in a correctional facility in Broward County, Father Anderson was the prison chaplain. He had suffered a devastating loss followed by more adversity, and He was struggling with his faith. We were very close, and he confided in me about it. He knew all about what I had been through, and he thought I might be able to help him deal with his crisis of faith."

"What happened?"

"Father Anderson had a nephew named Ted who was in the Army. He was very close to him. Ted's wife became pregnant and eventually gave birth to twin boys. Just after their birth, Ted got shipped over to Iraq. While on patrol, his unit got ambushed, and Ted was killed in a firefight. The entire family was overwhelmed with grief. To make matters even worse, a few weeks after his nephew was killed, one of Father's brothers, who had made millions of dollars in the stock market, made some very risky investment decisions and lost all his money. I knew I had to do something to try and help Father Anderson, so I prayed about it and ended up writing the prayer, "In Times of Trouble and Doubt." Father told me the prayer was a source of great comfort and peace to him."

"How did you come up with the words you used in the prayer?"

"The prayer is based on a combination of biblical principles, sermons by pastors, and discussions that I've participated in over the years. I tried to gel all those concepts together and put them in my own words as best I could."

"When was the last time you saw Father Anderson?"

"It's probably been a good three years. I sure would like to see him again."

"This coming Sunday I'll be going to Mass with Anna at Father Anderson's parish. Would it be okay if I told him you were here and would like him to visit you? I won't let on to Father anything that you just told me."

"That would be wonderful."

Just then Corporal Alexander announced that Anna had arrived and it was time for John to go. John's release had already been fully processed, and he only needed to change from his prison attire to the jeans and shirt Anna had brought for him. After saying good-bye to Robert and changing his clothes, Alexander led him out of the dorm.

On the way out, Carlos Delgado yelled to him, "Watch your back out there, Taylor. You never know what's coming next." John didn't take the comment as a threat, and Delgado didn't mean it as one.

John responded, "I will, Carlos. You take care too."

"By the way, Taylor," said Delgado. "If you come back here as a volunteer, I'm ready to get some help with my reading and writing."

"You got it," replied John.

As they entered the administration building where Anna was waiting for John, Alexander smiled broadly and then spoke to John. "Taylor, I've got to tell you. You are one lucky man getting to go home to a wife as pretty as yours. Make sure you take good care of her."

"Well, Corporal Alexander, I guess I better hurry up and get out of here. I don't want a 'Pretty Boy' like you trying to steal my wife."

"Cute, Taylor, real cute," said Alexander, as he tried his best to suppress the smile that had crossed his mouth.

As John and Anna exited the administration building and headed to the parking lot, John turned around and looked back at Newtown. "Anna, I've got a really good feeling about the programs at Newtown. Although it's certainly not perfect, they're off to a great start in reducing recidivism and turning inmates into productive members of society. Let's remember to keep them in our prayers."

"Absolutely!" Anna agreed.

They got into Anna's car and before Anna started it up, John leaned over and gave her the sweetest, most meaningful kiss they'd ever shared.

. . .

When they arrived back in West Palm Beach, John was anxious to see his new home. As Anna pulled into the driveway, she commented, "Here we are. Isn't it cute?"

"Yes, it is. I can't wait to go inside."

As the two of them entered the home, John was pleasantly surprised at how spacious it seemed and how attractively Anna had decorated it. He told Anna how much he liked it.

"It's almost 2,300 square feet, and everything is in great condition. We don't need any more than this, John, and I'm so thankful to God that we're back together again in this lovely home."

"Amen to that. There's only one problem."

"What's that," Anna nervously asked.

"Now we don't live two blocks away from the best surfing around here, and there's no public parking in that area. After I get my driver's license back, do you think that the Milans would let me park in their driveway so I can go surfing up there?"

"I'm absolutely sure they'd be fine with that!" Anna answered, laughing and hugging her husband tightly.

Chapter 40

Two days later, on Friday morning at ten, Anna was driving John to Good Shepherd Academy, a Christian-based, interdenominational high school, located on the outskirts of West Palm Beach. While at Newtown, the Chaplain had requested that John speak to the student body regarding his DUI conviction and subsequent imprisonment. John agreed, and they arranged for him to speak at ten thirty. Anna took the day off work, and after John and Anna met with the principal in her office, the three of them walked over to the school gymnasium where John would be speaking. John had spent several hours preparing his talk. Although accustomed to public speaking by virtue of practicing law for twelve years, the subject matter of today's talk, as well as his audience, was totally foreign to John. He had been pacing around the house earlier this morning in nervous anticipation of what lay ahead.

When the principal opened the gym door, his anxiety level

increased threefold. The building was filled with people, both students and adults, whom he thought must either be teachers or parents. Not only were all the bleachers packed to capacity, but chairs were also set up over the entire gym floor—and there was not an empty one in sight. Anna managed to squeeze into a bleacher seat, and the principal led John to the stage. After a short introduction, John cautiously approached the podium, removed his notes from his pocket, and took a deep breath before speaking.

"Good morning, everyone. I wish I could tell you that it's nice to be here, but I can't. However, there's a very good reason for me to speak to you today—and not just to you students, but to the adults as well. The reason I'm here is to share with you some terrible mistakes that I've made in my life, in the hopes that you'll avoid making such errors in judgment. The mistakes I made caused me to be convicted of driving a car under the influence of alcohol, seriously injuring another human being, and hurting his family. As a result of my bad judgment, my legal career went down the drain. I was put in prison, and I lost all my liberties. Eventually, all my material wealth—my house and my bank accounts—was also lost in order to make financial restitution to the man and family I hurt. I also came close to losing my relationship with my wife, the woman I have loved dearly and been together with for twenty-two years, since we were high school sweethearts."

John struggled to control his emotions and stopped speaking for a few seconds. He silently prayed, asking God for the strength to continue. All eyes in the gym were on him, and no one in the audience was talking or making any noise. John had this crowd's undivided attention.

"In order to explain my mistakes, I need to give you a little background about myself. Prior to my DUI conviction, I was a lawyer for twelve years in Palm Beach, and I lived on the Island in a very nice home. I drove an expensive car, took fabulous vacations around the world, and made a lot of money. After we had been married for a number of years, my wife and I decided it was time to have a baby. We were blessed with a beautiful girl and named her Maria. One night, when Maria was six months old, Anna got up and realized that Maria had not awakened for her normal feeding. When Anna went in to check on Maria, she was unconscious. We immediately called the paramedics. They did their very best to revive her, but they couldn't. Maria had passed away, and the only diagnosis we got was the label Sudden Infant Death Syndrome. To this day, we still don't know the exact cause of Maria's death."

There were gasps from many in the audience. Some of the girls sitting in front of John were crying. He could no longer hold back his tears and stopped speaking. Anna wanted to run up to the stage and embrace him but knew she couldn't. After a minute or so, John was able to regain his composure and continued on.

"As a result of Maria's death, I became angry and bitter. I started to lose my faith, and I felt like I couldn't trust God. That was really the first and biggest mistake I made. Then, I made my next mistake. One night, about six months after Maria had passed away, I was playing in a softball league. After the game, a bunch of the guys went out to a restaurant for dinner and drinks. While I was there, I drank beer, but I didn't feel like I was drunk at all, so I left and started to drive back home. On the way to my house, I struck another car, and the driver was hurt really bad. He had severe damage to his arms and legs and is confined to a wheelchair. He had no memory of how the accident occurred, and there were no witnesses.

"I maintained throughout the trial," John continued, "that I was not under the influence of alcohol and that the other driver caused the accident by running a red light. The jury disagreed and found me guilty. I was ultimately sentenced to eighteen months in prison. As a result of the conviction and my continued insistence that I was innocent, I lost all my faith in God. After I went to jail, my downward spiral got even worse, and there was nothing anyone could do or say to help me.

"Fortunately, for me and for my wife, that wasn't the end of the story." John now spoke with hope in his voice. "With the help of my wife and some great people at Newtown Correctional Institution, the prison where I was sent, my faith was gradually restored, and the fear, anger, and bitterness that had consumed me went away. My renewed faith and trust in God helped me accept responsibility for the crash. Although I had two large insurance policies that paid money to the other driver and his family, that wasn't enough to adequately cover his family's financial damages. So Anna and I decided to sell all our assets, including our Palm Beach home, and use the money to settle the lawsuit. Although that money will never adequately compensate the family for the life-long injuries the father suffered, at least they'll have the money they need to cover medical expenses and the loss of income since the father won't be able to work like he used to.

"I asked God to forgive me for the tragedy I caused, and I know that He did. Daily I ask Him for strength to bear the burden of what I've done. I haven't yet reached out to the other driver and his family to express my apologies and seek their forgiveness, but I will do so. I hope and pray they'll be able to forgive me.

"I have two primary reasons for coming to speak to all of you today. The first is to ask that you not lose faith and trust in God when the trials of life come your way. In that regard, I would like to read to you a prayer given to me by a very devoted man of God before my trial. The prayer is entitled 'In Times of Trouble and Doubt.'"

John then read the prayer in its entirety to the audience. "Although I would not accept this prayer when it was first given to me, nor for a long time after, with the help of Anna and a friend I made in prison, I have come to believe in the power of prayer. I hope and pray that each of you students and adults have or will find a similar prayer or Bible passage that provides you with peace and sustains your faith during difficult times.

"The second reason I wanted to speak to you today is to reinforce the dangers and foolishness of drinking and driving. Of course, the students who are in here should not be drinking alcohol at all, because you are not of legal age. But when you reach twenty-one, you may decide to drink alcohol. I hope you won't, but if you do, please don't drink and drive. Even if you've only had a little to drink, you never know how it could impair you or affect your response time in an emergency. The same applies to every adult in this room. Just because you don't feel intoxicated doesn't mean you're not under the influence of alcohol. I am a prime example of that. I never should have driven home that night. I should have called a taxi or gotten a ride from my wife or a friend. Please avoid my mistake and the heartache it has brought for so many. Thanks to all of you for listening to me, and I hope and pray that you will follow my advice."

The audience stood up and gave John a rousing ovation for several minutes. A large number of students and adults approached John to shake his hand and express their thanks. It was nearly thirty minutes before John and Anna could get out of the gym. On the way out, John told Anna, "I don't know what good, if any, will come of that talk, but if it keeps even one person from making the mistakes I did, then it will be well worth it."

"There's no doubt about that, John. I believe it will help many more people than you'll ever know."

As John and Anna headed to the parking lot, they were surprised to see the Old Man and Red standing by Anna's car waiting to talk to them.

"What are you doing here?" asked John.

"My grandson goes to school here, and he told me you were coming to speak today. So Donna and I decided we'd like to come and hear you," replied the Old Man.

"You did a great job, John. I'm really proud of you," Red told John.

"John," said the Old Man, "there's another reason I wanted to come here today. Jim wanted to come as well, but he was called out of town for a closing on a corporate deal. Jim and I both owe you an apology for the way we treated you before you left the firm. We should have been much more sympathetic to your situation. The purported deal with the other attorney never went through, and we're both glad it didn't. We now realize you could never have been replaced. You had become the heart and soul of our firm, and everyone misses you for a number of reasons, some of which I will admit are selfish in nature. But to get to the heart of the matter, all the partners have talked it over, and I'm here to ask you to come back to the firm."

John couldn't say anything. His mouth hung open in surprise. Before he could collect his thoughts, the Old Man continued. "Of course, we realize your license is suspended, but since you've served your sentence and made full financial restitution to the Lucianos, the suspension will be lifted in due course and your license reinstated. In the interim, although you can't practice law, you can work for the firm as a paralegal. What do you say?"

"Well, first of all, George, this comes as a complete surprise— but a very good one. Of course, I'll have to talk with Anna first about your offer. For now, what I really need to do is to ask you for a favor."

"What's that?"

"Right now, I don't know where God is leading me and what He may call me to do. Can you keep the door open? I really don't want to say yes or no right now, but I'd appreciate the opportunity to respond in the near future."

"Take as long as you need, John. The door will always be open. As I just said, you can't be replaced."

After they all exchanged good-byes, John and Anna headed to

their new home. They had a number of projects to work on, and they spent the rest of their day painting their kitchen.

On Saturday, John went to the food pantry with Anna to volunteer. Although, like Anna, John also found it hard to work there, he experienced the same sense of satisfaction, peace, and blessing as Anna did in working at the pantry. He committed to her that he would be by her side at the pantry every week.

Sunday rolled around quickly, and this time it was John hurrying Anna out the door for Mass. He wanted to arrive early to speak with Father Anderson. He was on a mission and didn't want to wait until after the service. When the Taylors arrived, John rushed right up to Father Anderson and gave him a big bear hug. Father was surprised, and when John finally let go, the pastor greeted him and welcomed him back.

"Father," blurted out John. "I have two things to tell you. First, I want to thank you for caring so much about Anna and me and always being there to help us. Although I never really appreciated it in the past, I do now. To prove it to you, I guarantee I'll listen to—and like—every word of your homily." John flashed his mischievous grin at Father.

"Okay, John," laughed Father. "What's the second thing?"

"While I was at Newtown, I became good friends with another inmate. He told me about a chaplain he met while in jail in Broward County, and it was you! He said the two of you became quite close while you worked at the prison."

"Don't tell me it was Robert Williams?" Father asked with a smile.

"Yes, it was! He said he'd love to see you again when you have a chance."

"I'd love to see him as well. I'll put that at the top of my to-do list," said Father Anderson.

...

After Mass, John and Anna got in the car, and Anna started driving toward their new home. John stopped her. "Wait! Turn that way," he said as they approached an intersection, instructing Anna to go a different route. She looked at him, confused. "I need to see Maria's grave," he explained to Anna.

Anna quickly complied, but she knew that this would not be easy for either of them, especially John. When they arrived at the cemetery, they slowly walked toward Maria's grave with their arms held tightly around each other. When they reached Maria's headstone, John fell to his hands and knees, unable to control his emotions. Anna had never seen John so emotional. She knelt down beside him, wrapping her arms around him.

While they were still kneeling, John told Anna, "I am so very sorry for being selfish and refusing to visit our baby's grave for so long. I know you needed me there, and I was only thinking of myself. I promise you will never have to visit here alone again."

"I forgive you, John. And let's move on from the past. The important thing is that we're both here now."

John sighed deeply. He couldn't believe God had blessed him with such an amazing wife. Who else would be so quick to forgive? Who else would have supported him so wonderfully while he served a prison sentence? John knew he had much to be grateful for.

John looked Anna squarely in the eye. He touched her face with the back of his hand. "Anna, thank you," he said.

He didn't need to say more. Anna knew what he meant. She simply said, "You're welcome, John. It's my pleasure and my honor to be your wife."

John took another deep breath. He continued staring at his beautiful wife, thinking back to how much baby Maria had looked like her mom. "You know, Anna, for the longest time I was tortured every time I thought of Maria's death. I still miss her terribly, but I am comforted by two things."

"What's that?" asked Anna.

"Well, first, I know Maria is in heaven with God. And there's no better place she could be than in the arms of the One who created her."

Anna smiled. "That's true," she said. "What's the other thing?"

"The second thing is something Dr. Mayne and I discussed in one of my sessions with him. We were talking about what heaven was like for Maria, and he reminded me that each of her four grandparents is there with her. I like to picture them taking turns holding her—caring for our baby—their grandbaby."

"What a beautiful thought, John. I'm glad you shared it with me."

They stayed at the gravesite a moment longer, and as they stood up to leave, they were comforted to see a rainbow directly over their heads. It seemed to stretch endlessly, and the colors in it were more vivid and magnificent than in any other rainbow they'd seen.

"John, this is absolutely incredible. I can't believe how brilliant this rainbow is!" exclaimed Anna.

John silently thanked God once more. "It's a sign from God, Anna. It's like a little kiss to let us know that Maria is okay."

"God is so good to us, John," said Anna wistfully as they walked back to their car.

"He sure is good, Anna. He sure is."

The End